Praise for *One Step Too Far*

"I didn't guess the twist… I simply had no idea whatsoever and when it was laid down in front of me I felt as though I'd been punched. The book's a keeper too. Next time round you'll know how it all works out but there's a great deal of pleasure to be had in re-reading."　　　*thebookbag.co.uk*

"The author reveals Emily's motivations for leaving her family with great patience and narrative skill… (there is) excellent dramatic pacing, dialogue and prose, culminating in poignant concluding chapters which examine Emily's decisions without sentimentality. An evocative, skillful novel about the price of escape. Recommended."　　*Kirkus Reviews*

"It's compelling, gripping, frightening, embarrassing, deeply sad and lovely all at once. Just read it. You won't be sorry. I loved this book."　　　　　*myzennana.com*

"WOW! This one is a winner! While the plot might seem like a "movie-of-the-week", the gorgeous writing elevates it to fine contemporary literature. By the end, I was truly aching for Emily/ Cat, desperate to know her secret. And when it was finally revealed I gasped out loud! This is an excellent example of how a book can play our emotions like an instrument… I am praying that someone options this for the big screen."　　*Suzanne Rogers, South Carolina, US*

"I would have to compare this favorably with *Gone Girl*. The pacing and suspense are great, and I definitely was hooked early. I liked it, and will recommend it to many, including book groups."   *Avid, goodreads.com*

"The author does a wonderful job of keeping the reader guessing and clueless until she's ready to let you in on the secret. And when she finally does, the reader should be prepared for a jaw-dropper. Seskis's book was a wonderful read that I fully expect to quickly rise on the list of bestsellers."
Catherine Armstrong, Rochester Public Library, US

"A highly enjoyable and compelling read with all the right elements of a page-turner – just the right amount of information dripped in to keep the reader interested."
Penny Faith, author, London

"Superb story. Budding authors should read this novel to see how a good book can be written. I give this 6 stars out of 5. It would make a great movie!"
Christopher French, Tauranga, New Zealand

"A compelling and intense novel. There was not one point in this brilliantly written story that I could clearly know what would happen to Cat. The world building put me right there, watching over Cat's shoulder, living her story along with her."   *Dii, Tome Tender*

Tina Seskis

Tina Seskis grew up in Hampshire and after graduating from Bath University spent over 20 years working in marketing and advertising. She is the author of two novels, *One Step Too Far* and *A Serpentine Affair*. She lives in North London with her husband and son, and is not planning on taking the train to Manchester.

Also by Tina Seskis

A Serpentine Affair
(DUE FOR RELEASE AUTUMN 2013)

One Step Too Far

Tina Seskis

KIRK PAROLLES

LONDON

First published in Great Britain in 2013 by Kirk Parolles.

A CIP catalogue for this book
is available from the British Library.

ISBN 978 0 9575443 2 1

Typeset by Ellipsis Digital Limited, Glasgow

Printed and bound in Great Britain by
CLAYS LTD, ST IVES PLC

Kirk Parolles's policy is to use papers that are
natural, renewable and recyclable products made from wood
grown in sustainable forests. The logging and manufacturing
processes are expected to conform to the environmental
regulations of the country of origin.

www.kirkparolles.com

For my mother

Part One

ep into the room.

1

The heat is like another person to push past as I make my way
along the platform. I board the train although I don't know
whether I should, after all. I sit tense amongst the commuters,
moving with the carriage and the crowds from my old life into
my new one. The train is cool and oddly vacant-feeling, despite
the people, despite the sweltering of the day outside, and this
emptiness calms me a little. No-one knows my story here, I'm
anonymous at last, just another young woman with a holdall.
I feel adrift, like I'm not really here, but I am, I can tell, the seat
is solid beneath me, the backs of houses are rushing past the
window. I've done it.

It's funny how easy it is, when it really comes down to it,
to get up from your life and begin a new one. All you need
is enough money to start you off, and a resolve to not think
about the people you're leaving behind. I tried to not look
this morning, tried to just leave, but at the very last second I
found myself drawn to his room and stood watching him
sleeping – like a newborn really, not yet awake to the first day
of the rest of his life. I couldn't risk even a peep into the room

3

where Charlie slept, I knew it would wake him, stop me going, so I'd quietly turned the latch and left them both.

The woman next to me is struggling with her coffee. She's wearing a dark suit and looks businesslike, a bit like I used to. She's trying to get the plastic lid off her drink, but it sticks and she tussles with it until the lid comes off with a shudder and hot coffee spurts over us both. The woman apologises noisily, but I just shake my head for her not to worry and look down into my lap, knowing I should be wiping the dark stains from my grey leather jacket – it will be ruined, it looks odd that I don't – but the eruption of coffee has upset me somehow and the hot tears mingle with the coffee ones and I pray that if I don't look up no-one will notice.

I regret now that I didn't stop and buy a newspaper but it felt inappropriate, on the day I was running away, to go into a newsagents and join a queue of *normal* people. I sit here and miss having one, miss having those closely packed words to dive into, concentrate on, chase out the evil thoughts in my mind. I'm agitated with nothing to read, nothing to do except look out the window and wish people's stares away. I watch forlornly as Manchester fizzles out and realise I may never see it again, the city I once loved. The train rushes through sunburnt fields and the odd unknown village and although we're going fast now the journey seems interminable, my body strains to get up and run, but to where? I'm already running.

I feel cold suddenly, the initially welcome cool of the air-conditioning has become a bone-withering chill, and I pull my jacket tighter. I shiver and look down and shut my leaking eyes. I'm good at crying silently, but the jacket continues to give me away – the tear drops land gently and spread generously across the fabric. *Why did I dress up, how ridiculous was that? I'm not on a day trip, I'm running away, leaving my life, surplus to requirements.* The sounds in my head and the rhythms of the train over the track fuse together. I keep my eyes shut until the panic drifts away like ghost dust, and then I stay like that anyway.

I get off the train at Crewe. I find my way to the newsagents, before the main concourse, and I buy papers, magazines, a paperback, I mustn't be caught out again. I hide out for a while in the ladies, where I gaze in the mirror at my pale face and ruined jacket, and I loosen my long hair to cover up the stains. I attempt a smile and it comes, twisted and fake maybe, but definitely a smile, and I hope the worst is over, at least for today. I'm hot, feverish even, so I splash at my face and the water adds new marks to my jacket, it's beyond repair. I take it off and stuff it in my holdall. I look absently at myself, seeing a stranger. I notice I quite like my hair down, it makes me look younger, the kink left from the French pleat renders it ratty, bohemian even. As I dry my hands I feel hot metal on my finger, and I realise I'm still wearing my wedding ring. I've never taken it off, not since the day Ben put it on me, on a terrace overlooking the sea. I remove it and hesitate, not sure what to do with it – it's Emily's ring, not mine anymore, my name is Catherine now. It's exquisite, the three tiny diamonds shine out from the platinum and make me sad. *He doesn't love me anymore.* So I leave it there, by the soap, in the public toilets next to Platform 2, and take the next train to Euston.

2

On an unremarkable day more than 30 years earlier, Frances Brown lay in a Chester hospital with her legs in stirrups as the doctors continued to prod about down there. She was in shock. The birth itself had been fast and animal-like, not at all typical of a first-born from the little she knew. She hadn't really known what to expect, they didn't tell you much in those days, but the one thing she most definitely had not been prepared for, after the head had crowned and the slippery red creature had flopped onto the bed beneath her, was that the doctors would tell her to deliver another.

Frances had known something was up, when the mood in the delivery room had changed in an instant, and all the doctors had come at once and huddled around her bed, conferring anxiously. She'd thought something must be wrong with her baby girl, but if so why were they poking around her instead of looking after the child? Finally the doctor looked up, and she was bemused to see that he was smiling. "The job's not over yet Mrs Brown," he said. "We've found another baby that we need to get out now."

"I beg your pardon?" she'd said.

The consultant tried again. "Congratulations, Mrs Brown,

you're soon to be the mother of twins. You have a second baby to deliver."

"What d'you mean?" she'd screamed. "I've had my bloody baby."

Now she lay there in shock and all she could think was that she didn't want two babies, she only wanted one, she only had one cot, one pram, one set of baby clothes, one life prepared.

Frances was a planner by nature. She didn't like surprises, certainly not ones this momentous, and apart from anything else she felt far too exhausted to give birth again – the first birth may have been quick but it had been fierce and traumatic and nearly three weeks ahead of schedule. She shut her eyes and wondered when Andrew would arrive. She hadn't been able to get him at his office, he'd been out at a meeting apparently, and once the contractions had quickened to every minute and a half she'd known her only option was to call an ambulance.

So her first baby had arrived in a gush of red and a gash of loneliness – and now she was being told to deliver a second and still her husband was absent. Andrew hadn't seemed too keen on having even one baby, so God knows what he'd think of this development. She started sobbing, noisy snot-filled gulps that rang through the little hospital.

"Mrs Brown, will you control yourself!" the midwife said. Frances loathed her, with her mean features and squeaky, grating voice – what was she even doing in this job, she thought bitterly, she'd suck the joy out of any situation, even the beauty of birth, like a malevolent pair of bellows.

"Can I see my baby?" Frances said. "I haven't even seen her yet."

"She's being checked. Just concentrate on this one."

"I don't want to concentrate on this one. I want my real baby. Give me my real baby." She was screeching now. The midwife got the gas and air and held it over Frances's face, pressing hard. Frances gagged and finally stopped screaming, and as she quietened the fight went out of her and something in her died, there on that hospital bed.

Andrew turned up just seconds too late to see his second twin daughter enter the world. He seemed flustered and awkward, especially when his hopes of a son were rewarded with not one but two baby girls. One was pink and pretty and perfectly formed, the other lay blue and grotesque on the filthy sheets, the umbilical cord stopping the air from entering her lungs and starting her life outside the womb. The atmosphere he arrived into was intense, critical. The doctor deftly unwrapped the cord from the baby's neck and cut it, and Andrew watched the blood swarm through her little body as the doctor took her across to the resuscitation unit, and one of the nurses held up a hoover and sucked the shit and scum from her airways. It was just moments before they heard the anguished angry howls. She was exactly one hour younger than her sister, and she looked and sounded like she'd come from a different planet.

"My poor darling, I am so so sorry," Andrew whispered to his pale bedraggled wife as he took her hand, red with new life.

Frances looked at him hard, in his Dirty Harry suit and

loosened tie. "What are you sorry for? That you weren't here or that I've had twin girls?"

He couldn't quite look at her. "For everything," he said. "But I'm here now and we have our ready-made family. It'll be great, you'll see."

"Mr Brown, you need to wait outside now," said the midwife. "We need to clean up your wife and repair the tearing. We'll call you when you can come back in." And she shooed him away and Frances was left alone again, with her guilt and her fear and her two baby daughters.

Frances had always assumed she'd be a good mother. She'd just felt she'd know exactly what to do – that it might not be easy but that she'd get through it, she had a handsome new husband, a supportive family, a maternal instinct. But when it came to it the trauma of the birth and the doubling of her expectations left her at a loss. She had two babies, not one – and they seemed to need feeding or rocking or changing *constantly* – and a husband who appeared to have drifted away from her whilst the baby (babies!) had been growing inside her.

They couldn't even think what to call their second daughter. They'd decided weeks ago on Emily for a girl, full name Catherine Emily – Frances thought the names sounded better that way round – but of course they hadn't known they'd need a second option. Andrew was pragmatic, and suggested calling one of the twins Catherine and the other Emily, but Frances didn't want to share the names out, they went so well together, she said, so they had to start all over again for the unexpected twin. In the end they settled on

Caroline Rebecca, although Frances didn't particularly like either name – but Andrew had suggested them, and anyway she couldn't face thinking of any others. She held that fact secret, one of the first of many, further proof that she wouldn't really have minded if the birth had been just a few seconds longer, if the cord had been that little bit tighter, if poor Caroline Rebecca had stopped breathing before she began. The effort of shoving that thought away (who could she ever tell?) took up years and years of Frances's life and turned her hard inside, right in the centre of herself where she had once been soft and motherly.

Frances spent the next seven days in hospital, and that gave her time to at least appear to recover from the trauma of the births, the absence of her husband, the fact she was quite unbelievably the new mother of twins. She decided her only option was to make the best of it, to embrace both girls, in fact maybe in the end it would be nice to have two. But it wasn't easy, Emily and Caroline were different from the start. When they were born you would hardly have known they were twins – Emily was pink and plump, Caroline thin and sickly and pallid, almost two pounds lighter than her sister. And then Caroline refused to take to her mother's breast, although Emily had no problems, and so Caroline's weight dropped as her twin's increased.

Frances was stoical by nature. She tried and tried and tried with Caroline, until her nipples bled and her nerves were ragged. She was determined to treat her two babies the same – she had to now they were both here. In the end it was one of the nurses who put her foot down and gave Caroline a bottle on the fourth day, she said they couldn't starve the child. Caroline gripped the teat in her tiny mouth ferociously, contrarily, whilst Frances felt like a failure, and another bond was broken.

In the months after that Caroline's weight caught up fast with Emily's, she absolutely loved the bottle. Her thin limbs filled out and she took on a puffy look – all creases of skin and fat red cheeks – that Frances tried hard to find appealing. It was as if Caroline couldn't grow up fast enough, couldn't wait to get one over on Emily, even at this age. She was the first to crawl, the first to walk, the first to spit her solids into her mother's face. Frances found her a handful.

The twins grew more physically alike as they got older. By the time they were three they'd lost their baby fat, their hair had grown thick and straight, and they sported matching blunt bobs that Frances did herself. She dressed them the same, that's what people did in the seventies, and it became hard to tell them apart.

Only their temperaments gave them away. Emily seemed to have been born happy and placid, able to simply go along with the world and make the best of what came her way. Caroline was strung out. She couldn't stand surprises, hated not getting her own way, went mad at loud noises, but most of all she couldn't bear her mother's easy love for her sister. Still a survivor in those days, Caroline turned to her father for support, but Andrew seemed rather vague and absent in his role as a parent, as if it all was a bit too *vivid* for him, and Caroline was left looking in on the family as though she wasn't really meant to be there. Frances was careful to never show any overt favouritism – the twins always had the same food, same clothes, same kisses at bedtime, but each twin sensed the gargantuan toll this took on their mother, and it left a burden on each of them.

It was a cold wet afternoon on a housing estate in Chester, and the five year old twins were bored. Their mother had gone food shopping and Andrew was meant to be minding them, albeit whilst half-listening to the football on the crackly Roberts radio he'd brought in from his shed. But Andrew had disappeared into the kitchen ages ago, to make another phone call they'd assumed, that's what he usually did when their mother was out, and they'd grown tired of their map puzzle, it was too hard without their father to help them. They lay now at each end of the brown velveteen couch, kicking each other's legs aimlessly, and not entirely painlessly, their matching red tartan dresses riding up their thighs and their knee-length brocade socks scuffing down their shins.

"OWWWW. Daddy!" yelled Caroline. "Emily just kicked me. DAAADDY!"

Andrew poked his head round the kitchen door, stretching the cord of the wall-mounted phone until its kinks were pulled nearly straight.

"I didn't do anything, Daddy," said Emily, truthfully. "We're just playing."

"Stop that Emily," he said mildly, and disappeared back into the kitchen.

Caroline disentangled her legs from her sister's and then launched herself across the length of the sofa and pinched her twin hard on the upper arm. "Yes, you did," she hissed.

"Daddy!" shrieked Emily. Andrew's head appeared again,

and he was cross now. "Just stop it the pair of you," he said. "I'm on the phone," and then he shut the kitchen door.

When Emily realised her father wasn't going to help her she stopped crying and padded across the expanse of neat beige carpet to the doll's house at the far end of the room, by the patio doors. This was Emily's favourite toy, but it was not exclusively hers – like most of her things it had to be shared, and Caroline loved to move all the furniture into the wrong rooms, or even worse take it out altogether for the dog to eat. Caroline followed her over and said coaxingly, "Let's play teddies," and so Emily agreed although she didn't entirely trust her sister's motives, and they'd set up their teddies for a tea party and even played quite nicely for a few minutes. Just as Caroline had tired of their half-game and stalked off to the kitchen to find her father, Emily heard a car pull up in front of the garage that formed the left side of the chalet-style house.

"Mummy!" Emily jumped off the couch and ran down the length of the living room as she heard her mother open the front door.

Caroline was on her way back from the kitchen, where she'd helped herself to a malted milk biscuit from the metal tin in the cupboard next to the cooker. Her father had quickly got off the phone and let her have one, which had surprised her, it was nearly tea time. She'd just bitten the cow's head off, planning to savour each body part, but now she crammed the rest of the biscuit into her mouth, eating urgently. As Caroline came into the hall wiping crumbs off her face she saw her twin hurtling down the lounge towards her, and her first instinct was to move, get out the way.

"Hello Mummy!" called Emily. Frances was putting down her shopping, ready to open her arms to both her daughters. But when Caroline saw Emily's joy and their mother's reciprocity she wanted to shut the scene out, it made her feel cross for some reason. As Frances set the last bag down on the orange shag rug in the middle of the sunlit hall, she looked up and saw Caroline slam the lounge door shut, hard, at precisely the right moment. And then she saw Emily come tearing through the plate glass towards her, and she heard the sound of a bomb going off.

Andrew had chased Caroline around the oval-shaped dining table whilst Frances picked shards of glass out of Emily's face and arms and legs. Miraculously, Emily's cuts were mostly superficial, but Caroline was still sent to her room until tea-time, despite Andrew trying to convince his wife that Caroline hadn't realised what would happen – she was too young, he'd said, she can't possibly have done it deliberately – and that they should let her come downstairs now. But Frances was unrelenting, she'd never been so furious in her life.

Later Andrew hypothesised that it was only Emily's speed at impact that saved her from Jeffrey Johnson's fate, the boy four doors down who'd been left with a livid two inch scar on his cheek from a run-in with his own glass door. There was however one deeper cut on Emily's knee which faded over time but failed to disappear completely, and she was never able to look at it without being reminded of her sister, and of course as she got older it reminded her of all the other things Caroline had done over the years, so the scar was

14

much worse than it looked really. The Browns replaced the door with a wooden one after that, and although the living room was always that much darker, Frances felt happier that way.

3

At Euston the heat is still waiting for me as I step down from the carriage. The train is leaking people out onto the platform and everyone is rushing, busy, knowing where they're going. I stop by a stanchion and remove my handbag from my armpit and shove it into my holdall, I can't risk losing it. My clothes are too hot for the day ahead but I'm not changing now, I have too much to do – I have to buy a new phone, find somewhere to live, start my new life. I'm determined now. I refuse to think about Ben or Charlie, I can't think about them, about how they'll be awake by now, will know I've gone. They have each other, they'll cope, in fact they'll be better off in the long run, I know they will. Yes, I've done the right thing.

I'd tried to research how to find somewhere to live in London, in those final unhinged weeks back in Manchester, back when I was Emily still. I'd made sure I always cleared the history on our computer so Ben wouldn't suspect what I was about to do. Until I get a job I can't afford too much on rent, I don't know how long my money will have to last me, so I'm going to try to find a shared house – the type where eight or nine people (usually Australians I think) live together and turn every room that's not a kitchen or bathroom into a bedroom. There's also less need for ID, for references in those kind of places, I mustn't be traced. I find the local papers in another newsagents, shuffle along another queue, and venture out into the hazy, infected sunshine.

Where do I go now? I'm lost and feel panicky, like I want to turn back the clock and run home to my boy, like this is all a horrible mistake. I look around blankly until eventually I can process the images, can see the big ugly road in front of me, snarled up with traffic, drowning in car fumes. Sweat is breaking out under my right arm and across my shoulder where the strap of the holdall is touching my skin, and the hot smell of myself reminds me that I am really here, I really have done this. I cross over at the lights and walk straight, down a long wide road, across a square, past a distant statue, of Gandhi I think, and I don't know where I'm going and it's taking me forever. Eventually I see a mobile shop on the other side of the street and I'm relieved, like I've succeeded at something. The shop is large and dreary despite the posters and the video screens showing the latest offers – the bright moving images make the shop itself feel more dismal somehow. It's empty apart from two shop assistants who eye me up as I enter, but then studiously ignore me for a couple of minutes although I can tell I'm being watched. The shop sells every network and I haven't got a clue what to go for, it's so confusing. All the phones look the same to me. A young man wearing a black uniform sidles up to me and asks me how I'm doing.

"Fine, thanks," I say.

"Is there anything I can help you with? What are you after

today?" His voice has a musical lilt to it and he has a handsome face with a neat black beard but he doesn't look at me straight and I don't look at him. We both stare at the shelves of phones, which are just dummy ones anyway and half of these are missing, there are just cables with nothing on the ends.

"I'm after a new phone." My voice is timid, unfamiliar to me.

"Certainly, madam. Who are you with at the moment?"

"No-one," I say, and I think *how true.* "I mean, I've lost my old one."

"Who was that with?" the shop assistant persists.

"I can't remember," I say. "I just want a cheap phone on pay as you go," and my tone is sharper than I mean it to be, and I didn't used to be like this. I pick up one of the battered looking dummy phones.

"This one looks OK, how much are calls on this?"

The man is patient and explains that it depends which network I choose, and I realise he must think I'm an idiot, but the truth is I've never bought a phone from scratch before, my mum and dad bought me my first one after college and I've always just upgraded or had work ones since then. The shop assistant makes me go through the rigmarole of saying how many calls and texts I'm going to use, whether I want access to the internet, so he can work out which package is best for me, and I really don't care after what I've been through and I don't understand any of it anyway and I just want to get out of this place and call some house-share ads before it gets too late, before I panic, so I have somewhere to sleep tonight.

"Look, all I want is the cheapest deal, can't you just decide for me," I say, and it comes out wrong. The shop assistant looks hurt.

"Sorry," I say, and to my horror I'm crying. The man puts his arm round me and in his beautiful sing song voice tells me I'll be OK, and through my embarrassment I wonder how I've become such a bitch. He finds me a tissue and then picks out something he says will be perfect for me and even insists on giving me a discount. When I finally leave the shop I have a working new phone, fully topped up and ready to make calls. He was so kind he somehow made me remember there's more going on in the world than my own misery – I must go back and thank him one day.

Out on the street I feel wobbly again – I need somewhere quiet to sit where I can compose myself, where I can make some calls, it's much too noisy here. I take a bus, any bus, from outside Holborn station, and it takes me all the way down Piccadilly and drops me outside Green Park. I only know this because I'm reading the street signs, but I'm pretty sure Green Park is somewhere in the centre, and if I'm in the centre I can head in whichever direction to my new home, it can be wherever.

I walk through the park and am surprised at how quiet it is, once you turn off the main thoroughfares, away from the deck chairs and the tourists. I find a banked area where the grass has been left to grow long and I walk up towards the top and set down my bag in the shade. I kick off my ballet pumps and lie down in the yellow grass and there's absolutely no-one around, just the low rumbling of the traffic outside the park to remind me I'm actually here, in the capital. The sun through the trees feels warm on my face and I shut my eyes and feel almost normal, content even. And then the image that has seared itself into my soul appears suddenly, vividly, and I shrink inside myself for the millionth time and open them again. It's weird that it didn't happen on the train when the grief of leaving was so raw. Just now I was almost feeling happy, from the physical tiredness, the thrill of the privacy, the anonymity, the promise of a new start, here in the middle of this great city. And happiness Catherine, that is *not allowed*.

I call nine or ten places, all over London. They're either already gone ("Oh, you came through Loot, love, that's a bit late, you need to call as soon as it goes online") or there's no reply, or the people don't speak English well and don't seem to know what I'm talking about. I can always get a hotel, but the thought is depressing. To go through with this I need to start *now*, today. In a hotel it would be too easy to dwell on what I've done, what I've lost – too easy to hole up quietly and open my veins. I don't trust myself.

I call the last ad on the list – room in shared house, Finsbury Park, £90 per week. I've no idea where it is. It's more than I wanted to pay. I'm desperate. I think no-one's going to answer and then at the last moment before I hang up someone picks up.

"Finsbury Park Palace," says a laughing voice. I hesitate. "Hello?" she continues, in some kind of Essex accent, or at least that's what I think it is.

"Uh, hello, I'm looking for a room, I saw your ad in Loot."

"Did you? There's no rooms here, babe." Just as I'm about to hang up I hear someone interrupt in the background.

"Hey, hang on," the voice continues. "Oh, it seems someone's moved out today, but it wouldn't be advertised yet. You must be answering the last ad, but that room went ages ago."

"How much is this one?" I persist.

"It's the size of a cupboard I warn you, and Fidel was a pig. £80 and it's yours – saves us advertising for it, and you sound more normal than the usual nutters who ring."

"It sounds fine," I say. "I can be there by six," and she gives me the address and I hang up.

I haven't eaten anything all day. Hunger forms like a fist in my gut and I leave the park in search of something, anything to eat. I'm not sure which direction to head in, I've lost my bearings, so guess and go right, as that's the way most people seem to be going. I pass a kiosk and buy a bag of crisps and a Coke, that's all they have and my dithering annoys the man, he must think I'm a tourist instead of a runaway. I stand in the street and eat and drink with my holdall gripped between my feet, I'm so scared of losing it. Then I make my way, with everyone else, down the tiled steps into the tube station, which is fortunately right there, right where I need it, towards my new home.

The area feels rough and the house is a total dump. I'm not at all keen to go in and I question just what I'm doing here. (*Have I gone properly mad at last?* I wonder how it's taken so long.) I have no idea what awaits me within but the outside is inauspicious – an untidy overgrown hedge, piled-up crates of empty beer and wine bottles next to three pungent over-filled wheelie bins in the garden, huge-patterned curtains hanging crookedly at the aluminium windows, chipped and dirty painted brickwork, a plastic porch. I think of our beautiful Chorlton cottage with its Chapel Green front door and geranium-filled window boxes, the scent of lavender, the trendy laid-back vibe of the neighbourhood. I realise I have little choice if I want somewhere to sleep tonight – I'm here now, it's getting late – so I take a breath, straighten my shoulders under the weight of my bag and walk up the path.

A surly black girl answers the door. "Yes?" she says.

"Hi, I've come about the room," I say.

"What room? There's no rooms here."

"Oh. I spoke to…" I realise I didn't get Essex Girl's name. I try again.

"I spoke to a girl on the phone this afternoon, she said someone had moved out, that a room had come up…"

"Nah, you must have the wrong house, sorry." She goes to close the door.

"Please," I say. "It was, er, Castro's room I think, apparently he moved out today. Is there anyone else I can talk to who might know?"

The girl begins to look annoyed. "There's no-one here called Castro. I've told you, you've got the wrong house." She shuts the door in my face.

As I turn away humiliated hot tears are seeping down my face. I stagger under the weight of my bag and put it down on the pavement in front of the hedge, where no-one from the house can see me. I feel like I'm going to pass out, from the heat and the hunger and the homelessness, from yet another loss. I sit on my bag and put my head between my legs, waiting for the swimming to pass, wanting to go home, wanting my husband. I hear the front door open and a girl is running down the path, calling for somebody called Catherine. I keep my head down, unresponsive, and then there's someone standing above me, so finally I look up. I look into the face of an angel and she says, "Are you here for Fidel's room? Oh babe, don't cry, she's a miserable cow sometimes, just ignore her. Come on in, I'll fix you a drink, it looks like you need it." And that's how I meet Angel, my angel, my salvation.

4

Emily met Ben on a parachute course, of all things. She hardly noticed him at first, he seemed so quiet, and when they were put in the same car for the trip to the tiny airport they didn't talk much. The other passenger was Jeremy, a tall thin pierced boy who seemed way too anxious and uncoordinated to throw himself out of a plane safely, and as they made the hour-long journey she kept wondering how she'd got herself into this situation. Her friend Dave had persuaded her, and it was meant to be for charity, but still, now that it came to it jumping out of a plane seemed like a crazy thing to do. And why was she crammed in the back of Dave's bashed-up old car with long folded-up Jeremy? Shouldn't he be in the front where there was much more leg room? It occurred to her then that perhaps Ben was embarrassed of her, maybe that was why he'd insisted on sitting in the passenger seat – and then she told herself not to be silly, no-one was ever interested in her, although the truth was actually the opposite. When she noticed an ugly red boil on Ben's neck, just below his hairline, she felt sorry for him – he kept shifting his jacket to try to cover it up, but he wouldn't just go for it and put the lapel up, it would be too obvious. She knew he could feel her staring at it, so she tried not to look, but somehow it was distracting her from the thought of what she was meant to be doing soon, and the more she tried to ignore it the more she felt her eyes drawn back to it, or maybe back to him, she realised afterwards. She shivered although the car was fumey-hot, there was something wrong with the heating. She wasn't feeling herself at all.

The airport was hidden down country lanes behind tall hedgerows amongst green and yellow fields. As they drove through the entrance the little planes looked cow-like, herded together as if for company. There were corrugated-roofed sheds laid out on three sides of a rectangle – one for packing the parachutes, one for keeping the planes at night and one that housed a recreation area for the hours and hours parachutists seemed to spend waiting for the cloud to lift. Emily was too nervous now to even think about playing games and instead she excused herself and sat in the corner with a mug of stewed tea and her book – thank God she'd thought to bring one with her, sometimes reading was the only thing that could distract her. Her friend Dave came over and sat with her and tried to cheer her up with a succession of terrible jokes ("What's the fastest cake in the world? Scone. What do you call a fish with no eyes? Fsh," etcetera) but although she tried to laugh she almost blamed him for getting her into this and so he took the hint and left her to it. She sat quietly, feeling trapped and lonely while the other would-be parachutists played pool or scrabble and seemed to enjoy the boredom. She may even have made her excuses and left if she'd been in her own car, but she was stranded in the middle of a field somewhere in the Cheshire countryside, she could hardly walk home, and anyway she had collected so much money for charity she really had to go through with it now, she couldn't let everyone down. She gripped her book tighter and tried to concentrate on the story, tried not to think, but her mind was catapulting – this wasn't a practice, she wouldn't be jumping off a platform in a sports hall this time, she'd be leaping out into air, and it all felt too real now she'd seen the planes.

"Hey Emily, d'you want to play pool?" She looked up to see Dave looking eagerly at her, his stubble over-long like cut up spider legs, his hair greasy, his ever-present leather jacket open over a black heavy metal T-shirt.

"No thanks, I'm OK, honestly Dave," she said, but he looked unconvinced. "Don't worry about me, I'm at a good bit in my book."

"Go on, you can't just sit there all day, it'll be a ball, ha ha. You and me against Jeremy and Ben."

Emily paused and looked across to the pool table, which was wonky and threadbare, in time to see Ben pot an impossible looking red, but he barely reacted, just moved around to the other side to take his next shot.

"I'm rubbish at pool, I'll let you down."

"No, you're fine," said Dave. "Come on," and he grabbed Emily's hand and pulled her out of her seat. Ben glanced up from his next shot as they came across to the table, before looking down quickly. Maybe he did like her, she thought again, but immediately told herself she was imagining it – and anyway she wouldn't really be interested, she tended to steer clear of relationships, she left that kind of thing to her sister.

Once Ben had finished thrashing Jeremy, who was so tall

he had to bend his knees to take his shots, they started their doubles game. When it was Emily's turn she leaned over and aimed for a ball down the other end of the table, but she scuffed her shot and the white ball skewed lazily off-course, just missing the yellow she'd gone for.

"Sorry, Dave," she said, but he just grinned and she handed the cue to Ben. For a split second they were both holding it, and it felt peculiarly intimate, so she let go quickly as he muttered thanks and looked away. He aimed at the easiest-looking red, but although he'd been potting everything before, he misjudged it and it bounced lamely out of the pocket.

"Damn," he said, blushing a little, and went to hand the cue to Dave.

"Two shots," Dave reminded him, so Ben went again and although this shot was even easier he missed it too. Dave took the cue and went on a massive potting spree, showing off, and as Jeremy was useless anyway and Ben seemed to have gone completely off the boil, when it came to Emily's turn all she needed to do was pot the black to win. She felt odd still and wasn't sure what it was – fear of the jump itself, embarrassment about Ben's apparent nerves around her – but she took aim and although it was tricky and she got the angle wrong, the table's crazy slant sent the ball dribbling inexorably into the far end corner.

"Whoops, sorry," she said.

"Yes!" shouted Dave and he went to hug her but decided at the last minute to high-five her instead, and Jeremy said well done and Ben smiled and looked sheepish, and then he wandered off to the canteen.

As the day wore on the cloud hung stubbornly, and the temperature dropped as if it would rain. Emily had retreated back to her corner with her book and yet another cup of tea, while Ben and Jeremy spent ages playing chess and Dave got whipped at table tennis by Jemima, a little ball of a girl who'd done over 300 jumps apparently. When Emily looked at her watch for the umpteenth time and saw it was gone four she put down the book and for the first time felt a glimmer of hope – maybe it was getting too late for them to jump now, it would be getting dark soon. Where was Dave – she'd go and ask him if they could think about leaving, surely there wasn't any point hanging round for much longer. Just as she stood up, feeling better at last, the head instructor appeared at the shed doorway and he was pumped up, as if they were at the Somme and he was about to send them over the top. "Cloud's lifted," he shouted. "Get kitted up *now*, quick!" As everyone ran like excited children Emily dragged behind, her legs feeling loose, as if they weren't quite attached to her body. Ben was already there, seemingly in charge, and he was more confident now, less shy and geeky, almost handsome in his black jumpsuit. He helped her into her harness, turned her round and hoisted the parachute onto her back.

"Bend over," he said. He tightened the straps at the top of her legs and as she stood up, somewhere in that 90 degree trajectory, she fell in love.

Emily didn't see Ben for another three months after that. She'd flung herself out of a plane with the memory of his fingers on her thighs, and she'd been shy, embarrassed afterwards. He was so unsuitable really, a chess-playing parachuting accountant, and she shuddered at what her sister Caroline would make of him. In the car on the way home, she'd gazed at his boil lovingly now, willing to lean forward and kiss it, convinced he could feel her lips hot on his neck in his mind. But when they reached Chester he didn't even look at her, simply said bye over his shoulder, and she got out the car and stood on the pavement, hesitant, until Dave revved the engine impatiently, and reluctantly she shut the door. As the car drove off, black smoke spewing, she stood watching the clouds dissipate, looking down the now empty road for long stretched out seconds, before she shook her head with frustration and turned away.

Emily assumed she'd bump into Ben at work, but so far she hadn't – nearly 3,000 people worked in the building, she'd discovered. She even considered another parachuting weekend, but held off (please God no), confident each Monday morning that *this* week she'd see him. His apparent disappearance made her more infatuated, more determined – which was quite unlike her – but then she'd never been smitten before. She even found she grew to enjoy the waiting – she'd wake up in anticipation, relish the daily thrill of scouring the basement canteen for his curly dark head, glance around reception on her way in and out, nerves on high alert, every day offering up countless possibilities for them to meet, every day thwarted.

Emily awoke late on a dark February morning where the rain was so heavy deep puddles gleamed orange from the street lamps. Either her alarm hadn't gone off, or she'd slept through it, she wasn't sure which, she was so hungover. Her head was killing her, but she had to go in – she had an important meeting that afternoon, and besides it was Friday, only one more day to get through before the weekend. She made herself a strong tea, ate a banana and took some pills, then stood for 15 minutes under the shower and although by the time she came out she felt marginally better, she was running horrendously late now. She threw on the easiest outfit, a plain red belted dress and boots, scraped her wet hair back and didn't bother with makeup, she could do that when she got to the office. She put on the orange anorak she usually wore for walking and it looked terrible with the dress, it was too short and the wrong colour, but she didn't care, it was raining for God's sake.

By the time she parked her car an hour later she was still feeling wretched. She didn't feel ready to face work, let alone face Ben walking towards her, away from the office, takeaway coffee in hand, girl in tow. This was not one of her many scenarios of how they might meet. She panicked, blushed, said hi and hurried off. He was more attractive than she remembered – his hair had grown, his suit was well-cut, shoes polished, dark brown wool tie not quite that of a newly qualified accountant. He hadn't seemed particularly pleased to see her – friendly but unmoved. The girl was not his girlfriend, she knew that much – not his type, not her! She'd convinced herself that once they did finally see each other again, it would all just happen – they'd stop, have a chat, arrange a coffee, and that would be it. Instead she'd looked about as awful as she possibly could have, and he'd been with someone else. It was a shambles.

For three months Emily had been fine, but now she wasn't – she just couldn't wait any longer. She threw off her revolting anorak, flung it on the back of her chair, sat down and considered her options. Visit the 17th floor expressly to see him – wander about until she found his desk, ask to talk to him privately, trawl around for an empty room, all eyes on them? Hideous. Pretend she had other business on the 17th floor, saunter up and say hello as she passed? Too contrived – and as she didn't know where he sat she could hardly saunter. Look up his number and call him? Better, less public. Or send him an email? The easiest but in a way the most tortuous – what if he didn't reply? What if he didn't get it? She needed to start this right now, today.

She looked up his email address in the directory. "Hi Ben," she wrote. "Good to see you today. Will you have a drink with me tonight? It's important. Let me know, either reply to this mail or here's my number. Thanks, Emily."

She hit send and sat back in her chair, relieved. She'd done it, it was happening at last. She felt absolute resolve that she'd done the right thing, after all it was obvious he'd liked her. She checked her schedule – nothing apart from the meeting after lunch that she'd come in for, he'd have called her by then.

By five o'clock Emily was desolate. She'd been so convinced there'd be an email waiting for her back at her desk that when there wasn't the doubt flooded in. What the *hell* had she been thinking, being so forward? She re-read her email: "It's important." OK, could be, maybe she needed to talk to him. About what? About parachuting of course. "Have a drink?" The connotation was unmistakable. My God, he'd think she was a maniac, a stalker. And anyway he had a girlfriend, she'd seen them together – and even if he was single she'd looked so utterly crap that morning he couldn't possibly have fancied her.

"EMILY?" Maria, who sat next to her, leaned over and made exaggerated crosses with her hands across Emily's face. Emily looked up, stricken. "Are you deaf? Can I borrow your stapler, someone's had mine. Hey, what's up?"

"Nothing, I've got a headache."

"You look like shit, why don't you go home?" Maria said.

"I've just got to finish this report, then I'm out of here. Here you go." Emily handed over the stapler and turned away, her eyes filling, tears dropping onto her keyboard. She checked her email one more time – nothing – and then pressed the computer's off key without bothering to log out. "Bye," she said to Maria, as she stood up and hurried to the lift.

At home Emily couldn't settle. She checked her phone constantly, as though the call could have crept up on her while she wasn't looking, despite it being in her pocket, despite her having changed the settings so it would ring and vibrate at the same time. Maybe he'd emailed her, she thought, if only she could check emails at home. But he'd call now instead, wouldn't he, she'd given him her number. *Why hasn't he called?* She felt nauseous in that over-hungry, post-hangover way, but she couldn't motivate herself to even make a sandwich. She looked in the fridge and found some cheddar, cracked with age, and some stale breadsticks in the cupboard, and she ate purely to take the edge off her hunger. She flicked through the TV channels, picked an old episode of The Simpsons she'd seen before, but she found she couldn't follow the plot. Her mother rang – the thrill of the phone going and the disappointment of it not being Ben meant she couldn't face picking up. She ran a bath, but lying there made her hot with shame. In the end she went to bed and finally found some solace, after ten o'clock, when she knew that he really wasn't going to call tonight so she might as well stop thinking about it, and she fell exhaustedly into the seventeenth century underworld of her latest book.

The buzzing and the ringing woke her. She grappled for the phone, on the table next to her bed – 11.28. "Hello," she said.

"Emily? It's Ben. Hello? Er, it's Ben – from parachuting. I'm so sorry to call so late, I've been on a course all day and then I was out at the pub and then for some reason I logged on when I got home and saw your mail."

"Oh," Emily said.

"What's important?" Ben persisted, and she thought he sounded a bit drunk.

"Oh, it doesn't matter now."

"D'you still want to have a drink tonight?"

"It's 11.30," Emily said. "It's too late. There's nowhere open."

"I could come over. Are you still in Chester?"

"Yes," she said. "Where are you?"

"Trafford. What's your address?"

"That's miles away. It would take you hours."

"I'll get a cab. I could be there in an hour..."

Emily was silent.

"If you'd like me to?"

Emily still hesitated. It was more than she could have hoped for, but now she was ambivalent. It was so late. She hardly knew him. What was she getting into?

"Yes please," she said, in the end.

"I'll see you soon," he replied, and the tenderness in his voice reassured her.

An hour and seven minutes later the buzzer rang. Emily had put on jeans and a slouchy jumper and piled her hair on top of her head. She was bare-foot and wary-looking when she opened the door. He was still in the same dark suit, his brown tie loosened. He smiled and moved past her, as far away as he could get in the cramped hallway and he smelled of beer and damp, it was still raining outside. They went into the kitchen, where the strip light was unflattering, made them both look pale, exposed.

"Sorry, after all that I've got nothing to drink," she said, and her voice was high-pitched, unnatural. "Would you like a coffee? Or I can make you Horlicks?" And she tried to laugh, but it wasn't much of a joke.

Ben said yes, coffee would be great, and then said nothing more as she made it, and she couldn't think of anything to say either. She slopped the kettle and swore gently as the water scalded her, but she continued pouring and stirring anyway. She took the milk from the fridge, offered him sugar and led him into the sitting room. She put the coffee on the table that she'd hurriedly cleared of the papers and books and crap that normally lived there and sat down on the sofa. Ben sat in the only other chair in the room. The distance ached between

34

them. She stood up again and put on some music – Radiohead. The notes sounded mournfully, expanding into the space. How could it be that she'd sent him a note effectively asking him to be her boyfriend, and he'd been so keen he'd rung her in the middle of the night and now he was here in her flat and they didn't know what to do, how to take it forward? Conversation eluded them – Ben was shy and Emily was teetering on the very edge of the next stage of her life. She literally didn't know what to do, how to take that step.

The body dropped like a stone under her. It fell maybe fifteen feet before wrenching violently to a halt, bouncing, then hanging from its ankles. The body writhed and wriggled, its long legs trying to untangle themselves from the ropes that bound them. She looked down, horrified. The shock completely overwhelmed the adrenaline that had been pumping through her and she was now rigid with terror. With a snap the body came free and it turned 180 degrees in the air, the bright red and yellow finally revealing itself, as Jeremy continued downwards away from the plane, slightly more gently now, a little more how she'd imagined it. She looked into the eyes of the instructor and understood now what the training had been about, why she'd been told to sit right at the very edge of the door, half in, half out. "Are you OK?" shouted Greg above the roar of the engine. Emily shook her head. She wished she'd jumped first, so she hadn't had to witness it from above, because now she couldn't do it. Greg smiled at her kindly, squeezed her arm, then shoved her hard into the void.

"What are you thinking about?" said Ben.

Emily remembered then where she was, here in her hastily tidied sitting room with this geeky parachuting accountant, how parachuting had caused all this trouble in the first place.

"I was wondering how you can bear to fling yourself out of a plane the second time, once you know what it's like."

"You just had a bad experience," said Ben. "Jeremy is 6'3" with zero coordination, he wasn't your best role model. He's not really cut out for parachuting."

"It wasn't just him that terrified me though," she said. "It was worse being pushed out of the plane – I can't believe the instructor did that, it's cruel," and even as she remembered it, from the safety of her living room, it reminded her of something long forgotten, made her feel unnerved, distressed all over again.

"He had to do that," said Ben. "Otherwise you'd have missed the landing area. It was actually perfectly safe."

"It really didn't feel it. I don't feel safe now."

"What do you mean?" Ben said, and he seemed alarmed, as if he'd made a mistake to come here so late after all.

"I don't mean like that." She hesitated for long slow seconds, took a gulp and paused again, and then she surprised herself as she looked straight at him and said it.

"I just mean I don't know how I'm ever going to go back to a place where I'm not totally crazy about you."

Ben smiled. "I was hoping you'd say something like that," he said, and he got up from the silver wicker chair that Emily had found in a junk shop and sprayed herself. She stood too and moved slowly around the glass coffee table towards him. They stood three feet apart just looking at each other,

36

still anxious, their bodies aching, and then – who moved first they never could work out – they were holding each other very tightly, and they stayed like that for a very long time.

5

I sit in the kitchen of Finsbury Park Palace, with its country style oak cupboard doors and marble-effect formica worktops, and I have a vodka tonic in front of me and I swear I've never had that drink before. Although the floor is gritty under the soles of my ballet pumps, the kitchen is cleaner than I'd imagined it would be, from the outside, but the sweet stench of bins is making me want to retch. *How much rubbish does this house produce,* I wonder pointlessly, thinking of the overflowing dustbins in the front garden. Angel sits across from me, too pretty and sparkling for these surroundings, and her fringed waistcoat over skinny jeans makes me feel dowdy and old. A thin swarthy boy with lank longish hair is cutting odd-looking vegetables next to the sink, his name's Fabio I think Angel said, but he keeps his head down and doesn't take part in our conversation. The surly girl from earlier is nowhere to be seen, and Angel says no-one else is back from work yet.

"You feeling better now, babe?" says Angel, taking a long sip from her drink.

"Yes, thanks so much for helping me."

"Don't worry, it was nothing," she says, and smiles her angelic smile. "Where are you from anyway?"

"I'm from near Chester, originally, but I've been living in Manchester most recently," I say. "I just split up from my boyfriend and felt like I needed a change of scene. I've lived round the Manchester area my whole life and so thought I should give London a go, before I'm too old." I giggle nervously.

I've rehearsed all this, have my back story sorted, close enough to the truth to feel authentic. I spit it out all in one go, before I've been asked, and it sounds fake, apologetic.

"Too old! You're never too old for London," laughs Angel. "You might be too old for sharing a crappy house with a bunch of lunatics though – you look far too posh for this place."

"No, no it's fine," I say. "I just can't afford too much rent until I get myself sorted, plus I thought it would be a good way to meet new people."

"I wouldn't go that far, babe. The people who live here you'd normally cross the road to avoid. Don't worry about him," she continues, nodding towards Fabio's bent head as I look over, embarrassed. "He doesn't speak English." Angel scrabbles in her bag. "Want a ciggie, babe?"

"No thanks. I don't smoke."

"You mind if I have one?"

I nod no, of course not, although the heat and the bins and the hunger and the vodka are making me feel increasingly nauseous. I realise I left the Chorlton cottage 14 hours ago and I've barely eaten. My jeans feel sticky and my feet hurt and I desperately want to lie down, but I don't want to be rude. I take a gulp of my drink.

"I love your name," I say pointlessly, trying to keep the conversation going. I find I'm still polite like that, now that I'm Catherine.

Angel laughs. "All I did was drop the 'a' babe, it's amazing what it's done for my image."

A thought enters my head. I feel silly but there's something about her that makes it OK to ask. "Angel, would you mind calling me Cat? I'm just totally stealing your idea, but I've always hated the name Catherine."

"Whatever babe," smiles Angel, and my name changes for the second time today.

6

When Ben woke early and Emily wasn't there beside him, he assumed she'd had another of her sleepless nights, and would be found downstairs on the couch, reading. She seemed to be re-reading all the old classics lately, Ben had noticed, absolutely ripping through them, and he wondered whether it was a way for her to escape out of herself, into a world so familiar (whether it be the American South or Hardy's Wessex or the Yorkshire moors) that she didn't need to think about her life, here, now. There were many different ways to block pain, Ben realised, and he felt it was best to leave Emily to it for now, to be there quietly in the background, helping take care of Charlie, until she was ready to come back to them both.

Ben shifted onto his side and managed to find his way into sleep again, a fidgety, disturbed, damp slumber under the heat of the winter duvet they hadn't yet swapped for the summer one, even though it was late July. That used to be Emily's job, and she was normally vigilant in her timing, providing a soft cashmere throw at the foot of the bed for those in between days when the lighter duvet was not quite protection enough from the cold. It was these small slippages that seemed to add to their pain – to the feeling that nothing was quite right nor ever would be again. The lack of clean shirts, the running out of breakfast cereals, butter, bleach, bread, the unopened post, the weeds in the window boxes. All these things Emily had taken care of, *before*, not because Ben was lazy or she was in any way a martyr, she just always had been the organised one, and Ben had been such a fantastic cook and tidier-upper they had each been happy with the arrangement. Now Emily did nothing, not that he blamed her, of course.

It was only when the alarm went that Ben stirred from these semi-conscious thoughts. He kicked his sweaty legs out from the duvet and lay sprawled there a moment, wondering what to say to his wife when he went downstairs. He decided to have a shower first, he felt so revolting, and then he'd go and get Charlie, and they'd go and say hi to her together. It still gave him a thrill of excitement, the thought of seeing her, despite all this time and all that had happened. He'd make her a cup of tea, and try to get her to eat some toast with heaps of butter and a smear of marmalade, the way she liked it, and then he would kiss her and Charlie goodbye and set off on his four mile cycle to the office. Life must go on, Ben told himself, although he sometimes worried that Emily didn't agree.

The shower was fierce and Ben had it at maximum temperature despite the weather, it was so hot already outside. He found that standing under the searing stream with his face turned into it helped him forget, for a second or two at a time, as if his brain was being cauterised. Emily never commented on his lengthy showers any more, even though she used to be so conscious about stuff like that. She seemed oblivious to what Ben did these days, as if she'd lost interest in even him now. Ben wondered whether they'd ever get back what they'd had between them, one day far in the future.

It first occurred to Ben that his wife was gone when he opened the stripped oak door to the living room and she wasn't there. He didn't need to check the kitchen or the downstairs cloakroom, he could feel the screaming emptiness throughout the house. He didn't know what to do next – call 999, wail, throw himself out the window? He went back up to their bedroom and opened the packed wardrobe. It looked much the same as usual. Maybe she's just gone for a walk, it's a lovely day, he thought. He decided to give Charlie his breakfast and then make himself a proper cappuccino, he could always ring the office and say he was running late, and by then Emily would be back, surely.

When Ben had finished his coffee and Emily was still not home he went back upstairs and knelt on the soft cream rug to look under their bed. Charlie trailed after him, crying now, but Ben ignored him. Good, the big suitcase was still there. He pulled it out and opened it up. The leather holdall they'd bought in Marrakech was gone from inside, where they usually kept it. It must be under there somewhere, Ben told himself, and he lay down flat and wriggled underneath the frame and pulled stuff out, frantically now – a blow up mattress, a small pull-along suitcase, a child's tent, a proper hiking backpack, a bag of jumble, a long-missing sock. Dust rose and hung suspended in the low shafts of sunlight. When there was nothing left to extract Ben lay quite still on the floor and let out a single defeated sob, and then he sat up and rocked poor Charlie in his arms.

★   ★   ★

43

PC Bob Garrison looked sympathetically at Mr Ben Coleman across the desk in the small windowless interview room. It was a sad case, he knew that much, and now he had to break it to the lad that they couldn't do a great deal to try to find his wife. High risk mispers don't clean out their bank account, pack a bag full of clothes and take their passport with them. Poor sod's got to face up to the fact that she's just left 'im, PC Garrison thought, but somehow, even though he'd dealt with cases like these a thousand times before, he found it harder to sit opposite this desperate man in his fancy suit and break it to him that, apart from log his wife as a missing person, there wasn't much else he could do.

7

Angel orders us a pizza and although it's revolting I devour it and it takes the nausea away. I know she can tell there's something very wrong with me, but despite her open manner she's too polite to ask, and I don't elaborate on the story about splitting up with my boyfriend, in case I'm tempted to venture anywhere near the truth.

Instead, Angel starts to tell me, poignantly, funnily, about herself, and in the past I would have been shocked that someone's life can be full of so much drama, but now I'm not, because so is mine. I can't believe that on the very same day that Mrs Emily Coleman left her home in Chorlton, Manchester, the day she left Ben and Charlie, she is sitting here, called Cat Brown now, in her new home with her new friend Angel drinking vodka and eating pizza, in Finsbury Park, which is somewhere in North London. And no-one knows how to find her. No-one knows how to find *me*. I realise I'm fortunate, at least in this respect: that although my given name is Catherine Emily Brown, for the last five years I've been known as Emily Coleman, my married name. The fact that I never got round to changing my passport is now very convenient in terms of getting a job, opening a bank account, living my life in my new persona. And Brown is such a common name there must be hundreds of other Catherine Browns. I'm safely gone.

As Angel and I chat various people get home (from work?) and come in and out of the kitchen paying me varying amounts of attention. First there's Bev, who I find out later is a roadie from Barnsley, with dreadlocks and a fierce under-bite who walks in, waves hi super-cheerfully, as though I've always been there, says, "Fucking hot, isn't it," goes to the fridge, rummages around for ages and then in an instant her good mood deserts her and she lets out an anguished roar, like a lioness with a missing cub.

"Where's my chocolate?" yells Bev. "Who the fuck has eaten my chocolate? Angel, have you eaten my fucking chocolate?"

"Hey cool down Bev, it wasn't me this time, I promise. Ask him," Angel says, as a very tall, unwieldy-looking man in dark blue jeans and an Abercrombie sweat-top slouches in. He's so big all over that his trainers are massive, like paddles, but his legs are too short for his body and with his sweet boyish face he reminds me of an over-grown toddler, and I almost want to hug him.

"Nah, wasn't me Bev, though you need to get a life," says Brad, with an Australian accent and an affectionate smile. But Bev is not in the mood to be placated. Instead she stops shouting and sits at the kitchen table and starts to rock to and fro, as though she's mad. "I've had enough of this fucking house. That was my chocolate," she says, pitifully now. "My fucking chocolate." The swear word is almost a caress, a

46

seduction, and I mourn Bev her lost chocolate and I don't know what to say, she seems so sad. I feel like I'm witnessing a bereavement.

Angel stands up and goes over to the iPod to put some music on, loud, I don't know who it's by but it repeats over and over, "Where's your head at?" which I feel is a bit taunting, but Bev doesn't seem to mind, the anger has passed now. Someone I can only assume is Brad's girlfriend bounces in. She's tiny, in a mauve patterned mini-dress, with a perfect little body and a plain face, like she got mismatched in the doll factory. She stops at Brad's side and looks at me suspiciously. "This is Cat, Erica, she's moved into Fidel's room," says Angel in her friendly easy way, but Erica just looks at me with undisguised hostility.

"Who gave her the room? We didn't even advertise it yet." Her voice is as ugly as her face, a brutal Antipodean twang that twinges my over-strung nerves.

"Yeah, well Cat was desperate, weren't you babe, and it saves us the hassle," says Angel implacably. I love Angel. She is kind and speechlessly pretty and gets away with everything. I wonder what she's doing living here. (*She should be a superstar*, I think, but this is before her fourth vodka and the tales about her crap upbringing with her feckless mother and various "uncles.")

"Well, does Chanelle know?" asks Erica and I wonder who she's talking about, until I remember the unfriendly black girl who answered the door to me three vodkas ago. I realise I haven't seen her since.

"Yeah babe, she knows. It's all cool."

Erica looks deeply pissed off and nudges Brad out of the

kitchen, as though his trip to the sweetie shop is up and it's time for him to go home for his nap. Angel snorts. I giggle. I don't know what it is – the vodka, the new beginning or these wildly eccentric characters, but I'm almost beginning to enjoy myself, for the first time in months. It's insane. I feel a searing of guilt, and remind myself not to look back, I'm doing the best thing for all of us, in the long run. And I have no other choice now.

The swarthy boy from earlier is back, at the stove this time, cooking his vegetables and he quite impressively manages to make the kitchen smell worse than it did with just the bins. A second boy appears from outside, bike helmet under his arm, yellow lycra body suit hot with sweat, and kisses swarthy boy number one. They say something to each other – in Portuguese I think – and ignore me completely. Angel smiles and pours us another drink.

I feel like I've known Angel forever. I think we've come into each other's lives at just the right time, we have a connection of sadness, and even though I can't tell her my story she doesn't mind, she somehow understands.

Angel works as a croupier in a West End casino and I don't know whether that's terribly glamorous or terribly seedy, I've never met anyone with that kind of job before. She's lived in this shambolic shared house for three months, she tells me in between kitchen interruptions, after her boyfriend beat her up and threatened to kill her and she had to find somewhere to hide. Before that she lived with him at Tower Bridge, and I've heard of there, it's on the river obviously, so I assume it must be posh. It was her friend Jerome who helped her move into this house, where her boyfriend wouldn't find her, just until she got herself sorted.

Jerome is a bouncer who technically occupies the final room, though it seems he's at his girlfriend's in Enfield most of the time. Chanelle is his cousin and she owns the house – she bought it off her parents and according to Angel is proving to be a right little entrepreneur, having turned every room except the kitchen into a bedroom, and what she says goes. Only Angel can get round her, and Angel says that although Chanelle can be a miserable bitch she's not a bad person, she's all right once you get to know her. I feel unsure and hope I don't see Chanelle again today. I'm feeling woozy from the vodka, exhausted suddenly, and I tell Angel I really have to go to bed. It's half past nine, just getting dark, but the heat is still thick and sickly-smelling.

"Babe, remember I warned you not to expect too much," Angel says as we go upstairs. The stair carpet is swirly, my head is swirly, the room is horrific. The mattress is foul, the walls are wood chip, painted in peach-coloured egg shell so they gleam in the dim in-between light. There is one empty beige and brown formica wardrobe. The room stinks of old take-away cartons and something unidentifiable, and the carpet is thick with dust and God knows what else. My good humour fades and I feel overwhelmed, desolate, like this is all wrong, I'm in the wrong place, again. I realise I have no bedding. I can't sleep on that mattress, I'm certain of that, but the floor looks almost as bad. *How has my whole life distilled into being right here, right now? How did it go so totally awry?*

Angel sees my face. "Look, babe, I hope you don't think

I'm being too forward, but I'm off to work later and I won't be back 'til the morning. Why don't you just use my bed for tonight? It's OK, I changed the sheets today." And she ushers me out the door and into a room along the landing that's messy but clean enough and has a duvet with embroidered daisies on it. I give her a hug and thank her over and over and barely wait for her to leave, I just throw off my jeans and sweat-soaked top and fall into her bed, my handbag full of money lodged safe between the mattress and the wall.

The next morning I wake early and don't know where I am. I rewind the events of the evening before and remember the vodkas, the cooking smells, the bins... the hovel which is my room. I remember that I'm not in that room, thank God, I'm in Angel's. That's right, my own room is uninhabitable. I haul myself out of bed, throw on my clothes from yesterday and go to take another look next door. In the sunlight the room is even more unpleasant than it was last night, if that could be possible, and although I try not to I think briefly of my lovely home in Chorlton, where I lived until yesterday. I decide I have to do something or I really will go certifiably mad. I go downstairs to make a cup of tea – there'll probably be no-one in the kitchen at this time, I can hopefully just steal someone's tea bags and milk for now, I'm that desperate. The red plastic kettle is disgusting – furred up on the inside and with grime so thick on the outside you could push your fingernail through to write your name. All the mugs are stained, most are chipped. I fish around in the cupboards above the sink and find a box of teabags. Just as I'm pouring the boiling water into the best mug I could find Chanelle, the girl who owns the house, comes into the room. She's wearing a short yellow towelling robe that looks threadbare and shows off her long thin marathon runner's legs.

"Oh," she says. "It's you."

This is awkward, I haven't seen her since she shut the door in my face yesterday. I feel like a burglar.

"Hi," I say limply. "Thanks for letting me take the room after all."

"Thank Angel," Chanelle humphs. "She fought your corner. I see she's doing her Good Samaritan gig again, must make her feel better."

I don't know what to say to this, so I just smile politely and squash my stolen teabag sheepishly against the side of the mug and pull it out and rest it on top of the overflowing bin.

"That room is a bit of a mess," continues Chanelle, a bit less hostile now. "Fidel left it in a right state. I was going to sort it out before someone else moved in."

"I don't mind doing it," I say eagerly. "I love doing that kind of thing. I need to get some bedding and stuff anyway, so I could pick up a few other things, and I'd pay of course. Is there an Ikea or something near here?"

Chanelle seems to like the turn the conversation is taking, and she's almost friendly now. She gives me detailed instructions on how to get to somewhere called Edmonton and even lends me some of her milk, which she'd brought down from the fridge she has in her own room. I consider myself blessed.

★　　★　　★

Ikea is just opening when I arrive and as it's a Tuesday morning it's virtually dead. I feel minuscule and alone as I head up the travelator into the vast blue building, pick up a big yellow shopping bag and head off on my retail adventure, following the arrows, Dorothy-like, past bright space-optimised kitchens, through ingenious storage solutions, skirting cosy inviting sitting rooms, and I'm doing OK, feeling almost normal, like I'm just another shopper – until I turn the next bend in the magical path and find myself suddenly, without warning, in the children's section. Car-shaped beds and dragon toy chests and pastel-hued wardrobes mock me from every angle, storage boxes full of cuddly toys are stacked high all around me. A little girl is toddling about, holding a monkey, grinning at her mother who's telling her to put it down. An image of my boy explodes into my mind, and the pain in my chest reminds me that I am still alive after all, not stuck in a primary coloured dream, and I continue along the path, fully running now, head down, and I don't look up until I've reached the end. I lean facing the wall next to the lifts panting, and yearn in this moment to give up, not be here, melt into nothingness.

It's all too much.

It seems I can only run away from myself if I keep tighter control, keep every aspect of my previous existence in the past, become immune to children. I stand up straight and square my shoulders and try to breathe deeply. Fortunately no-one has witnessed my panic attack this time, but I must be more careful, I can't keep acting like a maniac. The cafe's in front of me and despite the thumping in my heart I find that I'm hungry, so I load up my tray with a full English breakfast, a banana, an apple, a yogurt, some kind of Swedish pastry, a carton of orange juice, a mug of tea, and I sit alone amongst the stretch of tables overlooking the car park and devour the whole lot, every last bite. The concentration of eating helps me cope somehow, helps put things back in the past. When I return to the store it's busier than before: there are plenty of little children around now, but this time I'm ready. I study the map and head straight to the beds section, ignoring the arrowed path, cutting my own swathe through the sofas, short-cutting behind the mirrors, blanking out everyone. I pick out a cheap white single bed, too solid and stylish for the money, and I write down the code on my pad. I choose a mattress, then I look for wardrobes, and handily they're just a little further along the path, and I pick a simple rail with a white linen cover. I've been to Ikea many times before, so I know the routine, and I whizz through the marketplace filling my yellow bag with home-making essentials, and the more things I pick out the easier it becomes to do this – it's hypnotic, compulsive, supermarket-sweepish. I carry on to the self-serve warehouse, my codes ready, then head round to the large item pick-up area to get my bed, where a young Asian man with kind liquid eyes helps me load my trolley. I finally reach the checkouts and there's hardly any queue, it must be still early. My bed, mattress, clothes rail, bedding, cushions, rug, lamp shade, curtains (all in tasteful shades of white or cream), cost under £300. It has taken me a little over an hour and a half, including the breakfast. I feel absurdly pleased with myself. I leave everything, even the small items, to be delivered that afternoon, and catch the bus back to Finsbury Park.

I stop at a small scruffy hardware store and buy the biggest tin of brilliant white paint and a roller and some brushes. When I get home (home!) only Swarthy Boy One appears to be in. He's cooking something revolting-smelling at the stove again and he ignores me completely, as though he's deaf, as I gulp a glass of water at the sink. It's 1.30 already, I need to hurry. I gallop upstairs, change into a T-shirt and the only shorts I've brought with me, lug the old bed and wardrobe into the middle of the room, and start to paint.

It's hot again today and the room is stuffy, but I'm filled with abnormal levels of energy – I seem to have developed some kind of crazy nesting instinct, like when I was... I stop myself, carry on working, try not to think. The room is small and I paint over everything – I don't bother cleaning first, I just paint and paint and paint, over the grime and the dust, until the peach wood-chip becomes thousands of small flesh-coloured nipples, and then I go round the room again and again without stopping until they finally disappear – it's so hot the paint seems to be drying fast enough to just keep on going. I do the window frame too – in the same paint, it's all I have – but it doesn't matter, the effect I'm after is obliteration of what came before.

I hear the doorbell, one of those old-fashioned sing-song chimes. My Ikea delivery! I race downstairs and yank open the porch door. The man dumps the stuff inside the hallway and there seems to be so much of it I'm worried it'll annoy my new housemates if I leave it there. *I've got to hurry.* I run back upstairs and carry on painting, like my life depends on it, and maybe it does. When everything is white, I take hold of the revolting old mattress and drag it out the door, haul it along the landing and shove it down the long steep stairs from the top. As it gathers its own momentum the front door opens and a stinking stained mattress practically lands on the mountain of a man who enters.

"Shit, sorry," I say.

"What the fuck are you doing?" he says, but he softens as he sees me at the top of the stairs in my shorts, covered in paint.

"Hi, I'm Emi- I'm Cat," I say. "I've just moved in. I'm doing up my room a bit."

"So I can see," says the man and I realise he must be Jerome, Chanelle's cousin. "Here, let me help you with that." And he picks up the mattress like it's a box of cereal and throws it out the front, next to the bins.

"You got anything else you're planning on chucking down the stairs?" he asks and I think, thank God for that, and say yes please, a bed frame and a wardrobe. Jerome goes into the shed in the back yard and comes back with a sledgehammer. I'm feeling a little alarmed now, not because I'm wearing hardly anything, alone in the house with a titanic stranger, who incidentally is now wielding a hammer at me, but rather that I hadn't properly thought through how Chanelle feels about the old bed and wardrobe, we didn't exactly agree on me going that far with the room improvements. I decide that if she doesn't like my replacement furniture I can always offer to pay her, hopefully she'd be OK with that, so I let Jerome upstairs and he swings the hammer and he smashes up the brown and beige cupboard and dismantles the bed frame and slings the whole lot out into the front garden, just behind the hedge. It takes him ten minutes.

"You want some help with that new stuff?" he says, and I'm beginning to feel like I'm taking advantage.

"I'm sure I can manage," I say, but I'm tired now and I must have said it half-heartedly and Jerome takes the hint. He proves to be a whizz at flat-pack furniture and within half an hour my bed is screwed together and the mattress is taken out of its plastic sheath and tossed on top, as easily as if it were an air bed, just as I'm finishing off putting my three part clothes rail together. Jerome shrugs off my thanks and disappears to his own room and I unwrap my sheets and duvet and duvet cover and there's packaging everywhere. I make the bed, being sure to keep it away from the still damp walls. I even remembered to buy clothes hangers so I empty my holdall and hang the few clothes I have in my new covered rail. I still have Jerome's screw driver and although it takes me three times as long as it would have him I stand on a chair and manage to unscrew the curtain rail and I take down the mouldy faded apricot curtains and hang some full-length sheer white cotton ones in their place. The paint isn't properly dry yet but it won't matter, they barely touch the walls. I'm determined to finish this so I go and find the vacuum cleaner and get as much crap out of the carpet as I can manage. I change the lampshade to a plain white one. I take all the discarded packaging downstairs and shove it in the front garden with everything else. I'm dog tired now but I go back up to my room and unfold the cream shag rug and it's perfect, it takes up nearly the whole floor next to the bed, hiding the stains on the carpet beneath, so I can pretend they're not there. The transformation is complete.

In the space of 36 hours I have a new home, new friend, new name, and now a spanking white bedroom. *But no child, no husband*, says a voice out of somewhere. I ignore it and head for the shower.

8

Andrew woke suddenly and leapt out of bed all in one movement, the body next to him still and snoring lightly. He went straight to the small en suite bathroom and showered away the girl's bodily fluids. He was annoyed that she was still there – he normally made sure they left afterwards – but he'd been tired last night, and straight after he'd finished he'd rolled off and fallen into a heavy dull sleep. Maybe he was coming down with something.

It was only six o'clock, too early for breakfast, and day two of the conference didn't start until nine, but he didn't want to be there when she woke up, it was too intimate, embarrassing. She didn't look like she was going to wake up any time soon, she'd been completely plastered the previous night, and he realised with a shock that he couldn't remember her name although he kept trying. He decided to leave himself, go for a walk – hopefully she'd be gone by the time he returned, that would solve the problem.

He dressed quickly, trying not to look towards the bed as he did so. He made sure he opened the door as noiselessly as possible, and although she grunted and turned over, he made it from the room without her waking. He walked quietly down the long drab corridor of faceless doors, and outside a couple were trays of already rotting food from the night before. Andrew only relaxed once he'd made it to the lift and the mirrored doors had shut him in, offering up a golden reflected image of himself. Andrew knew he was a handsome man, but he could see his looks had dimmed of late, maybe it was his paunch or the fact his hair was showing signs of receding, or more simply that his internal misery was starting to be worn on his face.

As Andrew walked through the reception he looked straight ahead and ignored the night porter sitting behind the desk – it wasn't that he meant to be rude, he just didn't want the man to see the shame in his eyes.

Outside Andrew had no idea which way to go, it wasn't really a place for walks, so he arbitrarily turned left, along the already busy main road. He walked for maybe 500 yards, until he'd given up hope of there being a turn-off, but finally he found a smaller road on the left, which after a few more hundred yards narrowed and led into a neat housing estate, a little like the one where he and his family lived in Chester. Lights were just coming on in some of the houses and Andrew wondered what was going on behind those tidy front doors, with their high-end family cars in the driveways and the marigolds in the straight, unimaginative borders beginning to show their gaudy colours in the half-light. Were everyone else's lives as fucked up as his was?

It had all started going wrong early on, when Frances had announced she was pregnant: it was so soon after the wedding he simply wasn't ready for it. It was such a corny response, his attraction to the new secretary rushing him away from his expanding wife at home towards the office, to the exchanged looks and the thrill of the proximity as she leaned over his desk to take notes on his letters, and the knowing that he couldn't touch although they both wanted him to, it was *forbidden*. After a while the lunches started, then the staying late at the office, the intimate chats, as the tension grew between them. Andrew held out for as long as he could, but the day they'd had lunch and she'd broken down because her father was seriously ill, he'd offered to take her home, she was too upset to go back to work, he'd said, and he swore that at the time his motives had been honourable. She'd invited him in and as they waited for the kettle to boil she'd cried again and so of course he'd comforted her, and when they'd finally kissed the feeling had been extraordinary, like an adrenaline shot of danger and deceit, a physical reaction that had left him hooked – and wondering what hope his new marriage had.

When he arrived back in the office much later on that shape-shifting afternoon, there were three messages from Frances and then two more from the hospital. He felt sick. He sensed the disapproval from his colleagues as he rushed away, head down, to his wife. But afterwards his shock at having missed the actual births, but inexplicably was the father of twin daughters, just made his feelings for Victoria more intense. Within weeks he'd resumed the affair, despite the guilt, despite his promises to himself. It wasn't only his passion for his secretary, it was also the need to escape from his dowdy exhausted wife and their screaming babies. He began to "work late" more often, spend less and less time at home, and eventually Frances stopped asking him when he'd be back, where he was, she just seemed to accept it. So that must mean she doesn't really mind, he'd reasoned with himself, and this had made him feel better.

As Andrew continued his walk around the sad early morning Ways and Closes of the Telford estate he finally saw his betrayal for what it was. Abandonment. How could he have been married for less than a year with twin baby girls and become involved with someone else? He'd felt he couldn't leave Frances physically, it just wasn't done, so instead he left her emotionally, and in his place remained an insipid vague husband, an apathetic father, to babies who grew over the years into two very different girls, one calm and kind like her mother, the other flighty and neurotic.

It was only when Victoria finally put her foot down and ended the affair, after years and years of Andrew's broken promises of, "When the girls are five, six, seven," that Andrew had started his casual couplings at the dismal work events his sales job offered up. And if there was too big a gap between those opportunities he'd found himself turning to sessions in cheap Manchester hotels with middle-aged hookers. He despised himself.

Andrew checked the time – quarter past seven, he needed to start heading back. He really ought to call Frances before the conference started and see how Caroline was doing in the clinic – her weight had finally started to stabilise, and she was heading back towards six stone apparently. He felt such grief for his 15 year old daughter, *unloved* by her mother and *abandoned* by her father. The clarity of his realisation was as piercing as the fresh spring sunshine as he marched eastwards, along the clogged main road, towards the hotel.

* * *

Emily sat at her desk in her bright square bedroom trying to concentrate on her GCSE maths revision. The house felt strange, characterless, without Caroline there – her twin had always added a kind of electric zing to the atmosphere – but although she missed her Emily felt relieved that Caroline was finally getting some help. She was pleased with their mother's response too – Frances seemed to have overnight transformed into more of a proper, genuine mother to Caroline, as if a switch had been flicked on, and Emily had felt her mother's focus shift from her at last. It might even help hers and Caroline's relationship too – Emily had always done her best to get on with her sister, make allowances for her behaviour, after all it was no wonder Caroline was so jealous of her, considering how much she was favoured. It was weird how it was only now her twin wasn't here that Emily was fully aware of it.

Emily was a nice girl. She had inherited her father's whimsical nature but none of his weakness, along with her mother's strength and stoicism. It was a good combination. She was sweet, in both looks and nature, did well at school, was quietly popular, gently amusing, in fact all round sickening to her younger twin. Caroline was a harder, glittering version of Emily – prettier, cleverer, wittier even, but with none of the lovability, and the irony was that Emily seemed embarrassed to be liked and yet everyone loved her, and Caroline was desperate to be loved and nobody did.

Emily presumed that that must have been why Caroline had begun to starve herself, to try to take back some control in the midst of such isolation. She knew very little about the illness and was astonished now that none of them had noticed, but Caroline had been clever. When she'd refused to join the family meal times they all assumed that was just Caroline being Caroline; when she started covering herself from head to foot in black, that was Caroline going through her gothic phase; when her cheekbones shone brittle through her pallid skin it was her new choice of makeup. Emily felt ashamed. This was her twin sister after all, she couldn't believe she'd been so oblivious. She turned the page of her maths book – simultaneous equations. Emily enjoyed doing these, loved the solidity of them, the reliability, the fact that despite the complexity of getting there, there was only one right answer in the end. That's pretty much how she approached life, she realised, always looking for the right answer and it nearly always coming to her. Even with this situation, although Emily was sad for her twin she felt optimistic, sure that Caroline's cry for help had been heard and now she'd get better. They'd get on better too, Emily was confident of that; she was determined to try harder. She studied the question:

A man buys 3 fish and 2 chips for £2.80

A woman buys 1 fish and 4 chips for £2.60

How much are the fish and how much are the chips?

Emily half got up from her desk by the window and peeked down into the road – her father should be home soon. She turned towards the door and surveyed her room, with its neatly-made bed and over-sized cushions that Frances had covered in aztec-style fabric, arranged casually along the wall so she could lounge with her friends, like it was a sofa. She was happy with her new posters, of Madonna in a cone-shaped bra and Michael Bolton with his long angular face and flowing hair. She thought they were nicer than the ones Caroline had plastered all over her wall in the room next door, of grungy bands Emily had never heard of like Stone Temple Pilots and Alice in Chains, and shouty intimidating punk-rockers like The Sex Pistols – one thing she had been glad of in the past weeks was not having to listen to Caroline's music through her bedroom wall, she always played it so loud, particularly when Emily was trying to do her homework. She sat down at her desk again and studied the equation. She'd just worked out that the chips were 50p (finding the price of the fish would be easy now) when she heard her father's car in the driveway. She called downstairs brightly as she came out of her bedroom.

"Hi Dad! How was the conference?"

She paused on the landing, looking down into the open plan living room, with its new leather corner suite and sheepskin rug, as he stood there inert, shiny briefcase under his arm, desolation in his eyes. Then she came slowly down the two half-flights of stairs and put her arms around her father, as he buried his head against her shoulder, like she was the parent and he was the child.

"Oh Emily, what a pathetic father I've been to you girls. Seeing Caroline in that place is just..." Andrew stopped as his voice broke, and after all these years and years the release finally came.

Caroline looked hostilely at her mother, who sat at the end of the hospital bed in the institutionally-cheerful room, with its yellow painted walls and drab washed out pictures and vile green-checked curtains. A single vase of unopened daffodils stood nakedly on the formica table in the corner, beneath the window and next to the chair on which, in Caroline's opinion, Frances should have been sat and *not* on her bed. She was surprised at the strength of her anger. Over the past months her diminishing weight had seemed to diminish her senses too, and all the effort of planning her calorie intake had until now deviated her thoughts away from more dangerous areas where painful feelings lurked – feelings like resentment of her mother, derision of her father, hatred of her sister. It was easier to decide whether to have a quarter or a half an orange for breakfast than choose to wish her mother or sister dead first. And now here was Frances snivelling on the end of her bed about how sorry she was, how she'd let her down, about how much she loved her, and Caroline knew she was LYING.

Caroline felt tired within her own skin. She wanted the whole world to just fuck off and leave her on her own private island of meal planning and calorie counting, a place where for the first time ever she felt safe and in control. She didn't want to have to face her mother here in this revolting room. She'd spent so many years, tried so many strategies, yearned for Frances to focus on her instead of Emily, to accept her, to love her. And now that she, Caroline, had finally given up on the whole thing Frances was suddenly sniffing around, trying to be some ridiculous maternal saviour.

"I'm so sorry, my darling, I really had no idea."

"You have no idea about anything to do with me," said Caroline.

"I'm going to try harder, you'll see, we'll get you out of here, we'll get you better."

"Wouldn't you rather let me just waste away? Then you'd only have Emily to worry about. Isn't that what you want?"

Frances thought then of the dreadful day Caroline had entered the world, unexpected, alien, and how at the very moment of new life she had wished her youngest daughter dead. The memory had been buried for so long that Caroline's question invaded Frances's brain, hot and bright like a nuclear bomb, and jerked the whole horrible saga back to the surface. Caroline saw the expression on her mother's face and understood unequivocally that the answer was yes.

Frances felt denial, then shame, and then an overwhelming relief that at last she had shared her secret. The fact that it was with Caroline of all people didn't actually matter. The poisonous choking ball of hate in her heart was expelled into the room, as if physically, allowing the love to flood in. They looked at each other, Frances with love at last, Caroline with desperation. And then Frances fell into her daughter's bony arms and held her tenderly, for the very first time, 15 years too late to save either of them.

9

I wake up in my new room and it smells of paint. My sleep has been full of emulsioned visual canvases, splattered and raw, Pollock-like, and I can't seem to get rid of them unless I open my eyes. My bed is comfortable enough although I'm not used to a single, and it feels strange not to lie with my back to my husband, apart from him, not touching yet knowing he was there, our marital bed having felt like the loneliest place in the world by the end. I try not to think about him or our son, instead I focus hard on my new surroundings and notice that the bedding is still stiffly new and feels almost good. The sun is leaking through the sheer white curtains and when I check my new phone it's still only six o'clock – they may look great but they're useless at keeping the room dark. I wonder dully what I can do today. I've had such clear deadlines for the two days since I left – find somewhere to live, make my new room habitable – that today stretches in front of me, expansive, boyless, empty. I know I need to get a job soon, open a bank account, but somehow it all feels too much. My body tells me I'm tired, that I need time to recover from the upheaval and stress, from this latest trauma. I'm a survivor at heart, I guess. It's too early to get up but I'm wide awake, so I scrabble under my bed and find Monday's paper, the one I bought at Crewe. I prop up my new pillows against the white bumpy wall and open the pages. I read about a disease affecting yellow finches, making their throats swell so they can't eat: half a million of them starved to death last year, it says. I try not to think about this, try not to picture them, but still my eyes fill and so I move on to the next story. A man has raped and killed his twelve year old niece, she only went round to watch the football and her aunt happened to be out, surely she'd be alive otherwise. I turn the page. A merchant banker has been convicted of murdering his wife's lover, whilst they were all camping together in Brittany. A woman in a shop has been beaten by robbers with batons, it's been caught on CCTV – it's probably already available to watch on YouTube.

I stop reading. The news is making me feel depressed again, adrift. I try to go back to sleep but my mind is too active, wired, thoughts of my golden boy keep drifting in, uninvited, and I'm worried that any progress I've made in the last two days will be dissipated here, in this blank white room. I didn't bring a single one of my books from Chorlton and the novel I bought at Crewe is trashy, what was I thinking. I can't face the bathroom again, I'd rather not even bother this morning, although I'm sweaty from the night. I'll make sure I buy some flip-flops today to use in the shower, and maybe a wash bag that hangs on a peg and folds open, so I don't have to put it down on any of the surfaces – that will help make the bathroom bearable, give me something to do. I'm restless still so I try the paper's review section this time. My mind won't concentrate on any of the articles, but as I go to put it down I notice the Sudoku on the back, next to the crossword. I've never done Sudoku before, it always seemed such a total waste of time, yet that's exactly what I want to do now, waste time, help make the gaping minutes go by. The level is moderate, it says, but although I try and try I can't fill in a single number. It's something to do with patterns, I remember my sister telling me (*forget about her*), and I keep staring until the random numbers swim, and then finally I've got it and I fill in my first number and I'm off. I'm good at maths but this has nothing to do with maths really. It's strangely compulsive and I keep going and it takes me ages and I'm on a roll now and then in the very final box I find I have two 6's but no 3. I must have made a mistake, somewhere along the line, but although I try for ages it's too hard to unravel, and that's how my life feels – it was all going along so beautifully and then I got two 6's and no 3 and now it's fucked up, irreparable. The tears come again, silent, gliding, ominous, and I see the room for what it is – a grotty horrible little room in a grotty horrible house in a grotty horrible part of London. I see myself for what I am, a stinking self-centred coward who has run away from Ben and Charlie, rather than stay and face up to things. I miss Charlie in particular right now, the biscuit smell of him, the feeling of holding him tight, despite him trying to wriggle out away from me, and us both enjoying it anyway – me for trying, him for knowing that I've tried, that I love him.

There's a soft knock on the door. I startle and wipe my eyes, and Angel pokes her head around.

"Oh, you are there babe, just checking you were OK."
She looks around. "Jesus Christ, have you been on Changing Rooms? This place looks amazing. Can you do mine next?"

"Yeah, I went on a bit of a mission yesterday," I say, as brightly as I can manage. "Chanelle seems OK about it too – it's better isn't it?" I look at her glitzy top. "Are you going out?"

"No, I've just come in babe. I keep funny hours in my job. I'm starving, though. D'you fancy going out for breakfast – there's a cafe round the corner that's not too bad?"

"I'd love to," I say, instantly feeling better.

"I'll just get changed then, give me two secs." She disappears.

I jump out of bed and survey the clothes in my new wardrobe: two pairs of jeans, one interview outfit, two T-shirt dresses, some linen trousers, expensive belted grey jacket (ruined), a few tops, a denim skirt, a cable knit jumper. Nothing feels right anymore. I choose jeans and a mid-blue jersey cowl-neck top and I feel boring, un-Catlike, although I don't know who Cat is yet. Ten minutes later Angel reappears. She has changed from her short black skirt and red satin blouse (*is that her uniform?*) into a floaty white Indian cotton dress and she has tied her ash blonde hair back, it's just long enough, and gentle tendrils escape. She looks effortlessly casual and stylish and innocent. Her heart-shaped face is small and guileless and she doesn't look like she should work in a casino. I realise I don't know what a croupier does look like, apart from in Oceans 11 and that doesn't count.

"Come on, babe," says Angel and I follow her quietly, gratefully, down the steep threadbare stairs, through the trainers- and coat-stuffed porch, past the debris-filled front garden, onto the sallow early morning street.

10

Angela shoved her way through people's legs, past the stools that were as high as her, away from the bar, towards the stage. As she moved the odd hand came down and ruffled her hair affectionately, as if she were a dog. The punters were used to seeing a small blonde girl in here these days, and Angela had grown used to them, mostly. She still hated the choking smoke and the *adultness* of the club, dimly aware that this was no place for a child, and some of the men looked at her in a way she didn't yet understand but knew she didn't like, and sometimes they even squeezed her bottom as she passed. But she'd worked out how to pass the time in here now – sitting on a bar stool drying beer glasses when her favourite barmaid Lorraine was on, she seemed to really appreciate the help; or playing with her mummy's make-up in the tiny dressing room behind the stage, being careful to cover her tracks in the lipsticks and rouge so Ruth wouldn't find out and go mad; or sometimes playing dominoes with Uncle Ted, if she could persuade him. It wasn't fun coming here anymore though, she was bored of it and it made her tired for school – but now she was older her mother had started bringing her along to jobs more often, she wouldn't shell out for babysitters, and she supposed it was better than being left at home alone.

By the time Angela reached the front Ruth had disappeared and the pianist was already packing up his sheet music. It was quicker now for Angela to get to the dressing room via the stage than cut round the back of the bar. As she raised her arms to climb onto the too-high boards one of the customers said, "Need help, sweetheart?" and he lifted her above his head and she clambered up on her hands and knees. She stood up, straightened her red spotty dress to cover her knickers, and ran diagonally to the left, as fast as she could.

"Hello Mummy," said Angela shyly, as she poked her head around the dressing room's curtain. She adored her mummy but was never quite sure what mood Ruth would be in, what reception she'd get.

"Hello angel!" said Ruth, as she bent down and hugged her tight. "Have you been a good girl for your Uncle Ted?" She was wearing a tight sequined midnight blue dress and had big hair and kohled eyes and Angela thought she was the most beautiful mummy in the whole wide world, with the most wonderful heart-breaking voice that even Angela recognised cracked with sadness and a life lived.

"Yes, Mummy. Can we go home soon, Mummy? I'm tired."

"I know, sweetheart, I'll just get out of this dress and then we'll have one drink with Uncle Ted and go straight home."

"But I want to go home now, Mummy," Angela said.

"I told you darling girl, one quick drink and then we'll be off. Mummy's thirsty after all that singing."

"Please Mummy, I want to go home. I want to go to bed."

"I said no, Angela," said Ruth. "Shall I get you a lemonade?"

"NO!" yelled Angela, out of control suddenly as the tiredness took hold. "I want to go home NOW."

"Don't you talk to me like that, young lady," said Ruth. "We'll go home when I say so."

Angela stopped screaming and pulled herself up into the only chair in the room, a proper dressing table chair, with gold legs and padded arms, covered in faded pink velvet with a single kidney-shaped stain on the seat. She dangled her legs sullenly and stayed silent – she knew not to argue with her mother when she took that tone with her, she didn't want to get a whack.

Ruth changed out of her evening dress and stood before the mirror in her matching bra and pants, in lacy petrol blue, still wearing her high heels, still sexy. She wiped at her armpits with a damp flannel and sprayed antiperspirant under her arms, across her still-flat stomach and around the tops of her legs. Then she put on plain black Capri trousers and a cap-sleeved tight black top. She left her hair and make-up as it was, and in this light and with the way she walked she could have been a raven-haired Marilyn Monroe. She took Angela's hand, firmly rather than roughly, she obviously wasn't *too* cross with her this time, and they made their way along the corridor and out into the smoky club, where Ted was waiting for them at the bar. Ted bought Angela a lemonade and a packet of prawn cocktail crisps, and

Ruth's one drink turned to three or four, and Angela finally fell asleep, jack-knifed over a barstool with her head resting between her thin little arms on the beer-sopped counter top.

11

I sit in the cafe with Angel and I'm surprised at how hungry I am. It's run by a nice old Greek couple and the coffee is good but the food is great. It's like I haven't eaten in months, and I wolf down egg and bacon, mushrooms, beans, fried tomatoes, toast, my stomach telling me there's more living in store for me yet, even if my heart doesn't believe it. Angel seems tired when you look closer, but she retains that sweetness at the core that only some people have, and it transcends the bags under her eyes.

"What are you up to today, babe?" says Angel.

"I don't know, I need to go food shopping, maybe get to the bank if I can face it, and then tomorrow I need to start looking for a job." The tasks seem insurmountable.

I pause, try to lighten the mood. "One thing I must do today though is buy some flip-flops – how the hell d'you cope in that bathroom?"

Angel laughs. "I try to shower at work mostly. And anyway I'm not here for long babe, I just needed somewhere where my bastard ex-boyfriend couldn't find me. I wouldn't normally live in such a pit, but needs must and all that."

"Oh." I look down.

"What's your excuse, babe?" says Angel gently. The kindness pricks at my eyes.

"Same as you really, I suppose. And I don't mean to sound like a weirdo, I know we've only just met, but I thought it would be all right in that hideous house, with you there."

"Don't worry, babe," Angel says. "I'm not going just yet."

I feel ridiculous that I've formed such an attachment to Angel, but she doesn't seem to mind – I get the sense that she's used to looking after people, that she likes it, likes to feel needed. She seems in some ways more grown up than I've ever been, although I must have 10 years on her, and I used to be a wife, a mother.

"Well, we'll have to keep in touch when you do go," I say limply.

"Of course we will, babe. Anyway, I'm here for now and there's no-one else in the house I'd want to hang out with." She smiles at me and there's wickedness in her eyes. She puts on a terrible American accent. "Don't you worry Miss Brown. You and me, we're gonna have us some *fun*."

I cheer up, like a screaming child who's been given an ice-cream, and although Angel is done with eating she's happy to stay, and so we sit for longer and order more coffees and chat about everything and nothing, and I finish the buttered toast that's piled up between us, every last piece.

When we get home, Angel goes straight to bed, she's been working all night, and as I don't know what else to do I check out the kitchen, just to see if it's empty. I haven't yet sussed out who in the house does what, when or whether they work, who's going to be in when. As there's no living room I

77

assumed there'd always be plenty of people in the kitchen, but so far it's been fairly quiet. I've not seen Bev, the girl from Barnsley who had her chocolate stolen, since that first evening, but she's here now, busy at the sink. It's too late to not go in, she's heard me. She turns her head over her shoulder and beams at me. "Morning!" she says. "Fucking dogs, I've just stood in fucking dog shit. I don't know why people have the little fuckers, they could at least pick their crap up but people round here are so fucking IGNORANT." I realise that Bev has her wooden clog in her hand, and she's scraping at it with a table knife, over a stack of dirty dishes in the sink. She sees my face.

"Oh, don't worry, washing up liquid is fucking amazing stuff, it gets rid of 99.9% of germs. I read an article on it, it's all fine."

I'm at a loss how to respond to this. Australian Erica enters into the pause. She's wearing an aubergine skirt suit that shows off her incredibly petite figure and her plain face is thick with make-up and her dark hair is pulled up in one of those big hair clamps. I smile at her but she just scowls at me, then she goes over to the sink and sees what Bev's doing.

"For God's sake, Bev!" says Erica.

"Oh, get over it Erica, I'm going to clean up afterwards."

"That is DISGUSTING," says Erica, and although I don't much like her I have to agree with her on this.

Bev laughs and carries on cleaning her shoe. Erica turns on her kitten heels and stomps out of the kitchen, slamming the door.

"Good luck with the interview," calls Bev cheerily, then under her breath mutters, "You sour-faced cunt." I'm usually offended by that word, but I find myself empathising in this case, almost wanting to laugh.

I hesitate but she seems friendly. "Bev," I say. "Do you know where I can buy flip-flops round here, you know, the rubber ones?"

"What? D'you think you're in fucking Skegness love? D'you want a fucking rubber ring too?" Bev laughs at her own joke, but I don't mind, I like Bev, with her dreadful language and total disregard for social niceties. It's refreshing.

"Try down the Nags Head, there's loads of cheap pound shops, and shoe shops too, you might get something. While you're there, can you get some bin-liners, big strong ones, we're always running out." This is the first profanity-free sentence I've heard from Bev. I acquiesce meekly and leave the dog-shit stench of the kitchen.

As Bev predicts, I struggle to find rubber flip-flops in Holloway. I look for a hanging wash bag too but people don't seem to know what I'm talking about when I ask about that. Once I've exhausted my search I don't know what to do next – what are runaways *meant* to do with their time? I decide to explore, try to get my bearings in my new neighbourhood, take my mind off things. I head off the main road and walk for what feels like miles in vaguely the direction of home, through worn-out streets full of satellite dishes and crumbling stonework and wheelie bins. The odd house has full on bars on the windows and it seems to me like a horrid way to live, they must be in their own private jail too. As I meander aimlessly, I turn left out of another sad street and without warning find myself in a square full of grand well-kept houses with a beautiful garden

79

in the middle, and I sit on the grass and tilt my head to feel the sun on my face and it feels nice, bearable, it's not quite so hot today. A smartly-dressed mother sits on a bench and spoons a yogurt towards an invisible child somewhere in the depths of a bright red buggy, and her smile is wide and delighted and I find that I'm just about OK with this scene, if I look away quickly. Two perspiring young men in suit trousers and open shirts eat sandwiches out of thick waxed paper swilled down with cans of Diet Coke. I lie down with my head on my bag and I am so exquisitely tired it feels like I'll never get up again, it's like I'm being pulled through the grass to the earth's core, to the land of forgetting, into endless sleep...

I wake up with a jolt and have no idea what time it is and I'm panicky again. What the hell was I doing sleeping, especially with all this cash on me, how foolish is that? I decide I must try to open a bank account after all, I can't keep walking around with so much money on me, especially round here, so I head back roughly the way I came, through similar unloved streets, past more untaxed cars and scuffed front doors, feeling anxious this time about being mugged. I can't find a bank anywhere and don't like the look of anyone to ask, I'm being paranoid now, so I walk quickly, keeping going until finally I find one on the Holloway Road. I think I can open some type of pre-paid account which will do for the time being, and it should be easy enough: I really am Catherine Emily Brown, it says so on my passport. I'm oddly grateful to my mother now for being adamant my names sounded better that way round, as if she didn't have enough to worry about when she'd just had twins. It makes the practicalities easier at least.

The branch is small and dismal, and I wait for ages watching people come and go until a bustling woman in a black polyester suit comes out from the back and leads me to a dreary little office with a half empty leaflet dispenser drawing the line between me and her across the desk. She's cordial enough but I can tell she's suspicious that I have no proof of address and nearly £2,000 in fifty pound notes in my handbag. I tell her this rubbish story even though she doesn't ask, about how I've recently come back from living abroad and I don't think she believes me but she opens the account anyway, she must have seen all sorts in this branch.

I feel much calmer now and carry on with my aimless shopping, drifting in and out of stores, barely noticing what's for sale, oblivious to the other customers, but in one of the street's many charity shops I find a dusty old print of those men in New York sat on a crane, dangling their feet high in the sky, nonchalant, God-like. I'm not sure I like the picture much, it's a bit vertigo-inducing, but it's only £7 and I think of the blank bumpy wall above the length of my bed, and the proportions are right, so I buy it anyway. I go into the supermarket two doors down and it's busy, full of joyless people buying multi-packs of crisps and jumbo bottles of fizzy drink for their already fat children. *Look after them*, I want to shout. *You're lucky to have them*. I am officially a nutter.

I hold my nerve for long enough to buy cereal, fruit, salad in a bag, chocolate (will it be safe in the house, dare I?) and several ready meals, I'm not up to cooking from scratch yet. They have paper plates in the supermarket and I'm tempted, but I think that looks a bit weird, to use my own plates, so I try not to think about Bev and her unsavoury habits and resolve to get on with it – she's probably right about washing up liquid anyway. It's hard to carry my food shopping as well as the picture, it's heavy, I bought more stuff than I meant to. The plastic handles are digging deep into my wrists and I'm reminded of Caroline. I wonder fleetingly what she'll think when she finds out I've disappeared, whether she'll be upset, but it seems I don't care how she feels anymore, not one iota. I sit at the front of the half-empty bus facing backwards, in the seats you're meant to give up for disabled people. The other passengers look sad and hot, as if they're melting, and I remind myself that I'm not the only one with a history. The lady opposite me is swelling at the ankle joints and as she shifts in her seat there's a whiff of fresh sweat. She's wearing a Barry Manilow T-shirt, I didn't think they made them anymore, and then I wonder that I even notice. Maybe it's another sign, after the laughter with Angel and the thrill of my decorating frenzy, that I'm slowly waking up at last, getting my senses back, rearranging the threads of my personality so I can be Cat Brown now instead of Emily Coleman. I realise that Cat seems to be different from Emily already, brittler, perhaps more like Caroline? I shudder. It's all too strange. Here I am, Ms Catherine Brown, sat on a bus in Holloway. I officially live in London, it says so on my bank statement. Here I am, out here, alive and unfindable.

12

Emily had warned Ben about her family, and so he was prepared, to an extent. "My mum's lovely and I adore my dad,"
she'd said. "Although he does seem a little distant at times,
you'll see what I mean. But I'm afraid Caroline can be a bit
difficult if the mood takes her. She's great once you get to
know her though, and I'm sure she's going to love you."

Ben found it peculiar that Emily had an identical twin. He
found himself thinking weird things like what if he got the
two of them mixed up, what if he found Caroline attractive,
how can there be two Emilies in the world? As the car pulled
up he felt unusually anxious. He knew he was in love with
Emily, even knew he wanted to marry her one day – though
he hadn't actually asked her yet, it was still much too soon
– so meeting her family was a big deal. He needed them to
like him.

The house was steep-roofed and modern, built in the
seventies, with white-washed wood cladding, four bedrooms,
a neat front garden and a shiny BMW in the driveway. It was
a bit too *ordinary* for someone as special as Emily, he felt, and
he thought of his own family's detached house with crunchy
gravel and sweeping front garden, and decided that that was

the kind of place they'd have one day – what with him being an accountant and Emily a lawyer, they'd be able to afford it eventually. He found it odd that he was thinking like this, that it had still only been a month since the night he'd paid a fortune for a cab-trip from Manchester to Emily's place in Chester. But there again the parachute trip had been three months before that, and he'd thought about her pretty much constantly since then. He couldn't believe they'd never run into each other at work, he'd been on the lookout for her every single day. And then when he had finally bumped into her it had been out on the street and he'd been unprepared and, worse, on the way to a course with Yasmin, his deeply annoying colleague. So all he'd managed in his shock was to say hello – he hadn't even stopped to ask Emily how she was, whether she'd got over the trauma of her jump, anything to show that he liked her, as friends at least, that would have been a start. Ben smiled, as he remembered how pissed off he'd been all day at his course, how he hadn't been able to concentrate, how he might as well have not gone at all, he was so angry with himself for blowing it.

It was just so strange that now here he was in her car, about to meet her parents, and he'd assumed until he got her email that, whatever attempts he made, he actually stood *zero chance*, she was so insurmountably gorgeous. When he'd picked up Emily's mail, half-drunk from the pub, he'd jumped up and down and punched the air, like he was actually at Old Trafford instead of just down the road from it. He'd called her before he even realised what time it was, though he would have called her anyway.

Emily parked her car behind her father's BMW so its boot

hung just onto the pavement. Before Ben even had time to get out, the white plastic front door opened and Emily's mother waved hello. She was blonde, pleasant-looking, her face having lost the faint bitterness it had held for so many years. In its place was weary acceptance – of her characterless house, of her weak-willed husband (oh she knew), of her nightmare youngest daughter.

"Hello, you must be Ben," she said as she shook his hand. "I've been dying to meet you. Emily doesn't normally let us meet her boyfriends, so we've been terribly excited."

"Muum," said Emily, embarrassed, but it was true. Emily had never been interested in boys, largely because she couldn't bear fighting with Caroline over them. It was as if once Caroline had finally made peace with their mother, there'd become less need for competition over her, and so the next battle-ground she'd chosen was boys. It had put Emily right off the whole thing, and she'd left Caroline to it, preferring to spend time with her friends and her books. And as Emily got older boys never really approached her anyway – she didn't seem to know how to give off the right signals – and so she began to assume she just wasn't attractive. The few boyfriends she had had were kept well away from her family, just in case.

With Ben it was different, it seemed natural to bring him for Sunday lunch. She'd been scared at first to even ask, as though she was being too forward, too serious, but Ben had said yes immediately, that he'd love to. That was what she adored about Ben, that there was no side to him, just complete straight-forwardness and apparently genuine enthusiasm for her. She found it odd though how they were still too scared to spell out how they felt, where they saw it going, as if voicing it would spoil it, so for now they skirted around the words, and their eyes and their bodies told them instead.

"Emily, *hello!*" said Frances. "I said, do you want tea or coffee?"

"Oh, sorry Mum, coffee would be lovely."

"Come and sit down Ben, Andrew will be in in a minute, he's just finishing off in the greenhouse. He's looking forward to meeting you."

"Where's Caroline?" said Emily, changing the subject.

"Oh, she had to pop out love, she'll be back soon."

"How's it going having her back home?" Emily winked at Ben.

"Oh, you know, we can't get in the bathroom, she plays her terrible music far too loud, it's like she never left really." Frances paused. "But I think she realises it's for the best, just for the moment." She looked at Ben. "I expect Emily's told you Caroline had a breakdown?"

"Mum!" said Emily. Even though she had told Ben, she didn't know why her mother was being so indiscreet, it was most unlike her. Ben looked down embarrassed, at the thin lines of grey grout between the square white tiles, and he thought they looked too clean, too spick, like in a hospital perhaps.

"Sorry darling. I just thought it was best that we all know where we are, so we can have a nice lunch, that's all."

"How's she doing?" said Emily.

"OK under the circumstances, I think." Frances turned to Ben. "We thought she'd done so well – living in London, great job in fashion, but you never really know what's going on with some people, do you?"

Ben nodded nervously, not knowing what to say.

Has she gone stark raving mad, thought Emily. She'd never seen her mother like this, it was alarming.

"I just think Ben needs to know, that's all," said Frances. "If we're going to have a nice lunch together," and then Emily understood. Frances was warning Ben – she obviously still didn't trust Caroline not to steal her own twin's boyfriend.

The key scraped in the door. Caroline slouched in, looking amazing. She had streaks of amber through her hair and it was cut shorter than Emily's, a long asymmetric bob. Her style was distinct, all bold lines and sharp contrasts, and she looked sleek and dangerous. Her eyes glittered and Ben saw what the other two didn't, but said nothing.

"Hi Ems," she said and air-kissed her sister. "How's things? Is this your boyfriend?" And she said it like she was still 16, not 26, and Emily cringed.

"Hello," said Ben. "Great to meet you." He felt relieved to see for himself that she was so different from Emily, that they were definitely two separate people, and he caught Emily's eye to show her it was going to be OK, after all.

Caroline took off her blazer, ostentatiously, revealing a tight orange T-shirt with "Let's talk" in clashing aquamarine splashed brazenly across her skinny chest, and then she slung the jacket over the back of a kitchen chair and sat down.

"Hear you two really *fell* for each other," said Caroline. "Sweet."

Before Emily could think what to say in reply, Andrew came in from the garden. His jeans were ill-fitting, high-waisted, his hands were filthy, his hair had drifted out of place. He's almost got a comb-over, Emily noticed for the first time, with a stab of sympathy for him. Andrew had always been so handsome, it was a bit pathetic to see him like this.

"Hi, Dad, this is Ben," she said. Ben held out his hand instinctively and as Andrew shook it clumps of earth fell on the sparkling white floor. Everyone laughed, nervously, except Caroline.

"Come to ask permission, have you?" she sneered, and Emily wondered for the millionth time why Caroline went out of her way to alienate people.

"Not this time," replied Ben, and Emily thought that that was such the perfect answer, she loved him even more.

Over lunch Ben noticed that Caroline topped up her glass before Andrew offered and before anyone else was ready. He was surprised that they let her, but she was no longer a child, so short of having her sectioned again what were they meant to do? Caroline was a continuing shock to him. He'd been stunned when Emily had told him that first night in Chester that she had an identical twin. He couldn't believe that there was someone else out there, who looked like Emily, sounded like Emily but that he didn't know and wasn't mad about. It was freaky.

She'd told him it all in a rush then, as she lay in her bed beside him, their arms and legs intertwined – about how she and Caroline had never really got on, how at 15 Caroline had been hospitalised for anorexia but then had appeared to recover so quickly, her relationship with her mother somehow miraculously improved – how she'd sailed through all her exams and taken a place at Central St Martin's, studying fashion. She'd told him how they'd all been so proud of Caroline when she'd done her final show and had sent the models down the catwalk dressed as exotic giant spiders, and it had even made the press. She had glamorous boyfriends, trails of them, and she got herself a trendy flat near Spitalfields and everyone thought she was *fine*. It was her friend Danielle who had finally found Frances's number on Caroline's mobile, and begged her to come down – *now* – as Caroline was convinced there were terrorists in the walls and fist-sized spiders down the plug-holes. Frances hadn't seen her daughter for a couple of months, and she'd been shocked by her state. Frances had put it down to Caroline witnessing that horrendous nail-bombing in Soho a few years earlier (and of course she couldn't bear to think of any other reasons): Caroline and her boyfriend had been caught right in the middle of it and she'd still been so young. It had taken time to take a toll on Caroline's mind, but the years of hard living and the brittle relationships and her tendency to melodrama anyway had all come together to send her quite mad, and Frances hadn't known what else to do but call 999.

The ambulance drivers were unsympathetic, unmoved, they just recommended she take her daughter and get her assessed ("It's for the best love"), and anyway they were about to go off shift so they needed everyone to hurry up. Caroline was in the hospital for just eight weeks, and when she came out she seemed fine again, a little subdued maybe, but definitely on the mend. Frances wouldn't let her stay in London though, she put her foot down for a change and made Caroline move home again – just for a while, she'd said, just until you get your strength back.

Ben had been stunned. The only histrionics that had occurred in his family was when his mother had reversed his father's beloved Rover into the garden wall, and, oh yes, one of his cousins had shockingly left his wife within a year of marriage. But that was about it. His family didn't do drama.

"What've you been doing in the garden?" Ben asked Andrew, as he took the last mouthful of his Sunday dinner.

"Oh, you know, a spot of weeding, pricking out my tomato seedlings, watering the nasturtiums, just a bit of a spring clean now the weather seems to have finally turned." Ben didn't know what pricking out was or what kind of plants nasturtiums were, and he nodded politely, unsure what to say.

"More potatoes, Ben?" Frances asked.

"Yes, thanks, they're great, really crispy."

Caroline smirked. "Have some more gravy, Ben," she said, and she shoved the oval gravy boat with the brown flecked pattern that matched the plates, across the tablecloth, over the placemats, towards him.

"Thanks," he muttered, and her fingers brushed his as he tried to take it by the small looped handle and the boat tipped dangerously.

"So what is it you do for a living, Ben?" Andrew asked, although he already knew, Frances had told him that morning.

"I'm afraid that I'm an accountant," Ben said.

"Wow, that sounds exciting," said Caroline. "You two must have so much to talk about."

Emily scowled at her sister. "The beef was nice mum, where's that from?"

"Oh, I got it from the butcher in the town, darling, I find it's so much better than what the supermarkets sell."

"Oh, I agree," said Caroline. "I find dead meat is so much nicer when it's local, don't you?"

"Caroline," said Andrew, mildly. No-one spoke. Ben's fork scraped agonisingly on his plate. Emily took a sip of her red wine.

"We thought we might take the dog out after lunch," she said, to break the silence. "It's such a lovely day, we could take him down by the river."

"Good idea, mind if I join you?" said Caroline.

"Of course," said Ben quickly. "In fact, we could all go."

"Oh, I need to get cleared up," said Frances. "And Andrew is bound to need to finish up in the garden." She hesitated. "You youngsters go."

"OK, it's just us three then," said Caroline. "Super."

"Actually, thinking about it, maybe we should give it a miss if that's OK," said Ben. "I've got some work to do, so we probably need to be getting back quite soon anyhow. D'you mind, Emily?"

"Of course not, whatever," said Emily.

"Shame," said Caroline, toying with her vegetables, pushing them around the plate as if she was tormenting them. "I do love a nice Sunday afternoon stroll."

Ben looked across the table and wondered again how Caroline could seem so normal – a bitch certainly, and well on the way to being drunk – but not mad, not anorexic. She caught Ben watching her and raised her glass to him with a mocking smile. "Chin chin," she said, and took a long swig.

13

As I open the gate to the house I see that the bin men must have been, the front garden has been cleared. Only the wheelie bins and the smashed up furniture remain and it's at this point I realise that I've forgotten the bin bags. Shit, I don't fancy a tirade from Bev, but I can't face turning round again with all my shopping and my bulky new picture, so I steel myself and go in. There's laughter coming from the kitchen – loud machine gun blasts that I haven't heard before. I plonk my grocery bags down in the hall and run upstairs with the print. I prop it on the bed and I quite like it now, the men look so carefree lunching in the sky, as casual as if they were on a park bench, and it makes me wish that I could be more like them again, less terrified of life. I go down to put my shopping away and flat-pack Jerome is in the kitchen with an exotic Hispanic-looking girl, it's her laugh that I could hear earlier. She's all boobs and hair extensions and chunky gold jewellery, and she's warm and friendly and says, "Ello darleeng," in a fierce unidentifiable accent. She's laughing at something Angel has just said, who sits in the corner and looks soft and pink in a white fluffy dressing gown. Her hair's still damp, she must have just had a shower, and she looks way too clean for that bathroom, this house.

"Hey Dolores, this is the girl I was telling you about, she tried to kill me with a flying mattress." Jerome winks at me and Angel giggles, and Dolores lets off another military round of laughter. Swarthy Boy One or Two is at the stove, this time attending to an acrid-smelling stew, I think that's what it is, or is he boiling his cycle suit? "Let's Dance" is playing, I used to love that song, and I realise I've not listened to music for months. There's lots of people here and I feel hopelessly shy. I check my watch, it's nearly six o'clock, where has the time gone today?

I open the fridge and it's stuffed with jars and bottles and God knows what and there appears to be no room for all the food I've bought. I didn't even think of that, but it's too hot to leave it out. I start trying to shift things around to make some space. As I rummage I discover a liquid courgette wrapped in cling film, a quarter of a tin of beans covered in a thick layer of spawning green mould, a stray cooked sausage of indeterminate age, naked amongst the sad-looking vegetables in the crisper section, a curled up slice of ham. There's a thick layer of grease on all the surfaces, and a deep burgundy stain across the once-white back wall. Although it's gross I feel it's rude to start throwing things out, especially after what I've done to my bedroom, so I just pile in my things as best I can and ram the door shut.

"What've you been up to babe?" asks Angel and I tell her about my day, trying to make it sound interesting, but I feel timid, self-conscious with everyone here.

"So today was my rest day, tomorrow I need to start looking for a job," I say at the end, embarrassed to be the centre of attention.

"What is eet you do, Keetty Cat?" asks Dolores with a killer smile.

I have this all worked out, I even did my CV in secret back in Chorlton, before I left, although I hadn't printed it out – I hadn't known my new address or phone number then, obviously.

"I'm a receptionist," I say. "I used to work in a law firm, but I fancy a change now, something a bit more exciting hopefully."

"Dolores is a receptionist, aren't you babe?" says Angel. I look at Dolores in her tight sexy clothes and she's bubbly and sunny-natured and I can't remember now why I thought reception work would be a good job for me. Something to do with it being easy to pick up (surely), not having to think too much, not making myself conspicuous. Not being found.

"Sure I am. I loooove it, ees dee best job in dee world – HA HA HA."

I wonder how good a receptionist Dolores actually is, with her hard-to-understand accent and idiosyncratic command of the English language. Still, she's warm and fun and she looks good, and I'm aware that I don't really have the look of a receptionist, I lack that kind of glamour. My interview outfit is formal, lawyerish, I don't wear much make-up, and I have no jewellery any more, not a single piece, not since I left my wedding ring in the station toilets at Crewe.

The swarthy boy moves from the stove and gets two bowls from the draining board, I really hope for his sake Bev did as she promised and cleaned up properly from the shoe incident earlier. He dollops foul-smelling ladlefuls of greeny-brown stew into the bowls. He gets two forks from the drawer and two glasses from a cupboard, he fills the glasses with water from the tap, he puts the forks in his back jeans pocket, prongs pointing upwards and outwards, places one bowl on his right arm, waiter style, pinches the two glasses between the thumb and forefinger of his left hand, so his long dirty nails go in the water, and finally takes the second bowl of stew with his free right hand. He walks tentatively across the kitchen and hooks his right foot round the door and pulls it towards him, to open it, and stew slops on the floor which he swipes at with his trainer. By the time he's done all that I think he would've been quicker to have taken the bowls and come back for the water and the forks, and I'm sure there's a lesson in there somewhere but I can't think what it is. The last song finishes, a loud crashy number I hadn't heard before (I think the iPod must be on shuffle or else it's a very eclectic playlist) and then "You are the sunshine of my life," comes on, and when Stevie Wonder sings the second line my eyes fill up and Angel notices so I immediately look down into my hands, to where my ring used to be.

"How you gonna get job, darleeng?" asks Dolores, and I pull myself together and tell her I'm planning on registering with a temp agency to see what comes up. Dolores tells me to go to one her friend runs, just behind Shaftesbury Avenue, which specialises in jobs in media companies. She says to ask for Raquel and say that I know her, Dolores, and although I'm grateful I wonder if saying that is a good idea. She gets up off the chair, bends down and kisses Angel on both cheeks, twice, pulls Jerome to his feet by his shirt, says, "Bye bye – you tell Raquel dee great Dolores sent you – HA HA HA," and totters off on her heels, her big sexy bottom swaying behind her. Jerome follows meekly, like a giant puppy on a string, and I hear them leave the house, and I presume they're off to Dolores's place in Enfield, wherever that is.

It's just me and Angel left in the kitchen now. Angel sees my face and knows not to venture anywhere painful. She yawns. "Ugh, I need a night off," she says. "I'm wrecked." She pours herself a vodka tonic and offers me one too, and I wish I'd thought to buy a bottle at the supermarket, I can't keep drinking hers. I don't really want one, but I say yes and then offer her one of my ready meals and she says yes too, so I put a lasagne and a cannelloni in the oven and I get out a bag of green salad. I go to the sink and look in the cupboard underneath and it smells of damp, but I find some bleach and I empty the sink of dirty crockery and cutlery and pour neat bleach in the sink and wipe all around. I rinse the sink, then do it all again and then I fill it with hot soapy water and I wash the rest of the plates that were already washed and stacked haphazardly on the draining board. Angel watches me, but seems to think I'm just a clean freak and so I tell her about Bev and the dog shit and we both laugh until we can't breathe in the hot sickly air. My hands feel tight and dry from the bleach and I lick my finger-tips to moisten them, which is a revolting habit that I thought I'd stopped. I have another vodka and eventually confess my worries about my clothes for tomorrow, and Angel says to come with her and she takes me upstairs and although I can't borrow her clothes, I'm so much bigger than her, she lends me a silver belt and bag and a black and silver skeleton print scarf that transform my black shift dress. Angel goes to get ready for work and I can think of nothing else to do now but lie down on my bed. These are the worst times, alone in my room, worrying about how Ben and Charlie are, whether I've done the right thing after all, but it's too late now, I've left them, I can't go back. I try instead to prepare mentally for tomorrow; I lie still in the half-light and force my thoughts away from the past towards the future – along tangling telephone wires, through beeping fax machines, across expanding internal directories. I crowd out old memories with wanton switchboardery, until at last sleep comes.

14

Emily found out later that the house had been built in 1877 for a gentleman's mistress, the great love of his life. The story went that she'd adored the view from there, and so he'd made her throw a stone down towards the sea, and where it landed he built the house, even though it was an engineering night-mare. It was situated in the depth of the trees, completely hidden except from offshore, and if you looked from out there in the waves it appeared to cling to the cliff, almost desperately, as though it might fall off. It didn't feel like it was even in England, the vista was serene and expansive, just yellow-green trees and flat blue sea, Mediterranean perhaps. Ben and Emily had found it that first New Year, when to escape the sniping at Frances and Andrew's house (after all, Caroline was still living there), they'd packed up his car and headed south to the Devon coast, trusting that where they ended up was where they were meant to be. As they drove along the coast through little dead towns, past winter-sad hotels, Emily was losing her nerve – maybe they'd been mad to not find somewhere decent in advance, especially as it was their first New Year's Eve together, she didn't want it to be a disaster. She was about to suggest that maybe they'd be better off heading inland and finding themselves a little country pub – they were usually packed on New Year's Eve, she'd said, that might be a fun place to see in the new year – when Ben wound the car up a steep tree-covered lane, zigzagging away from the sea, and as they rounded the last turn they saw an old-fashioned sign: Shutters Lodge, Accommodation, Evening Meals.

"Shall we try in there?" said Ben. Emily nodded, doubtful, and he turned the car into the gate and followed a driveway, up into the trees, for what seemed like forever, but eventually it opened into a clearing and there stood a vast old country house: perfect, ethereal, as if it had been magicked there. Ben parked the car and they got out. There was no-one around. There was no obvious entrance, it didn't even seem like it was a hotel, maybe the sign on the road was old or something. The air was sharp and freezing and Emily huddled into her cardigan. It was four o'clock and the sky was high and hungry, eating up the last of the winter light. They walked towards the far end of the house, and entered a stone portico, feeling like intruders. There was no bell, so after a few fruitless knocks Emily tried turning the bronze ring on the giant oak front door. It creaked open and a gush of warm air came towards them.

"Hell-o!" called Emily. As they were about to give up, they finally heard footsteps and a proper old butler appeared from nowhere and ushered them into the warmth as if he'd been expecting them, and he served them tea and fruit cake by the fire in the great hall, and that's how they found the place where they would one day get married.

*   *   *

99

That first New Year's Eve was in every way but one the best Emily had ever spent. She normally hated the forced jollity of the occasion, and she'd long ago given up going to the local pub with her old school-friends, where people thought that just because it was New Year's Eve it was OK to ram their tongue down your throat. The previous year she'd spent it at home in her flat with Maria from work and a couple of other girls, and they'd cooked a huge meal and watched Jools Holland and Out of Africa which happened to be on the telly, and as far as Emily was concerned that had been perfect – no trouble getting home, no yobbish behaviour, no Caroline prowling around being drunk and obnoxious. She hadn't even felt obliged to invite her sister – Caroline wouldn't have dreamt of doing something so boring, and anyway she'd gone clubbing in London.

Emily and Ben had dinner in the hotel and the food was fancy in a self-conscious, second rate way, all oddly cut carrots and balsamic dribbles across over-cooked lamb, but it didn't matter, the restaurant was wood-panelled and charming and the wine was good. She and Ben just talked and talked, it seemed they would never run out of things to say, sharing childhood anecdotes, laughing at how they'd met, it was as if they were never tired of going over it. Emily loved that Ben was the first person she felt able to confide in about her family, knowing he didn't judge her, or them, realising that before she'd met him she'd spent her whole life feeling lonely, although she hadn't even realised it at the time. It was insane when she thought about it, twins weren't meant to be lonely.

"...and so just as I got there," Emily was saying. "Caroline slammed the glass door and I went headlong through it, like it was made of paper, like at the end of It's a Knockout or something. And then my dad started chasing Caroline round the dining room table, and he couldn't even catch her, and my mum was just shrieking like a mad woman, and all the while I was quietly bleeding to death," and she started to giggle and then Ben was laughing too and although he'd asked her before about the scar on her knee, she hadn't told him the truth at the time, but she hadn't been sure why. It wasn't like Caroline had been trying to kill her or anything.

"I think I'm glad I'm an only child," said Ben. "The worst thing that happened to me at that age was when my spout fell off while I was doing "I'm a teapot" during assembly. I've never got over the humiliation."

Emily looked at Ben and she wondered again how different his life growing up must have been, with his kindly older parents who had showered him with love, and no-one to torment him.

"Was it odd not having siblings?" she asked. "I think I'd have had to watch Eastenders if I'd been an only child, my life would have been so boring without Caroline."

"No, not really. I had my cousins just down the road so I'd spend loads of time with them, and we had our dog of course." He paused. "It's odd though, I've never felt so *complete* as I've felt since I met you. I don't mean it in any weird way, like you're my sister or anything," and they mock-grimaced at each other. "But from the minute we met I felt like I knew you, even though you weren't particularly friendly at first..."

"I'm sorry about that," she said. "I was so terrified at the thought of jumping out of a plane... I don't know what I was thinking when I agreed to do it, I bloody hate flying *and* heights – Dave must've caught me at a weak moment. I should never have done it."

"Yes, you should," Ben said, and she smiled at him. He carried on. "I don't know why, but you just made me feel so aware of myself in a way that no-one else ever has." His eyes narrowed. "Particularly about the boil on my neck."

Emily laughed. "Sorry, but it was unavoidable from where I was sitting. I thought it was going to spit at me."

"I wish it had, you rude cow," he said, and took her hand across the table.

"Have you finished, madam?" said the waiter, who although smart in his waistcoat seemed too frail and ancient to still be of this life, let alone be working. There didn't seem to be anyone young who worked here, the whole place felt from another time somehow. He picked up the plates and his hands were doddery and Emily and Ben smiled small smiles at each other, and Emily found her eyes filling with tears for some reason.

"Let's go for a walk later," Ben said then, urgently. "It's such a beautiful night."

"It's dark, we'll kill ourselves up here," Emily said.

"No, we won't, there's the most enormous full moon, let's go up on the cliffs for midnight. It'll be good."

Emily looked at her boyfriend in the Christmassy glow and wondered how she could have thought he was a geek before, he was *gorgeous*. She loved his passion, his enthusiasm for life, the depth in his eyes, loyal like a dog, and she knew, just knew, sat there in that moment in a hotel in Devon, that she would never let him go, not ever.

★   ★   ★

They had wrapped up warm: Emily had put on every item of clothing she had with her under her coat, it was so freezing outside. They had to beg the butler for a key, the door was locked at this time of night, and although he'd obviously thought them mad he gave it to them, a big single old-fashioned one, like for a prison, and as they ran down the drive, half-drunk already and with three-quarters of a bottle of red stuffed inside Ben's coat, they felt like naughty children running away from boarding school. Ben had been right – the moon was peerless, like it had been cut out with God's own scissors into a perfect circle of luminescence, just for them. They walked up to the cliff where the wind was still, and the water was calm beneath them, and the earth rather than the sea seemed to be moving, in and out gently, as if it were snoozing.

"Come on, let's go closer," said Ben.

"Are you sure it's not dangerous?" Emily felt nervous and although she didn't like heights anyway, it wasn't just that, it was something else, long forgotten.

"Of course it's not, as long as we don't get too near the edge. Don't worry, I'll look after you."

Emily stood safely away from where the grass ended and the air began, and as she looked out across the moon-lit expanse of silvery sea into her head appeared a series of scenes – confused, out of sequence. *Emily sobbing; Andrew shouting; Caroline skipping along beside her, holding her hand; castle battlements; Frances pale and stony silent; ice cream, there was ice cream somewhere; a tussle, Emily fighting with her twin, as if for her very life; a warm bath.*

"What is it, Emily?" Ben said then, hearing her breath

change although she hadn't said anything, hadn't moved. His words unlocked her from the past and she ran, ran back twenty feet at least, away from the precipice and she flung herself onto the concrete grass and lay there panting, until the spinning stopped.

"No wonder I freaked out when that instructor shoved me out the plane," she said eventually, and tried to laugh but instead she cried and then Ben was holding her, and between howls she told him what she'd remembered, and Ben wondered if he could love her more, or like Caroline less, and how with such an evil twin Emily could have turned out so sweet, so normal.

15

I wake up crying, it seems my dreams have followed me. I stay in bed for now, it's too early to get up. I find my old newspaper, the one from Crewe, under the bed and I lose myself in Sudoku, the hard one this time, and I manage to finish it and I'm vaguely pleased with myself, as if I've achieved something. I force myself down to the kitchen to have breakfast and then I shower and dress in my jazzed up outfit, still feeling self-conscious, it doesn't look quite right – not Cat-like enough maybe, whatever that is. It's drizzling when I eventually leave the house, but as always I feel better for being out. It's such a relief to be anonymous here, not having to worry I'm being pointed at, whispered about. Angel has told me to take the tube to Covent Garden, that from there it's an easy walk to Shaftesbury Avenue and it saves me having to change lines. She's lent me a pocket sized A to Z so I feel more confident today, I'll know where I'm going.

Under ground it is gross. The tube stinks of sweat – fresh sweat from over-heating office boys, stale sweat from people who probably have to put up with bathrooms like mine so haven't washed for a while, and deep ever-present sweat that has drained down into the seats for days and months and years and is now rising up again in this extraordinary heatwave. It's the latter type that repulses me the most so I stay on my feet although there are places to sit down, and I grip the vertical yellow pole, my hand just above a well-groomed black one with butterflies on its fingertips. The owner of the hand seems agitated – maybe she's late for work – and she taps and flutters her butterflies, and checks the watch on her other wrist, and makes little stamps with her beautifully-shod right foot, willing the train to go faster through the deep black hole.

I look for an internet cafe so I can update my CV. I have to add in my new address, my new mobile number, shorten my new name. I'm finding it frustrating that I don't have access to the internet, and I regret my insistence at the mobile store that I take the cheapest phone, I should have listened to that lovely assistant instead of being the customer from hell. My lack of access to Google feels like another loss, another absence, and I decide that if I do manage to get a job quickly, I'll just have to splash out on a laptop or some kind of fancy internet phone. *If only I could ask Ben, he'd know what would be best for me.* I stop myself. I have to keep it up, the forgetting.

I can't find an internet cafe, I thought it would be easy, and so I try stopping a few people to ask but no-one knows, most people don't need them, they have their own wired up homes and offices to connect them to the world. I give up asking and wander up and down random streets, searching lamely, aimlessly, tears threatening yet again, until I see some girls with dirty-looking tangled hair and rings in their noses, in short ra-ra skirts over leggings and Converse trainers, and I don't feel up to it but I ask them anyway, and they don't speak very good English but they know where one is, and they send me back towards Leicester Square.

I sit at one of the screens at the back of the functional room full of computer terminals and robotic people, and I wonder what lives they're living in cyber space, how different they are from their flesh and blood reality. How has history moved so fast to create this in the last ten years, what has happened to human interaction, what impact will it have on the future? Why do I even wonder? I've always disliked internet cafes – the name is a misnomer for a start, there's no attempt to make the surroundings pleasant, there's no-one to serve me coffee – and in this one in particular I feel like I'm in some kind of doom-ridden sci-fi movie. A loud clunk sounds over the low whirring of hard drives and the tap tap tap of keyboards, and I startle, but the noise is just someone buying a Coke Zero from the vending machine in the corner.

My CV is contained in the only email – apart from all the junk ones – that I've received at my new Hotmail address, the one I'd set up for Catherine Brown while I was Emily still. I'd stayed up late one night to type it out, telling Ben I wanted to write some thank you letters, one of the many lies I'd told him in those final weeks before I left. (And to think that *before* we had always been so open, so able to tell each other anything.) I'd sent the CV as an attachment in a mail from my old self to my new one, and then I'd deleted the word file and the sent mail, and emptied the wastebasket and deleted the history. A couple of clicks of the mouse, it was that easy to cover my tracks. I'd hated myself.

I look up a major temp agency and find a branch in

Holborn, in case I get nowhere with Dolores's friend – I'm not at all confident about that lead, although I feel I should give it a try, Dolores was so insistent, so keen to help me. I finish updating my CV and press save, and then send the file to myself again, so I've got it. I press print, and print out ten copies. It costs me a fortune but at least I won't have to come to one of these places for a while, hopefully never again. I watch the clean white paper get sucked into the machine and come out covered with beautifully formatted lies, and I pay the boy on the till who stinks of weed, and he doesn't even look at me as he gives me my change.

My A to Z sends me up Charing Cross Road and then left into a narrow street that smells of air conditioner fug and Chinese food. It's almost midday and I'm hungry, I seem to be always hungry now, but I decide to go and get it over with, while I still feel brave enough. I find the right street number and the door I'm after is a solid metal one, with various buzzers down the right hand side. The middle button says Mendoza Media Recruitment, that must be it, so I press it and wait.

I'm aware that I'm shaking. I've run away from my family. My CV is completely made up. I've changed my name, my occupation, where I've worked. I have no idea how to work a switchboard.

"Come on up," says a thickly accented voice, and the buzzer goes so I push and the door is heavy. I find myself in a scuffed entrance hall – there's a door to the left with a sad peeling sign for Smile Telemarketing, and some grey painted stairs in front of me which I take as there's no other option. At the next landing a dark-haired girl is waiting for me.

"You for MMR?" she says, and I think that's an odd abbreviation and it gives me a tiny stab of pain, but I nod. "Have you got an appointment?"

"No, uh, a friend sent me, she said to ask for Raquel."

"OK, who can I say is here?" asks the girl. She's a little overweight and her skirt and blouse are too tight, but her face is pretty and I think she's probably younger than she looks.

"Cat Brown," I say confidently. "Dolores sent me."

"Dolores who?" she says, and I don't know her surname, and the girl raises her eyes, just a little, but I notice and she's right, I'm an idiot. She ushers me into a small reception area with a once-trendy grey sofa, and a low level glass table that has a dying fern in the middle of it. It doesn't feel very media to me, not that I'd really know, but she motions for me to sit down and I do so obediently, and she disappears through a door behind me.

After 20 minutes I'm ready to leave. The girl hasn't returned and Raquel hasn't shown up, and I'm sat here, hungry, anxious, feeling that this has been a waste of time after all. Just as I go to get up I hear the downstairs buzzer and heavy clumping on the stairs and eventually I see a very large woman panting on the landing. She's wearing a kaftan and her skin glows orange, presumably from all the facial peels and sunbeds, and her hair is long and platinum blonde and it doesn't suit her colouring. She invites me into her office and above her desk is a large framed picture of her much younger self, one of those studio shots, and she looks slim and beautiful and I sit down opposite her and mourn her lost looks, my lost empathy. I try my best not to think any Muppet-related thoughts, and hand her my CV.

"So, you know Dolores, yes?" She speaks with a very faint accent and I think she's Middle Eastern, maybe Israeli.

"I live in a shared house with her boyfriend," I said. "I've just moved to London, I'm looking for reception work."

She asks me what I like most about being a receptionist, how I deal with difficult clients, how I manage when there are five calls waiting, that sort of thing. I try to forget that I'm lying and answer as best I can. She shuffles some papers on her desk.

"Are you available tomorrow?"

I panic inside. "Yes."

"I have a temp position, a couple of weeks, an ad agency in Soho." She looks at me doubtfully in my skeleton scarf. "I suppose you'd be OK. Do you have references?"

I have ready two printed references, both made up, both from big firms in Manchester where I've never worked. I assume that Raquel won't check, and I give her the best smile I can manage.

Raquel makes a phone call. "Hi Miranda, are you still looking for someone for tomorrow? ..... Yes, her name's Cat Brown ..... 8.45? Super .... She'll be there. Bye bye, bye."

She gives me the details for Carrington Swift Gordon Hughes, top ten advertising agency, Wardour Street, Soho, and I leave her office stunned, amazed at how easy, in practical terms at least, this is turning out to be.

16

Emily had found it hard to concentrate on her job after she'd finally got together with Ben. He'd invade her thoughts at inopportune moments, and she'd find herself smiling inanely, or even drifting off completely, during important meetings where she needed to concentrate. She felt like she'd been punched alive. She felt now like everything that had ever happened in her life before had been experienced through a veil, as if it had all been just a little out of focus. Ben made life dazzling and sharp for her, and it made the day to day business of being a lawyer an inconvenience, a distraction. She'd had to ban him from texting her at work in the end, as her concentration would vanish completely as she typed her wittiest reply and then waited for his response, and then she'd reply again a few minutes later, and then she might have to wait three minutes for his next text and her stomach would be turning back flips with the excitement of it all. Although they rarely met for lunch (Emily didn't like to be too public about it all) she would usually text him when she was going down to the canteen, and he'd be sure to saunter past to have a chat and smile his shy smile and that would keep her going for the afternoon. Eventually of course, she settled down and regained her focus, but she never quite regained her passion for the job she'd worked so hard for.

A few months later Ben and Emily were sat in the canteen early one Monday morning, drinking revolting coffee, the canteen's speciality. They were both tired, they'd climbed the two highest mountains in the Peak District at the weekend, and had barely got any sleep in between – it had rained and their tent had leaked, and besides they'd been too ecstatic. They sat comfortably together at a table near the entrance, on show to anyone who might be interested – they'd long since given up pretending they weren't a couple, and fortunately people had long since stopped teasing them about it, telling them they shouldn't jump into anything, about how great it was they'd fallen for each other, ha ha, yawn yawn. Now people simply accepted them as a pair, even called them Bemily, and they didn't really mind, they were too happy to mind about anything much these days.

Emily was embarrassed all over again today though, and despite usually holding her mug in both hands, chin resting above it, elbows planted on the melamine table top, this morning she kept her left hand firmly out of sight.

"Go on, flaunt it," whispered Ben. "Get it over and done with."

She looked down into her sparkling lap and she couldn't help her heart taking another little canter around her insides, down past her lungs, along her kidneys, over her large intestine. And then she remembered that she hadn't even told her own twin sister yet, maybe they should wait until she'd done that before letting anyone else know. She looked up. Ben was still watching her expectantly, and she didn't want him to think she was being reluctant – after all, she could always ring Caroline later.

"Why does it have to be me who does it?" she said in the end. "It's so bloody sexist. I'm not your property or anything. You haven't won me in a raffle."

"Woo-ooh, Little Miss Touchy," said Ben. "Here, give it to me then." And she took the ring off and mock-threw it at him, and he caught it smartly, just above his coffee, and then he rammed it onto the little finger of his left hand and it was so tight it would probably get stuck, and he stood up and flounced over to the breakfast bar, wafting his hands around, John Inman-like, he was much less reserved these days.

"Sit down, you bloody idiot," she hissed, only half-joking, but it was too late, a couple of colleagues were there getting breakfast and one of them squealed and went, "Is that what I think it is?" and then Emily's boss heard, over at the toast machine, and before she knew it there was a whole group of people around her and Ben, oohing at the ring, congratulating them, hugging them, and although Emily usually hated being the centre of attention, in this instance she found she didn't really mind.

17

On the first day of my new job I re-wear my black dress – I don't have anything else suitable for an advertising agency – and Angel lets me borrow her accessories again, in fact she says I can keep them but I tell her not to be so daft. I get up early but still have to wait for the bathroom, Erica just beats me to it. When she eventually comes out, the bathroom is steamed up and stinks of sulphur and mouthwash, and I wonder if she's as poisonous inside as she looks on the outside. Although I try to smile she scowls at me as she scurries past, wrapped in a short faded towel that shows off her perfect little legs.

I still don't have flip-flops, but I'm getting used to my bathroom regime now – trying not to touch any of the surfaces, trying to avoid the mouldy shower curtain slithering against my body, then once I'm clean standing on one leg whilst I hold the shower head to rinse the bottom of the other foot, drying it with the towel I've hung over the shower rail so it doesn't make contact with any of the surfaces, easing my dried foot into my waiting slipper, showering my other foot, half in, half out the bath, drying it and sliding it into the other slipper. I'm sure eventually I'll get used to it, lower my standards, but at the moment this is the way I can cope.

Brad and Erica are in the kitchen and he's friendly but she's not. Why is such a nice guy with such a bitch? I try not to let her bother me, I should be used to it from growing up with Caroline, and I sit quietly at the table with a bowl of muesli and a mug of strong sweet tea like my mum used to make me.

I leave before I need to, I mustn't be late, and it's just one line to Oxford Circus and it only takes me half an hour. I walk along Oxford Street and then turn right up Wardour Street and find the office a hundred yards up, on the right. It's 8.25, I'm too early. I look at the shiny plate glass windows, through which I can see furniture shaped like internal organs, and the fancy sign above the double doors, and I look at my dreary dress and boring ballet pumps, and know I don't look good enough. It's Day Five, Friday in my first week in London and I stand outside this gleaming tribute to four people's egos and find myself wanting to turn and run – but to where? Maybe I should have moved to the sea, I used to love it there. *Get a grip, Cat. You've already run away, you can't do it again. This is it now.* I shove away memories from happier times, smooth my dress and adjust my scarf, and lurk outside for a few more minutes, until it's time to go in.

18

Caroline adjusted Emily's veil for the final time and they both looked in the mirror as two very different girls stared back. The bride was open-faced, natural-looking, with dark blonde hair piled up high above her long neck. She wore a white satin jacket with fitted sleeves and tiny buttons down the front. Her matching skirt was panelled and kicked out just at the knees, and her shoes were high and forties style. The short veil finished the outfit off, and Caroline thought she'd never seen her twin look so glamorous. Emily had been worried about her sister doing the dress, she really wasn't sure she could trust her, but Caroline had seemed so eager she thought it would be rude to say no, she was a designer after all – and besides she might react badly, get really upset. But Emily needn't have worried, she was delighted with the result.

Caroline was wearing hot pink, daringly short, and she had clashing bright auburn hair, cut into a geometric bob with a thick fringe, like when she was three years old. Her make-up was garish. You could hardly tell they were sisters.

Frances came into the room and saw her two girls standing together, and she noticed how happy they both looked, and yes, even close, like twins should be, and she hoped that maybe they could be more of a proper family at last. Even Andrew seemed a bit more available to them these days, slightly less vacant. It was weird to think it, but perhaps Caroline's stay in that mental hospital had done them all good, one way or another. The staff had done a marvellous job in coaxing Caroline back into sanity, and then Frances's insistence that her daughter move home for a while had been a surprising success. After the initial shock of the loud angry music and the bathroom-hogging and Caroline's natural obnoxiousness, it had been cathartic for all of them. For the first time ever it was just Frances, Andrew and Caroline. Emily had already moved out to her tiny flat on the other side of Chester, and Caroline no longer felt in competition with her twin, at least not on a day to day basis, and it had been good for her. She'd been back with her parents for over two years now – none of them expected it to last anywhere near that long – and she'd appeared to soften, Frances thought, to finally gain some lovability. She'd got an admin job at a fashion house in Manchester and seemed to be doing well – Frances was thrilled for her. Caroline even seemed to hate Emily a little bit less these days, and she'd made her look so *beautiful* today. Frances felt her eyes fill unexpectedly with tears and she pulled herself together, in case she ruined her make-up.

An hour before the ceremony, Ben was getting dressed in his best man's bedroom, which was at the back of the hotel and was one of the few that didn't have that expansive sea view. He was pleasantly surprised that everything was going so well

– dinner last night had been seamless, entirely devoid of bad behaviour – but he was still wary, he knew better than to assume Brown family events would be incident-free. He still found Caroline prickly, and she had that knack of making people so nervous of what they said that they said silly things that she then took pleasure in mocking – but she had definitely improved, and there was nothing concrete that she'd said or done over the wedding to upset anyone. She'd even made Emily's wedding dress which had secretly worried him, but Emily seemed pleased with it, so he shouldn't fret. Ben didn't know why he felt so anxious. This was meant to be the happiest day of his life, they were getting married in the most romantic hotel in the world, with its heady setting and improbable back story, and he knew that Emily was the most unbelievably perfect girl for him.

There was a knock on the door. Good, that must be Jack with the waistcoat, he thought. He finished tying his tie and was tucking his shirt into his trousers as he opened the door.

"Oh. Hello," said Ben. There was something about Caroline that always made him uneasy, and seeing her now looking absolutely stunning propped up provocatively against the doorjamb made him shift his gaze quickly from her startling blue eyes to her vivid pink mouth, down the length of her silk dress and smooth exposed legs, towards the floor.

"Here it is, Benny boy," said Caroline and she held out the magenta waistcoat she'd designed for him. "Sorry it's late, I was just doing some last minute adjustments." Ben didn't like the waistcoat much, but he was happy to wear it for Emily, as long as she thought it looked good. He reluctantly let Caroline help him into it, and then she insisted on doing up all the tiny buttons, protesting that his fingers were too big and that he would mark the silk. She seemed to take ages and when she'd finished she looked him up and down slowly, as if he were naked.

"Wow, you scrub up well," she said. "My darling twin sister has certainly hit the jackpot." He went to move away, embarrassed, but she leaned into him then and whispered, "Good luck, Ben, I hope you and Emily will be very happy together," and before he could stop her she kissed him, right on the mouth, very gently, and for a nano-second Ben felt his body respond, and then he pulled away and muttered thanks and shut the door.

He put on his new shoes and they pinched a bit, and his cheeks were flaming, but he was ready. His best man, Jack, poked his head around the door. "You nearly ready, mate? Hey, you're looking terrible, are you OK?"

"I'm fine, just last minute nerves I think."

"Well, everything's cool, the registrar's here, I just saw Frances and Andrew, they're dressed, and people are beginning to arrive. I've given the hotel the music, it all works. Everything's going to be fine."

"I hope so," said Ben.

"Oh Christ, you're not having second thoughts are you? I need to get you a drink."

"No, no, it's not that. I'm certain about Emily, I'm just not so sure about her family."

"Well, be grateful it's that way round," Jack said and laughed. "Come on. There's nothing a beer won't settle," and he took Ben by the arm and the two of them walked together to the bar.

Andrew had noticed Danielle as soon as they'd arrived the previous evening. Caroline had moaned on and on that she didn't have a boyfriend to bring, how she hated coming to these things on her own, and so in the end Emily and Ben had asked if she'd like to invite a friend instead. She and Danielle had been close in London – it was Danielle who'd called Frances the night Caroline had her "episode," as they now called it, if *it* ever needed to be referred to. Danielle was still living in London, but she'd travelled all the way down to Devon specially, and now she was here she was glad she'd made the effort. She thought the hotel was splendid, a Gothic extravaganza with a huge flower-filled terrace and a view to die for. There was an immense great hall that was so chilled, even on a summer's day, that it had real fires blazing in monster fireplaces on either side of the room. Creaky creased leather Chesterfields made three sides of a square around each fire, heavy mud-coloured curtains flanked the windows, rendering the room pleasantly gloomy. A sweeping staircase led up to the minstrels' gallery that went the whole way round the hall, and it was off here that each of the hotel's 12 rooms was found. The bedrooms themselves were in direct contrast to the great hall: bright, sunny, sea-soaked, with dove grey walls and white Egyptian cotton sheets and bolster cushions, and bathrooms with fancy soaps and clawed foot silver baths. Danielle absolutely loved it here, and everyone had been so friendly, in Andrew's case a bit too friendly, but Danielle was used to dealing with that sort of thing, and besides he was actually quite dishy for his age. She was the type of girl that men found attractive although women often didn't see it, and she was cheerful and open which she knew sometimes sent out the wrong signals, but that's just the way she was, she didn't see why she needed to change.

The doleful notes of Fake Plastic Trees by Radiohead played as Emily walked down the makeshift aisle created between rows of cream fabric-covered chairs in the garden overlooking the sea. Frances had thought it was a strange choice of music, but only Emily and Ben knew its significance, how it had framed their first tentative embrace, and they were happy. They'd decided on a small wedding, only 40-odd people, where everyone they'd invited would come because they loved them and were happy for them, where there was no backbiting about the bride's dress or how the marriage would never last. In the beginning Emily had even wondered whether they should run away and get married on a beach somewhere, she didn't want to upset Caroline, she'd said, but Ben had put his foot down for once. He'd reminded her of the amazing hotel on the cliff in Devon, of how they'd talked hypothetically of what a great place it would be for a wedding, and how they'd both known at the time but hadn't dared acknowledge that they were referring to their own. Caroline would be fine about it, he'd said, it wasn't their fault she hadn't met anyone, and anyway she was much better about things like that these days. And so far, Emily thought, Caroline had been more than fine: she actually seemed happy for them, which was lovely.

Andrew and Frances stood together watching their eldest twin take her vows, and it made them think back to their own wedding day and how long ago that was. Had Andrew meant his vows at the time, they both wondered, and neither knew the answer and they each supposed it didn't matter now. As she faced the flat still water Frances's thoughts kept drifting away to earlier times, to their honeymoon, the awful births, the exhausting early years of their daughters' lives – to how she'd been surprised that Andrew hadn't left her once the twins had grown older, she'd known all along there'd been someone else. Andrew was thinking about how different his life may have been if it had been Victoria he'd married, if he'd met her first, and he wondered for the thousandth time why he hadn't just upped and left his family, surely love is more important? But it was too late now. He thought about how he'd tried to have it all, to keep Victoria, keep his family, and he saw how instead of making everyone happy it had damaged all of them. Victoria must have felt used, strung along by the end, he knew that. After she finally finished it he'd been so utterly bereft that what else was there to do but slide into his pattern of one-night stands and dispiriting affairs? He'd found then that he needed Frances after all, needed her steadiness and calm, someone to come home to.

And what was Frances's excuse for not going? She stood close to Andrew, willing him to take her hand, knowing that, despite all his lies and flakiness, she still loved her husband – he was in many ways a good man and still so handsome, and besides how would she cope on her own?

"So I now pronounce you husband and wife," said the registrar, a gentle-toned Welshman who'd managed to make the short wedding service meaningful, perfect, as his words hung on the breeze. "You may kiss the bride."

As Ben leant forward and gave Emily the tenderest of kisses, Caroline shifted in her seat and yawned.

The wedding breakfast was served outside on mismatched china plates and was a simple buffet of rare roast beef and an enormous whole salmon, with eight different salads and freshly dug new potatoes. Pudding doubled as the wedding cake and was the biggest pile of profiteroles Emily had ever seen, even better than she'd imagined. The weather was faultless, and as it was July she hadn't even bothered with contingency plans, she'd been that confident that the sun would shine on her and Ben, on their happiness. All she wanted was for everyone to eat lovely food, drink champagne and enjoy the view, and she wasn't too fussed about anything else. "Right people, right location, how wrong can we go?" she'd said, and Ben had loved her even more that she wasn't one of those women who turned tedious over their wedding plans, agonising over the colour of the ribbons on the menu cards or which flowers to have in the table sprays. Caroline swanned about with a glass in her hand, flashing her dancer's thighs, going on about how she'd designed all the outfits, annoying Jack's wife by continuously flirting with him, paying people compliments that sounded like insults. As the afternoon wore on, she became that bit louder, that bit brittler, and when she started saying loudly how she wished she could find herself a nice husband too, but one who wasn't a doormat like Ben, Frances took her to one side and suggested quietly that maybe she'd had enough.

"Had enough of what?" sneered Caroline. "Of my goody two shoes sister or her puke-inducing husband?"

"Caroline!" said her mother. "This is Emily's wedding. I thought you were pleased for her."

"Mum," said Caroline wearily, through the champagne. "Of course I'm pleased for her, she's my twin sister, she's in lurve, I just wish she didn't have to ram it down my throat." Caroline's words were slurring now, and Frances knew she needed to get her away from the party – people were listening, she didn't want any trouble. She looked anxiously for Andrew – there he was talking to that busty friend of Caroline's again, surely breasts that size couldn't be natural? Frances had been grateful to Danielle for looking after Caroline the night she'd been sectioned, and for staying in touch afterwards while all her daughter's other so-called friends had drifted away, but she didn't like watching her giggling at Andrew's jokes, they'd been chatting together for far too long, people might talk.

"Andrew," she called. "*Andrew!*" He ignored her the first two times, until eventually he couldn't pretend he hadn't heard her any longer, and when he finally looked round he saw his wife with their beautiful pink and orange daughter, who appeared to be holding onto her mother, her legs long and bendy, her eyes glassy, unfocussed. He sighed and thought, what now? Why couldn't they all just have a good time for a change? And then he went over and it was clear that Caroline was awfully, hideously drunk. It had all happened so quickly, maybe it was the sun, but they needed to get her out of there before she caused a scene. Andrew took Caroline by the shoulder and with his wife tried to prop her up, help her to her room.

"But I don't want to go to my room, Mum, I'm having such a great time, it's my twin sister's wedding, I want to catch the bouquet," she slurred.

"Come on, darling," cajoled Frances. "Let's get you out of this sun and get some water, you'll be fine then."

Caroline's legs splayed as her new magenta heels dug deep in the grass. She yanked at the left one but it stayed stuck where it was whilst her foot came free, and she nearly fell over. Andrew pulled the strappy shoe out from the turf and picked it up, and then he took Caroline under the arm, more firmly this time, and as he did so the thin stiletto heel poked into her bony ribs.

"OWWWW. Get off me, you stupid fuck," screamed Caroline. "Why don't you just leave me alone and go finish feeling up my friend, you loser?"

The hillside went quiet and you could almost hear the lapping of the sea even though it was far below, the endless in and out of the waves, the earth breathing ominously. It was humiliating for all of them, in their different ways. No-one spoke.

It was Ben who finally broke the silence. "It's getting late now," he announced, as calmly as he could. "Why don't we all go inside, the band will be starting soon, and there's plenty more champagne." Everyone moved at Ben's instruction, relieved to get away from having to witness the stricken look on the bride's face.

Later, much later, Caroline lay passed out, still in her fuchsia dress, on her single bed in the pitch darkness. The other bed in the room creaked wearily as Andrew lay with his face beneath Danielle's breasts as she rhythmically moved against him until they both finished, after which Andrew's self-loathing was able to seep in, gently, like the sea far below them, as the tide turned.

19

As I wait outside the agency, an immaculate girl shimmies up the street and wafts into the building. She has long dark hair like in a shampoo ad and her clothes are obviously designer – a red shift mini-dress with gold gladiator sandals. She makes me feel even more of a frump, and I know she must be Polly, the girl I'm meant to ask for. I don't know why I feel so inadequate, I used to be quite happy with my appearance, but today I feel like I'm auditioning for a role and I don't fit the part. When I finally go in, I can tell that she'd clocked me, out in the street, and that she thinks I'm not quite glamorous enough too, but she smiles and offers me coffee and takes me behind reception to show me what to do. Polly is stunning, cool, one of those girls that terrify you, and I find it hard to think what to say to her, I seem to have forgotten how to do small talk. As she goes through who the partners are, how they like to be contacted, who's happy for their mobile number to be given out, what the top clients' particular neuroses are, I look in on myself and feel even more out of place here than in a shitty house in North London. I'm aware that I'd previously taken all this for granted – getting phone calls, being told clients are in reception, having meeting rooms booked for me, I'd had no idea there was so much to it. The receptionists at my company in Manchester were normal, like me, not trophies on display like exotic flowers. As Polly is briefing me, people start arriving for work and they are achingly trendy – there are boys in the latest brand of jeans and statement T-shirts with mussy hair, they must be the creative types; others wear thick-rimmed glasses and narrow-leg trousers with polished squared off shoes, glossy leather satchels slung across their chests. The girls wear high heels and clothes I might at a push wear to a party and they carry over-sized designer handbags. Despite everyone looking different it's almost like they're in uniform. They arrive in dribs and drabs, lattes in hand, and no-one seems in much of a hurry, it's Friday after all. At 9.25 an older guy in a well cut suit and white plimsolls saunters in, says, "Morning Polly darling," then looks at me without interest and just about nods. I smile back and he takes the lift and Polly says, "That was Simon Gordon and he is GOD." The phone goes and Polly answers and she listens and says, "OK, give me two secs," then she disappears off somewhere and leaves me behind the desk and the switchboard starts blinking and I forget what to do. I press the button that's flashing and say, "Good morning, Carrington Swift Gordon Hughes, how can I help?" and by the time I've finished this mouthful the person at the other end is impatient.

"Is Simon there?" says an *extremely* well-spoken voice.

"Simon who?" I say, noticing two Simons on the laminated list Polly has given me.

"Simon Gordon," she says, with a "dumb-fuck" tinge to her tone.

"Who shall I say is calling?" I reply, and she snaps, "His

wife." So I look up Simon's extension, 224, and I press 224 and it connects and after a couple of rings he picks up and I say, "Your wife is on the line, Simon," and he says, "Oh," and he pauses and then says, "Thanks," and I press the transfer button and a loud angry continuous beep sounds through my head-piece.

Fuck. My arm-pits are growing hot. The switchboard blinks again and I know who it is but I don't know what I did wrong so I'm too scared to pick up in case I do it again and I don't know what to do and I'm beginning to really panic now, maybe it's better to just not answer than cut her off again. I'm desperate for the flashing to stop, it feels ominous, like a warning, and I know if I screw up this time I'll probably be fired, and then at last Polly shimmers gracefully round the corner, so I beckon frantically at her and she comes across to the front of the desk just as I answer.

"Hello, is that Simon's wife, I'm so terribly sorry," I say in my best voice, trying to disguise my flat Northern tones. I press 224 again and look helplessly at Polly, and as Simon says, "Where's my wife gone?" Polly drapes herself over the wide glass desk, leopard-like, and with the end of her long manicured nail she connects the call.

Polly is surprisingly a really nice girl. We have little in common and she's way too trendy for me, but she has a good heart and shows me exactly how the switchboard works, and although it's not hard it's unfathomable if you've never been told. Simon has forgotten his mobile today, so all the calls he would normally get direct are coming through me, Simon's wife has somehow managed to redirect his calls. I spend half the morning focussing on not cutting people off and managing people's confusion that I'm not Simon when I answer, but after a couple of hours I've got the hang of it, and Polly has told me that I don't have to say Carrington Swift Gordon Hughes each time, but that CSGH will do fine. Fortunately Simon found the incident with his wife funny ("It depends what mood he's in, Cat," said Polly), and it has given us a little bond ("Ha ha, I'm glad I'm not the only one who's pissed my wife off this morning") and Polly tells me it's because he has a long lunch at the Ivy to look forward to, not with clients or anything boring like that, but an over-due jolly with his best mate who runs one of the satellite channels.

Friday is definitely the best day to have started this job: there's only one day to get through before the weekend, and everyone is either in a good mood anyway or massively hung-over, and so (apart from Simon's wife obviously) they're a bit more forgiving than they might have been in the earlier part of the week. It was a good decision, in terms of timing at least, to run away on a Monday, not that I knew it at the time of course. It's meant I met Angel for a start, plus it's given me the whole week to sort myself out, and although at night my soul still screams through the dark for my boy, for how I've let him down, lost him, I'm otherwise oddly proud of my achievements. I've done it, I've made it here, I already have a home, a job, a head-start on forgetting.

20

Uncle Max took Angela by the hand and led her across the busy road. Angela liked him better than she'd liked any of her other uncles, even her Uncle Ted, but she still wanted to go home, she didn't really like these trips, and she absolutely hated being forced to dress up smart. They walked further along New Brook Street and after hanging around for a while entered yet another jewellery store. Uncle Max asked to look at some rings, a whopping sapphire one and another with a sizeable solitary ruby surrounded by miniature diamonds, as well as all the more traditional engagement rings. If Angela stood on her tiptoes she could just about see them winking on the glass counter, but she couldn't be bothered, she was bored, and she didn't see why she was having to be dragged around like this *again*. Uncle Max had promised her a milkshake later, if she did well, so she did as she was told and stood quietly and waited.

The door to the shop opened and a woman entered. She wore black Capri pants and a big fur coat, and she had dark cloudy hair, steep black eyebrows, heavy make-up. She had a look that demanded attention, like a film star. The man serving Uncle Max looked up briefly and acknowledged the woman. The other assistant was already busy with another customer, and so the woman stood impatiently, reeking of perfume, tapping her shiny high heel. Angela ignored her and started to take more interest in the rings Uncle Max was being shown. The woman became increasingly annoyed, presumably at being made to wait, and she started huffing and pacing, taking stompy half-steps around the little shop. As she turned back towards the main counter for a third time she appeared to stumble. She let out a soft gasp and fell, elegantly, to her knees, her head flopping to the floor as if in supplication, her fur coat splaying open like an animal pelt. The staff looked on in horror, but they were on the other side of the glass counters, they couldn't get to her immediately. It was Uncle Max who reacted first, and he rushed to help her. The shop workers stood transfixed, it was the most exciting thing that had happened in ages. Max bent behind the woman and put his hands under her armpits. He hoisted her up from the floor and helped her onto a chair and put her head between her knees, so the blood could return, he was sure she'd just fainted. By then another assistant had appeared from the back of the shop and she gave the woman a glass of water and fanned her with a store brochure until she felt better. Angela stayed where she was at the counter and did what she'd been told. The whole thing was over in a few seconds, and then Uncle Max returned to looking at the rings, although in the end he didn't buy anything. Afterwards he was in such a good mood he took Angela to the cinema to see Home Alone, and he even bought her popcorn.

21

Angel offers to take me clothes shopping. I've told her about my new job and my wardrobe problems but I say that I can't really afford to buy much at the moment, I only have two weeks' work and I don't know where my next job's coming from. Angel laughs and says she's good at finding bargains, and besides she's off on Saturday night, so she suggests we go late afternoon and then stay out for a few drinks afterwards. I find myself saying yes, after all there are two whole days to get through, to try not to think through, before I'm back at work on Monday, and I have no other plans – but I hate the thought of going out enjoying myself, especially when I think about everything that's happened. I wonder if the guilt will fade, one day.

Angel says she'll be sleeping until around two, she was working last night, and as it's a nice morning I think I'll go for a walk – it will help kill some time, and maybe the fresh air will clear my head. I miss our garden in Chorlton now, miss the opportunity to potter around when it's too nice to be indoors, weeding the pots, dead-heading the roses, or best of all putting a blanket on the grass and playing trains with my little boy.

Stop it.

Brad tells me about a disused railway line that's been turned into a country walk through the city and goes the whole way from Finsbury Park to somewhere nice, I forget the name. It's lovely, Brad tells me, and you can carry on to Hampstead Heath from there, and I've heard of that. Erica looks annoyed, as if she resents me for knowing and Brad for telling, I don't think she likes to share anything, even stuff that's free, and she reminds me again of my sister.

I definitely need some exercise after the stresses of yesterday – cutting people off, getting their names wrong, having to say CSGH a thousand times, watching the clock as the week winds down and the call volumes dwindle. And smiling had felt like especially hard work. But Simon Gordon seems to have taken to me fortunately, despite my shaky start, and I like him, he's nice underneath all the bullshit he's surrounded himself with. There's something about him, he seems to have seen right through me, almost as if he knows what I've done and wishes he had the guts (or the cowardice, depending on which way you look at it) to get the hell out of his life too. Two of the other partners – I haven't met the Carrington yet (first name Tiger!) – are less charismatic: Simon appears to have been the driving force behind the agency, but he seems tired of it all to me. As he was heading out yesterday on his way to his fancy lunch he asked me if I could organise a car for him later, to take him out to Gloucestershire somewhere, and I said, "Away for the weekend, Simon?" and he said, "No, I live there, I just stay in town during the week," and he seemed so sad and lacking in enthusiasm that I wondered whether his wife was a bitch to him too.

"Oh," I'd said, trying to be polite. "It must be lovely to have a London crash pad and a proper place in the country," and Simon had looked at me funny, and Polly told me afterwards that he has a whole house in Primrose Hill, he is *loaded*. I wonder how he can make that much money from daft commercials about aftershave and crisps, and how it can make you so joyless. I feel sad for him somehow.

I'm surprised by the Parkland Walk. Although I struggle to find the start of it, once I'm on it all I have to do is follow it straight and I'll get to where I'm going, and that to me is perfect, I wish life could be like that. It cuts a thin green swathe through North London and because it's summer the leaves are thick on the trees, and I can barely see the backs of the houses that remind me I'm even in the city. Every now and again I pass through a tunnel that is livid with graffiti, or an overgrown playground that nature seems to be reclaiming and is too dangerous now for the little children it was meant for. As I pass some railway arches my eye is drawn upwards and above me is a stone creature, some kind of sprite I think, climbing out the wall at me, like it's trying to get me, and it gives me the creeps. I suppose it's meant to be art, but I don't like it and hurry on.

Today is Saturday and I can hardly believe how far I've come in less than a week, how bizarrely simple it has been to start my life all over again, and how maybe I'm going to be all right after all, now that I've done it. I'll be OK as long as I don't think about Ben or Charlie, and what they might be doing now, on their first weekend alone, or how they're coping. I try not to acknowledge that what I've done is mad, unforgivable – that although Ben may not love me anymore,

I've still disappeared, he doesn't know where or how I am, whether I'm alive or dead. Charlie won't understand properly yet of course, his pain will come later.

Instead I concentrate on the business of keeping my feet moving, on everything that's happened this week – I try not to think of *before* again – and I get lost in the rhythm of the soft soil and the swaddling trees and my steady certain steps, and before I know it I find that I've been walking for nearly an hour. I've almost reached the end of this tunnel of countryside and it has helped reconnect me to the earth, helped ground me again. The sun must have gone behind a cloud and the colours switch from cheerful yellows and bright new greens, to sullen browns and dullard greys. The temperature drops. I turn left, my steps quietly snapping the dead rotting twigs beneath me, and I walk up the narrow path through the trees, towards the sound of the traffic.

I stand with my back to the lake and stare across the lawn at the vast white Regency house, and I had no idea that London was so beautiful. I've walked the whole way here, it must be maybe five miles, and I've managed to screen out for the most part all the well-heeled families with their kids and dogs and unbearable innocence I've encountered along the way. Maybe I'm starting to forget that I used to be like them, perhaps I'm already easing into my new self, becoming Cat – and I stand here feeling properly alive for the first time in months. There's a tingling again, where my heart used to be. The day is hot but nicely so, the air feels clean and untainted, the world feels like maybe it's an OK place to be, after all. I begin to think not only can I survive here in London, maybe I can even dare one day to be happy again. Happy in a different way certainly – but six days ago I was focussing on raw survival, today I'm looking at beauty and serenity as a possible way forward (I've forgotten for a moment the horrors of Finsbury Park Palace, the vainglorious CSGH). As I gaze around me in wonder, as if seeing the world for the very first time, I find myself smiling like an idiot, and I want to spin across the lawn in an absurd expression of my relief and joy, that I've survived, that I'm here, that I've done the right thing after all, that all three of us *will* be OK, one day, and just as I begin to raise my arms skywards I notice there's someone staring at me. The man looks at me, not as in what's that mad woman doing grinning at nothing, but in that way people do when they're sure they know you, and he starts to move towards me and smile as if to say hello, and I panic, *I've been rumbled*, and so I turn and run, along the fence next to the lake, down over the bridge, through the sun-starved woods, and although I'm blinded and stumbling I don't stop until my breath tells me I have to.

I'm lost. The heath is enormous, mapless, and I walk for ages, head down, not noticing where I'm going, not caring, as long as I don't have to see that man again. I finally reach a road and a bus is stood at the stop there and I don't know where it's going but I get on it anyway and sit stiffly, staring out the window, anxious, disorientated, until it eventually stops outside an underground station, I've no idea where, I've never heard of Archway. It's a tortuous tube route back to Finsbury Park and it takes me ages, but at least I don't have to ask anyone the way, I feel too ripped apart. At the house I sneak upstairs to my clean white room and lie face-down on the bed and sob and sob for myself and my husband and son, for all our lost lives. I feel worn out, depleted, sick of myself. I've made a hideous mistake thinking I could just run away, that it would be that easy, the kindest thing for us all. It's a relief, when the crying stops at last, to just lie there, quietly and alone.

The knocking stirs me and it's hours later, and Angel is at the door, in her white fluffy dressing gown. "Oh, sorry, did I wake you babe? Do you still want to go shopping? We need to go soon if you're – ." She sees my face, it's like all the pain of the past three months has settled onto it in my sleep, like a misery mask. I don't know what to do, I'm not sure why the man at the heath has unhinged me but he has. He KNEW me. Is there nowhere for me to hide? Angel sits on the end of my bed, and I sit up and start sobbing again, heaving animal rasps that sound through the house, and for once I don't care that people can hear, what people think. I lean into myself, bend double and press hard to try to contain the pain, and all Angel can do is sit and watch, and when at last the grief subsides a little she takes my hand and holds it, still saying nothing. We sit like that for a very long while, and then I dry my eyes and say, as brightly as I can manage, "I can be ready in ten minutes, if it's still OK with you?" Angel says, "Of course, if you're sure, let's go babe," and I'm amazed that she doesn't try to fix me, just accepts me, flawed and raw as I am.

We head "up West" as Angel calls it, and it reminds me of Eastenders and I didn't know people really talk like that. I'm trying hard to feel normal, be normal, let the apparent normality of other people rub off on me. We make our way along Oxford Street, past the discount stores and the bemused tourists (*this* is London?) and the chain stores and the mobile shops, until we reach Selfridges and it's so much bigger and busier than the one in Manchester. Angel seems to know her way round, and we go up the escalator to the second floor and she picks out clothes for me that I wouldn't dream of choosing myself. Her judgment is good, and despite myself I find I'm looking in the mirror and thinking, yes, maybe Cat Brown would wear that, but I'm still anxious – I feel oddly disloyal for doing something so frivolous, for trying on clothes, and I'm stressed about spending the money I need to survive. The shop assistants are uninterested in us, it's late, they're all bored, examining their perfect nails, waiting to go home, and we're largely left alone. Angel keeps bringing piles of clothes into the little fitting room, it's one of those old-fashioned ones hidden behind a full-length mirror, Angel knew where to find it. The tiny drab room seems out of place here, a throwback to another less showy time, before there were voluptuous changing rooms with huge ornate mirrors and thick brocade curtains, full of skinny girls in expensive underwear. Angel keeps coming back with more outfits in various sizes for me to try on, and soon the room is stuffed full of clothes, and after my initial reluctance I think to hell with it, and try on everything, whatever Angel brings me, however daring. The sobbing earlier seems to have been cathartic, maybe it's done me good to let it out at last. And then out of nowhere I remember the last time I went shopping, just *before*, with my mum, and it hits me: my God, I've abandoned her as well. I can't believe I haven't even thought about her and Dad until now, not even back in Manchester when I was planning it, of how they'll be devastated too. All I've thought about up until now is Ben and Charlie, and mostly myself of course. What the fuck is wrong with me?

I've lost the heart for shopping, although perversely I'm worried I'll offend Angel if I don't buy anything, she seems so keen to help me. (What about breaking my loved ones' hearts, shouldn't I be more worried about *that*?) Angel senses my reluctance, and suggests we go for a coffee and maybe come back later, when I've had time to decide what I really like, she doesn't want to rush me. So we leave the little room, with all the clothes piled up for the shop assistants to sort out (although I try to do it Angel tells me not to be silly, it will give them something to do, she says) and we make our way back down the escalator, through handbags, into perfumes and out onto Oxford Street, and despite all the people I calm down a little, the movement seems to help somehow. As Angel sashays through the throng I notice again how fragile she seems, too tiny and fresh to be a croupier, too innocent to operate in a night-time underworld of hope and fecklessness and loss. She bemuses me. We find a bar nearby – I hadn't realised what the time was, it's too late for coffee, too late to go back to Selfridges today, and I find myself worrying what I'll wear on Monday, as if it matters. I don't need to ask Angel what she wants, I order two vodka tonics and they're served long and cool with ice and lime. The bar must be new, it's expensively decorated, and it has an interior-designed feel to it, as if it's trying too hard, like me. We sit at the back, near an allium-papered feature wall, on identical shiny chairs, listening to unidentifiable music probably approved by management somewhere, and I mourn proper cafes with rusted Martini signs and mismatched tables and maybe even candles in bottles, naff though they are. Why has the world become sanitised, homogenised, boring? I could be in London or Manchester or Prague, bars like these are all the same. *You should be in Manchester*, says a voice and I suck through my straw, hard, to drown it out. Angel looks pleased with herself, and she rummages in her capacious Mulberry handbag (is it real?) that makes her seem even more diminutive, doll-like, than she really is and hands me a plain plastic bag, under the table. It feels weird, metallic, and when I open it inside is the orange silk dress and denim kick-skirt I'd coveted earlier but been too anxious to buy, along with a blue sequined top and silver shirt-dress that I'd loved but dismissed as too expensive, too daring. It takes me a moment to understand, the tags are still on, and then I look up into her face and I'm appalled.

Angel smiles sweetly. "Oh, babe don't worry, they can afford it, places like that budget for it."

"That's not the point," I whisper, bundling the clothes back into the foil-lined bag and shoving them under the table. Angel looks hurt.

"I was only trying to help," she says, and she looks downcast, like a child.

I don't want to hurt Angel's feelings, I've grown absurdly fond of her already, and so I buy her another vodka tonic and tell her thank you, that I'm touched after all, but inside I'm churning. I've never stolen anything, I don't even know anyone who has – apart from Caroline I expect. Angel realises she's misjudged me and seems ashamed, so I resolve to keep the clothes – what else can I do with them, what else can I wear on Monday? When we're on our third vodka a group of men come in and the bar is soulless and empty still, and Angel smiles and giggles at them and before I know it they've sent champagne over. I don't want to talk to them, they're way older than us, in expensive shirts with fading hair and a look of expectation in their eyes, as if the champagne is a transaction and now we owe them something. I want to leave, but Angel's enjoying herself, her eyes are flashing with the alcohol and the adrenaline. One of the men is not bad-looking and he obviously fancies Angel, so I sit like a lemon while they flirt with each other, and because I can't think of anything to say the others give up on me and go back to the bar. Maybe I should go home and leave her to it. Angel tips her head back and exposes her long white neck, which shimmies as she drinks, and I can see for an instant the desire in the man's eyes, reflected in mine. As Angel finishes the drink, she brings the champagne flute down on the dark wooden table, hard – I think she misjudged it, we're both quite pissed now – but although the energy shudders through the glass, it doesn't break.

"Ooops," she says. "Thanks guys, lovely to meet you." And she swings in one motion from the chair, puts her arm through mine, pulls me to my feet and we sway gently across the empty floor towards the door. As I glance back Angel's suitor looks annoyed for a second, as if he's been done, but Angel waves flirtily and he smiles acquiescently, devotedly even, and then he goes back to his mates and orders another drink.

Angel suggests we check out a bar she knows in Soho. I'm tired and miserable and want to go home, even though I know she'll be disappointed, she says it's her first Saturday night off in weeks. "Please go without me, I'll be fine," I say, although Angel is insistent she'll come back to the house, she's obviously worried about me, but her phone goes twice and I can tell that someone really really wants her to stay out. I feel awkward now. Even though we've become such good friends so quickly – it's largely because of Angel that I've settled as well as I have into that house, this life – it feels different out here in the West End. I'm still freaked by the shopping incident, by the expensive stolen clothes that are hidden in her handbag, and although I admit she'd already told me all that crazy stuff about her brazen scams with her mum's gangster boyfriend, how she used to steal diamond rings off shiny counter tops while all eyes were on her mother, I thought that was in the past, when she was just a little girl. I find myself grappling in new territory, with someone who's seen life and lived it, and despite everything that's happened, until a few days ago I was still just a boring lawyer from Chester. I'm suddenly wrung out from the events of the past week, the past months, and I feel weak with the need to rest.

"Come on babe," says Angel. "Let's just go for one drink and see how you feel. We'll have a good time, I promise," and she takes my hand and smiles a smile of such delightfulness that I find it impossible to deny her. We walk the whole way up Oxford Street (how does she walk in those heels?) and then we cross the road into my street, where I work, where I have a job! I point out the agency to Angel and she says, "Blimey, that's a bit posh innit?" and then we carry on along Wardour Street and across Old Compton Street and by this time my feet ache and my desire to go home (which home?) is overwhelming. Angel is practically towing me now, and we go down some narrow steps that I would never have noticed and it all feels a bit dodgy, but as we go through the entrance it opens into a gigantic bar, with high ceilings and bare brick walls and colossal chandeliers. Hard core porn is being projected onto a screen which covers the entire back wall. There's no sound to go with the blown-up images, thank God, just pumping loud techno-music, is that what it's called? The bar is heaving with beautiful trendy people and I feel embarrassed of my jeans and boring shirt. My eyes don't know where to look – I've never seen such an enormous penis or what he's doing with it – and so I stand with Angel at the bar waiting for one of the frantically busy yet coolly aloof bar-staff to notice me, and I realise that no-one else is looking at the screen either, it's as if it's not there at all. A gargantuan act of sexual liaison – and it may as well be a ranting man with a placard, people are so studious in their ignoring of it. What's it there for – is it art, is it fashion – and then I wonder why I care. As I wait to order two vodka tonics, I hear across the music a showy sing-song voice yelling, "Angel, dar-ling! You made it," and I turn to see an immaculately monumental black man, in a tight banana-yellow T-shirt stretched wide across his sculpted chest, embracing her, wrapping her against him like she's a little child just out the bath. Angel grins and looks up flirtatiously at him, although it's obvious to even me that he's gay. I've lost my place in the dubious queuing system, and I stand waiting again, convinced now I'm being deliberately ignored. When I'm finally served, by a beautiful young girl with rings through her eyebrows, I order three doubles – Angel's friend is too far away to ask what he wants and I can't face coming back. I'm charged an unbelievable amount of money, I had no idea three drinks could cost that much. As I reach Angel through the crowd she says, "Dane, meet my fab new flatmate, Cat, I found her under a bush," and she giggles.

"Hi," I say, smiling shyly. "I'm afraid I didn't know what you wanted, so I got you a vodka." Dane squeals and says, "Ooh, I'm more of a mojito man myself, don't worry darling, Ricardo's getting me one," and I look over and coming towards us is another divine-looking man, perfectly formed, dark and diminutive, with two frosted green drinks, fancy like ornaments in his manicured hands. Angel takes her drink, and I'm left with two double vodkas. I drink the first as fast as I can, mainly so I can put the glass down, and soon feel a warmth oozing through me. I try to offer the spare drink to Angel, but she shakes her head and says, "You have it, babe," and within 15 minutes I've finished them both. I feel light-headed now, as though I'm not really here, but I do my best to follow the conversation above the head-throb music, try to ignore the unimaginable genitalia, try to forget just how out of place I feel.

I have no idea what time it is. I'm standing on a table (am I somewhere different?) and I'm wearing the silver shirt-dress that Angel stole for me earlier. My feet are bare, I know this because the table is sticky and wet beneath me. Angel is next to me, dancing sexily, while I sway around drunkenly, my long legs bending to the music, my feet planted firmly on the table top. I have just enough presence of mind to realise how ridiculous I must look, before I'm swept away again on the euphoria of freedom and release and alcohol, and I throw my head back and whoop with relief, not caring what anyone thinks anymore, dancing still, vaguely in time to the music.

"Let's get another drink!" I yell above the noise to Angel, and then I leap Dirty Dancing-style off the table and my legs crumple beneath me. Someone (Dane?) helps me off the floor and then Angel is by my side and they drag me to the toilets, my legs don't seem to be working now. I lean on Angel and we manage to enter a cubicle and I sit fully clothed on the seat with my head between my legs, and I don't even feel sick or repulsed by the filth or the smell, I just feel exhausted. All I want to do is go to sleep, today is officially OVER. Angel is slapping me, shaking me, saying, "Come on babe, wake up," and at long last I rouse myself and I sit up and stare vacantly at her, and then that dreadful image appears in my head from nowhere and I'm crying hysterically again, like I'll never ever stop. Angel strokes my hair and says, "Come on, babe, I'll look after you, it's all going to be OK," and then she moves next to me and starts doing something on the cistern behind me.

"Have some of this babe, it will help, honest," she says. I stagger to a kneeling position on the toilet seat and stare blankly at the long straight line. I know what it is but I don't want to know. I've been offered before, at university, but I have never ever been tempted, not even slightly. I'm vaguely aware of my silver shirt-dress, open almost to my navel, my naked feet on the cubicle floor in the worse wet now, my long hair ratty around me, and all I want to do is go home, properly home, to Ben and Charlie and – and what? I just feel so tired. I pull back my hair and take the rolled up note from

Angel, my friend, my saviour, I can trust her, surely? My eyes droop towards unconsciousness again and Angel shakes me, harder this time. I don't know what to do. I just want everything to stop. If only I could sleep here but it seems I can't. And so in the end I lean forward defeatedly, decision made, and enter the next stage of my very strange life, the one I'm most ashamed of.

Part Two

22

The doors jolt open and people flood off, and then more miserable people swarm on like liquid, filling every available gap, pushing right past me, rubbing against my beautifully-cut nude coloured coat. I left the flat earlier this morning and the tube is more crowded than I'm used to. I stand amongst my fellow commuters, moving with the carriage and the crowds from the west of the city to the centre. No-one particularly notices me, I'm just another girl in designer heels, with a hole where her soul used to be. I went "shopping" yesterday, Angel said I should treat myself, and I have a new silk scarf slung gracefully round my neck. The tube is warm and cosy-feeling, despite the sad-mouthed strangers, despite my having to stand — it's comforting down here after the freezing cold wind of the May morning outside.

I'm determined to be in a good mood today, even though I'm being jostled and squashed, even though it's a Monday. It's my first day at work since my latest promotion, so I have a duty to be cheerful. In the nine short months I've been at CSGH, I've moved swiftly from holiday cover temp to permanent receptionist (the old one never came back from Bodrum, she fell in love with a Turkish soldier apparently), to office manager (sweet vacant Polly wafted off to a rival agency), then to Account Exec and now Account Manager! Even I'm astonished at the speed of my rise. Last July I would have thought an Account Manager balanced ledgers, not oversaw the process of making 96 sheet posters and extortionate TV commercials. I guess it's partly because I'm older, used to be a lawyer (not that anyone knows that of course), so I carry a bit more gravitas than the other Execs – but it obviously also helps that I'm Simon's little pet. I know people in the agency talk, and they probably think I'm sleeping with him, and I have thought about doing so, it's true, probably would have done under other circumstances – after all I do find him attractive, I have no allegiance to his bitch of a wife – but I cannot, despite everything else I've done, quite bring myself to sleep with someone who's not Ben. I don't know why, I've been so spectacularly drunk and high enough times to just fall into some stranger's bed, or have a messy coupling in a dingy club's toilets, but it's the one area of my life in which I've retained some standards, that I've not been prepared to shift on.

As we reach the next stop, more people shove themselves on, no-one gets off, and there's no room at all now. It's not cosy anymore, it's grim and unpleasant, rammed up as I am, over-intimate, against these random strangers. Fortunately it's just one line, no changes, straight through from Shepherds Bush, so there are only three more stops until I get off.

The flat that Angel and I share is a definite improvement on Finsbury Park Palace. We pay quite a bit more each month and we have a newly white-washed conversion in a large Victorian villa. We have a living room now, nice kitchen (no dodgy bins or Brazilian cooking smells) and the bathroom is newly fitted, completely devoid of blossoming mould and slimy shower curtains. That's why we went for it, because it's clean, neutral, the antithesis of our old house, plus it's handily close to the tube. At last I've thrown away my flip flops, and all my toiletries are stacked neatly in the mirrored cabinet above the sink, no longer carted round in my wash bag. Angel and I are happy, in our own ways. She still works in casinos and operates a weird upside down life, she still has a massive shoplifting and cocaine habit, but there again I'm not too far behind myself these days. I'm a million miles from the girl I used to be – maybe snorting coke was the only way I could cope, once the adrenaline of that first agonising week had faded. It's weird how I seem to have become so like my twin lately, perhaps bad behaviour's in my genes too. I just never understood before what she obviously knew all along – how drugs and alcohol can numb you, help you forget.

It's ironic that that was another reason things started looking up for me at work – once I started dressing right, doing the after work drinks thing, the sneaky trips to the toilets behind clients' backs, and it has made the new me shiny and sparkling, my wit sharpened, almost like Caroline's, but without so much hatred. It's hard to fathom, but people find me glamorous now, funny even. In my old life I had quiet confidence, unremarkable prettiness, easy popularity, but now I am super-charged, sleek, seductive. And although I know in my heart I take too many drugs and steal too many clothes I've convinced myself it's OK for now, it's all part of the process, part of the forgetting. I won't do it forever.

Although I love our new flat I almost miss my old

housemates, no matter that they drove me mad — entrepreneurial Chanelle and flat-pack Jerome, foul-mouthed Bev, the taciturn swarthy boys, giant-baby Brad and even the loathsome Erica. They became like family to me, and, let's face it, they were no more nutty than my real one, once you get beyond appearances. Although now it's just myself and Angel we have a constant stream of visitors, so I never get too lonely — Angel's various dealers; her dear friend Rafael, who she met at the casino; the adonis-like Dane and Ricardo; and sometimes even Angel's mother too.

Ruth is a remarkable-looking woman. She's only 47 and looks maybe ten years younger, and she still plays the clubs and has at least one boyfriend on the go at any given time. She lives in a mansion block in Bayswater, council I think, and she turns up every now and again to sleep on the couch, after yet another fight with the latest man in her life. Angel treats her like a little sister or even a daughter and, as with me, she doesn't judge her mother or try to change her, but just accepts her with the sweetness she has always shown me. I love Angel. It's almost as if half the love I had for my husband has transmuted into a platonic love of this waif-like beauty with her flawed genes and bad habits. The other half has gone to successful sad Simon, sat in his gleaming office managing tantrums and egos, making expensive commercials for cornflakes and cars. I feel lucky to have them both in my life, they've helped me move on from the desolate broken person that left home one stinking hot morning last July, to the successfully still-alive girl I am now.

Despite how close I've grown to both Angel and Simon I'm surprised that I've never ever been tempted to spill my secret – that I was once blissfully married, had a beautiful little two year old boy with sunshine in his eyes and spun gold for hair, another baby on the way. Until very recently I'd managed to transform my life so dramatically as to put all that firmly in the past; sometimes I'd even forgotten it was ever true.

I've never felt like telling Simon or Angel that I'm one half of a set of twins either – the supposedly normal, uncomplicated half at that – and this too has liberated me. Being a twin makes you seem odd in people's eyes, you're different, you're half of a whole, not an individual, you have between the two of you a bond that no-one else can feel or understand. If only they knew the truth! I'm glad to be rid of Caroline, to have finally given up on her at last, she deserves it after what happened. *I hate her now*.

As the tube rumbles eastwards my thoughts go where they like, free of their tracks, although I half-heartedly try to stop them. I find myself thinking of my poor parents, for the last 30 odd years having to manage Caroline's moods and willfulness, her latest condition (anorexia, madness, alcoholism, she certainly kept them busy), the destruction she has wreaked. With the distance of time it all seems like an episode of one of those chat shows, not real or in any way part of me. I've never quite understood Mum's role in it all, how Caroline got quite so screwed up, but I'm sure it's mainly to do with her. I was always aware, even when we were tiny, that there was something not quite right between them, even aware that Mum preferred me – it's only now I'm so far away I can properly admit it. And when they seemed to finally sort their issues out, resolve things, during my sister's stay in that eating clinic,

155

I guess it was already too late for Caroline, the damage had been done.

I don't know why, but I've rarely tried to analyse any of this before – although I always tried to get on with my sister, she was mainly someone in my life to be wary of, managed, even when we were little. I think I was a bit scared of her, looking back. Even when she almost ruined our wedding I forgave her – after all I still had Ben, he'd still married me – and at the time I was sure she hadn't meant it, it was par for the course, just "Caroline being Caroline." But after what she's done now I'm glad to be free of her, that's one thing I definitely don't regret about leaving.

How I feel about deserting my parents is different, and thinking about them from afar, from the safety of a new life makes me feel sad for them both. My poor pathetic father. He thought none of us knew that he'd slept with Caroline's friend at our wedding, but the look on Danielle's face the next morning, the bleary bewilderment of Caroline – she must have been in the same room for God's sake – meant that nothing needed to be said. I think it was that final very public humiliation that gave Mum the courage to leave at last, and after that it all came out, all his grubby exploits that Mum had spent years ignoring. I was appalled, couldn't believe it of him, I'd adored him so. Mum came to stay with us at first, Ben didn't mind even though we were only just married, and it would have been fine, apart from that it meant Caroline came around more often, flirting with Ben, and Dad was on the phone *every day*, crying, begging to speak to Mum, although she refused him. Ben was an absolute saint, looking back. He must have really loved me then.

As the train rushes forwards I find my thoughts rampaging backwards even faster now. Out of the blue I'm thinking of pretty much everyone I've left behind and wondering what they may be doing right this minute: Ben and Charlie of course, Mum and Dad, my lovely in-laws, Dave and Maria from work (have they got it together yet?), my bridesmaids, my friends from ante-natal classes, our next door neighbour Rod and his ancient hopefully-still-alive spaniel, my friend Samantha up the road, the canteen lady who used to make us undrinkable coffee. I keep thinking that exactly a year ago it was still *before*, just about, and I feel desperate all over again.

As the tube storms into Oxford Circus I physically shake my head to rid myself of these thoughts, and my expensively-streaked bob swings into my eyes. I smooth my hair, compose myself, put the past back where it belongs. I battle my way off the train, shuffle with the throng along the crowded platform, glide up the escalator (on tiptoes to protect my heels, mentally practising my cheery hellos all the way) and then I step out into the too-bitter Spring day.

23

Caroline looked at the thin blue line on the white plastic stick and she let out a soft breath of – what? Fear, or anticipation? She was still only 22, but she'd just graduated from St Martin's, had a flat off Brick Lane, a good-looking boyfriend, a promising job in fashion. She'd been pregnant twice before, and neither time had felt right, but this time? She wasn't sure. It surprised her how fecund she'd proven to be, despite having starved her body as a teenager, and she resolved to be more careful in future, she couldn't keep having abortions. Dominic was taking her out later, maybe she could sound him out then on how he'd feel about having a baby. She put the cap on the pregnancy test and stored it at the back of the bathroom cabinet, then she showered and put on her favourite outfit, she found she wanted to look her best today. She felt close to this starter-baby, unlike the others – maybe because she could see herself loving its father this time, after all he was her boyfriend, not just some random sexual partner where things had got out of hand. Caroline looked down at her belly, beneath the orange pop art T-shirt, and imagined it swelling and rounding with a beautiful little baby inside. Someone for her to love, who would love her back, unconditionally. She found she liked the thought.

Caroline finished dressing and smoothed the silver eiderdown over her bed instead of leaving it unmade like usual. The walls were painted fuchsia pink and were covered in pictures she'd bought off friends from art college: abstract naked women with their legs apart, black and white photos of muscly men wearing sadomasochistic collars and belts, a blood-spattered sunset. She loved that the pictures were so outrageous, and who knows they might be worth something one day. Although the room was nice enough the bed was so huge she would barely fit a cot in there. She'd probably need to move before the baby's born, she thought. Maybe she and Dominic could get a place together, somewhere a bit more child-friendly, Islington perhaps, or even Ealing. Caroline put on her shoes – gold platform trainers that were almost impossible to walk in – and went into the kitchen. The flat was in the eaves of a converted house, so the walls sloped into her and the cabinets were at crazy angles, but the room was bright and light and Caroline felt blessed, euphoric, as she looked out to the Virgin Mary-blue of the sky. She put some coffee on and went to light a cigarette, and then remembered herself – she was *pregnant* – and so she picked up yesterday's newspaper instead, and even the bad news seemed good today and she thought about ringing her mother.

No, she'd wait to tell Dominic first, she thought, in fact she'd call him now. She dialled his number, and it rang and rang but didn't flip to voicemail. She checked her watch, still only 9.30, she'd try him again later. She settled down to watch daytime TV, she didn't need to be at work until 12 today, and she flicked channels until she found her favourite show — uncouth people screaming and shouting at each other about falling out with their sister, or sleeping with their mother's lover, or their boyfriend not being the father of their child. Caroline may have developed a hard persona, a "don't fuck with me" veneer, but somehow when she watched these shows she always cried, it seemed the distilling of human emotions into these undignified shouting matches moved her in a way little else did. Glen from Sheffield was just about to find out whether or not he was the father of his two year old daughter when Caroline's phone went and she hesitated to pick up, and then she saw who it was.

"Hi Dom," she said, and her voice was free of the sarcastic drawl that so alienated people, put them on high alert for attack.

"Hi gorgeous, saw I missed a call from you?"

"Yeah..." She went to speak, blurt it out, and then she changed her mind. "Er, I was just wondering what time you were coming over tonight?"

"About 7.30? Is that cool? I thought we could get something to eat in town and then head over to Danielle's birthday drinks."

"Sounds great," said Caroline. "See you later." As she hung up she thought how much better it would be to tell him to his face, after all. She turned back to the TV but it was too late. She'd missed poor weasel-faced Glen's fate – proud father or humiliated cuckold? – but as she lifted the strong black coffee to her purple-glossed lips she found she didn't even mind.

24

As I cut through the back streets, past Liberty's, along Great Marlborough Street (I long ago learned to avoid the tourists on Oxford Street) I try again to ignore why I'm thinking about my old life today, why although I have tried and tried and tried, now it is actually May I cannot forget that the anniversary is *this Friday*. That's why the timing of this new promotion has been good for me in some ways – I'll have three accounts to manage, two people reporting into me, and I'll have to work directly with the fearsome Tiger Carrington. I won't have time to dwell on what happened almost a year ago.

"The cat and the tiger," Simon had laughed over lunch the day it'd been announced, and I had shushed him crossly. "It's not funny," I'd said. "I'm sure she hates me."

"Cat Brown, no-one could hate you," Simon had said, and I'd known that wasn't true, what about all the people in the office who thought I'd shagged my way up the agency? What about my husband?

As I arrive in front of the soaring glass doors, with the four names etched high above my head, I no longer feel intimidated, out of place, like I did that first Friday, in my dreary black dress and borrowed scarf. Now I can sashay as well as the other girls, I'm fully made up, my look is expensive and sleek, I've been seduced by the gloss in a way that surprises me. Yes, I'm a fully-fledged fake these days.

I walk like I own the place into the lobby, past the weird-shaped furniture, past the latest beautiful receptionist, and I take the glass-walled lift up to the third floor. I'm the first one in, and I sit down at my desk, power up my laptop, check my schedule although I already know what it says. Deodorant client status meeting this afternoon, creative presentation for car account Wednesday morning, awards do Friday.

Friday.

I don't want to go but I know that I have to, Tiger will expect it and I can't think of an excuse, not one I can tell her anyway. We're up for an award for Frank, the deodorant brand, for a TV commercial we shot in Spain, up in the hills behind Malaga. I'd been glad then that I'd stayed legitimate, had chosen to go back to my maiden name – it meant I could use my passport, after all it said Catherine Emily Brown already. I'd still been a wreck going through customs though.

That trip to Spain had been the first fun – proper, memory-free fun – I had had in months. The sun had shone, and everyone had got along, helped by the Sangria of course, and on the last day the main character (the sweaty one) had been dumped into a bush by the pony he was meant to be riding, and once it was clear he was OK we'd laughed until it had hurt, especially as it had all been caught on camera.

I feel rather than see Tiger stalk in. She has silver lowlights and surely her tan is fake, but she manages to look classy, groomed, in fact she looks absolutely great, she must have had Botox. She wears designer classics rather than the latest trends and they suit her – in fact I'd like to look like that at her age. I find these days that I often think quite freely of the future, assume that I will still be in it after all, and again I wonder at how I've turned my life around, over that first week, these past months – although I don't like to think too much how, into what.

"Morning," snarls Tiger.

"Hi Tiger," I reply, more cheerily than I feel. I try to think of something to say, she still makes me nervous. "How was your weekend?"

"Fine," she snaps and I know that it wasn't and regret asking. Although she's never told me of course, Tiger is going through her second divorce and I think she's in the process of moving house, out of the family home in Barnes into a swanky apartment block behind Harrods. I feel sorry for her, but I can't say anything, I'm not meant to know. I only do know because Simon has told me, it's not common knowledge in the agency, but I'm good at keeping my mouth shut and so Simon tells me most things. I'm like his stand-in wife these days, the person he should be able to share his hopes and fears and office gossip with, someone who can comfort and counsel him. But his real wife seems so selfish she's only interested in her latest renovation project in one of their homes, or her twice-weekly tennis lessons, or what new car she should get to replace her year-old Porsche. I've never met her, only spoken to her on the phone, but Simon tells me all this and what with how she speaks to me I assume it's true. Their eight year old son is at boarding school so she doesn't even have to worry about him, and I wonder at a 21st century mother who can leave her little boy alone, fending for himself in an out-dated institution — and then the irony bites and the tears stab, and I'm back in Monday morning.

"... so they'll be expecting to see the first concepts today," Tiger finishes, and I've not heard a word of what she's said or even know which client she's talking about.

"Huh? Yes, sure, of course Tiger," I say, and it's clear to us both that I'm clueless. Tiger roars.

"For God's sake Cat, do I have to say that all over again? I warned Simon it was too much for you, you've got virtually no experience."

"Sorry Tiger," I say. "It's not that." I try a jokey tone but the way she's looking at me is scaring me shitless and it comes out high-pitched. "I haven't had a coffee yet and I'm afraid I'm a bit Monday morningish still. Would you like one?"

"OK," she says, after a pause, and I think I've got away with it, this time.

25

Emily came back from the hospital in shock. She'd gone that morning for an investigation into an abnormal smear test, and although Ben had offered to go with her, she'd said no, it was fine, they wouldn't tell her anything today, he didn't need to miss work. That was where she'd been wrong. She'd been sat nervously on a sage vinyl chair in the harshly-lit waiting room, flicking through an ancient copy of Reader's Digest, when the receptionist came over and asked her to fill in a form: they needed some information before she saw the consultant. Emily took the black plastic clipboard and chewed ball point pen, joined together with greasy string as if in punishment, and whizzed through it. Name, address, date of birth, any current medication (no), any other illnesses (no), any operations in the last five years (no), date of last menses (?). Emily looked at the question and her mind wouldn't respond. When did she have her last period? She couldn't remember. Before their summer holiday or after? Definitely not while they were actually in Crete. She just couldn't think. In the end she put a question mark and handed the form in at the desk. She sat there, worried now, her mind trying to work back over the weeks, but she'd been so busy at work lately, she couldn't remember having had one at all. She consulted her diary. They'd got back from holiday, what, five weeks ago, and no, she definitely hadn't had her period since. So it must have been more than five weeks ago. A lot more than five weeks ago. She picked up the magazine again and flicked through the grimy pages. She couldn't concentrate. She opened her bag and took out her mobile and wondered whether to call Ben to ask him if he knew, but there were other people around, she didn't want them to hear and she couldn't risk leaving the waiting room, in case she was called. She thought about sending him a text, but he'd think she was mad, he'd have less of an idea than her.

"Mrs Coleman," called the consultant, and Emily jumped up and followed her into the room, and she tried not to look at the chair with cold metal stirrups, and she tried not to think that she'd be sat there soon.

The consultant sat and worked through Emily's form, swiftly, perfunctorily, and then she came to the final question. She looked up quizzically and Emily said, "I know, I'm sorry, it's ridiculous but I've got no idea." She paused.

"I've recently been to Crete," she continued, as if that explained it, and maybe it did.

The consultant smiled.

"Would you like to do a pregnancy test?"

"What, now? Would you be able to tell me if I was?" And as soon as she said it she felt silly, everyone knew how to do pregnancy tests. Except that Emily had never actually done one, she'd always been careful, paranoid even, about birth control. After all she didn't want to end up like Caroline.

"Of course we can do one. Can you manage it now?" Emily nodded. "Good. Let's do that first, and then we'll do the examination."

A nurse took Emily into a small anteroom where she changed out of her black trousers and bright white underwear, put on the robe she'd been given, went to the lavatory next door – and then returned to the examination room clutching the jar, evidence or otherwise of potential new life.

"Up you get Mrs Coleman." Emily climbed into the chair and reluctantly opened her legs to put her feet in the stirrups.

"I know this isn't pleasant but can you open them a bit wider for me?" said the consultant. "That's better. Now, this may be a bit cold."

Emily grimaced. She hated this more than anything, not so much the pain but the feeling of vulnerability. She shut her eyes and breathed in deeply, trying to quash her need to close her knees.

Two minutes later the nurse bustled back into the room. The consultant paused and looked up. "Well, is she?" she said, as casually as if she was asking whether Emily was parked in the hospital car park.

"Oh yes!" the nurse replied, and Emily gasped and then she put her hands over her face and started to cry and go, "Oh, oh," in a strangled little voice. The consultant and the nurse moved either side of her then, saying, "That's wonderful news, don't cry Mrs Coleman," and they gave her a hug even though her legs were still in stirrups, and through her anxiety and panic Emily thought two thoughts at the exact same time – how wonderful they were being, and what on earth she was going to say to her sister.

26

I make myself and Tiger really good coffee, I even warm the milk in the microwave but she barely looks up as I give it to her, she's reading her emails now. I decide to leave her alone for now rather than risk annoying her further, and so I go back to my desk. By this time the rest of the team are in, and they're comparing notes about the weekend: who shagged who, what clubs they went to, whether the latest cheated-on celebrity should leave their partner. I feel a bit awkward joining in, not because I find their conversation puerile, I quite enjoy this kind of chat these days, but because on Friday I was their peer and today I'm their boss and I'm not sure how they feel about it.

"Nice shoes," says Nathalie. "Bet they were expensive?"

"Thanks, they were a bit," I reply, thinking of the three hundred pounds I spent on them last week, to celebrate my promotion, and how nine months ago I'd bought a whole bedroom for the same money. I feel a tiny stab of shame.

I try to settle at my desk while the Monday morning banter continues, feeling nervous, uneasy, not really knowing what I'm meant to be doing. I decide to email Tiger to clarify what she'd asked me earlier, I don't want to get it wrong and I'm still too scared to talk to her.

"Hi Tiger," I write. "Just to confirm, was it for Frank that first concepts are due today?"

I press delete, in case it's not for Frank, my deodorant client. I try again.

"Hi Tiger. I'm sorry, I know this is crap but can you confirm who's expecting first concepts today?" Too brutally honest, too apologetic, on my first day post-promotion.

"Hi Tiger. Please can you confirm who's expecting first concepts today. Thks, Cat." To the point, economic with words, not apologetic, hopefully least likely to annoy her. I hit send.

I spend the morning chasing down what I need for my client meeting, haranguing laid back creatives, arguing with planners, amending photography briefs, putting together agendas, making sure Nathalie has ordered the lunch. By 12 I'm still feeling nervous, edgy, and although I'd sworn not to, in this week of all weeks, I find myself in the ladies, with its sleek frosted doors, white shiny surfaces, fancy liquid soap. I only have half a line, it's all I need to get me through the afternoon, but I hate myself inside. I come back to my desk glittery and jittery. There's an email reply in my inbox, from Tiger. All it says is, "You're fired," but I'm feeling sharp and invincible and assume she's joking.

27

Andrew sat at his grey empty desk and looked at the monthly sales report in front of him and none of the figures made any sense at all. Although he was well aware of his reputation as the office sleaze-bag – his affairs had always been so blatant – until recently he'd always been well-regarded as far as his ability went. These days though he was barely making it through the day, and he knew his boss would have to do something soon if he didn't sort himself out.

Things had started going wrong for Andrew years ago, ever since his wife had finally upped and left him. He'd become so blasé about her acceptance of his carryings on that even her disgust at his behaviour at Emily's wedding hadn't registered. So when in the car on the way back from Devon Frances had matter-of-factly told him she was leaving, he hadn't believed her. And when she'd packed a suitcase and left that same night, the night after the wedding, he'd been certain she'd come back, after all where would she go? And when she hadn't come back he'd found he didn't know how to cope: how to work the washing machine, how to cook a meal, where the dishwasher tablets were. He didn't even know where Frances had gone, and he rang round everyone he could think of – all her friends, her sister Barbara, Caroline, but she wasn't with any of them. Eventually he worked it out, and he turned up at Ben and Emily's place although they were still on honeymoon, pleading, banging on the door, but Frances refused to let him in. Andrew found out too late that his wife was the type of woman who could be pushed and pushed and pushed, but once she reached her limit that was it, over. OK, she had a spare key, but even so it wasn't like her to be so presumptive, and he'd realised she must have been desperate.

Andrew had grown more depressed the longer he was on his own, especially as Frances seemed to thrive, come out of herself, and according to Caroline had had her hair cut trendily short and was off doing charity mountain climbs in Kenya. He'd even tracked down Victoria – after all it was her he'd loved all along, wasn't it? – but his once-smitten mistress had ignored his increasingly desperate approaches online, and in the end had emailed to say she'd call the police if he didn't stop stalking her.

Even sex had lost its appeal to Andrew. The irony was that when it had been forbidden, clandestine, it had been worth the risk, even worth paying for. But now he could do it whenever he liked he'd stopped wanting to, and he began to realise just what he'd done to his wife for so many years. He took to doing little more than working and coming back to his small rented flat, eating takeaways and watching movies, loads of them, on Sky Plus. He developed a recurring pain in his arm and eventually went to the doctor and during the consultation he broke down and it all came out – his failed marriage, his depressing new home, his loneliness, his stress at work. The doctor prescribed both antidepressants and talking therapy, she was that concerned, and although Andrew had to wait three months he went along reluctantly, and the therapist was dark and gorgeous and Andrew perked up a bit, decided it might do him good after all.

After a year or so Andrew had finally got his life back on track, eating more healthily, taking up badminton, regaining his appreciation of a nice smile or a fine pair of breasts. The years ticked by. Both his daughters seemed settled at last, and he even became a grandad, which was lovely. But then he received the call that sent him to a place in his mind that he'd never visited before, not even when he'd missed the birth of his twins, or realised his uselessness as a husband and father early one morning on a Telford estate, not even when Frances had left him. The spreadsheet swam as his eyes filled – an almost daily occurrence now – and he bent lower over the useless, indecipherable figures, and his scalp shone lurid under the office lights, through the remains of his hair.

28

I see out my clients and sit down in reception, flicking through Campaign, relieved that my status meeting went well after all. Jessica and Luke, my two main clients on Frank deodorant (tagline "Be fabulous, be Frank"), had already been emailed about my promotion and they'd been delighted for me, very well deserved, great news etcetera, so that was nice. The new creative concepts had been well-received (they were for Frank, thank God, although I never had had clarification from Tiger), the photography brief was spot on and the planners had had a breakthrough on how to position Frank's new multi-particle formula that stops sweat at even higher temperatures. I think I could have got through it without the coke after all, and in a rare moment of self-awareness I wonder where my heart has gone. The effect has worn off now and I feel a bit lethargic after the stress of the day, so I lean my head momentarily against the alien lump that is the sofa's back rest and think yet again how ridiculously uncomfortable the reception furniture is. I'll get up in a sec, but I do feel sleepy and the late after-noon sun shines through the plate glass and warms my face. It feels nice. I shut my eyes.

I hear the doors go but I don't register, I'm feeling too

warm, too snoozy, in this 60 seconds of respite from the day. "What the hell do you think you're doing?" a voice growls, and before I open my eyes I know it's Tiger and that I've really had it now. How have I managed to get off to such a bad start with my new boss? *Because you were foisted on her, because she thinks you're sleeping with Simon*, a voice dimly tells me. I remember the email from this morning ("You're fired") and I sit up abruptly and there's fear in my eyes.

Tiger is standing tall in her heels, Amazonian-like, looking down on me sprawled helpless on the kidney shaped couch. She has a beaming smile on her face, and it doesn't look right.

"Well, well," she says. "I just bumped into Jessica and Luke and they were singing your praises after the status meeting. Perhaps there's more to you than being just a little arse-licker after all." And with that she turns on her heel and stomps off to the lift.

I'm woozy now so I catch a cab home. Tiger had been so pleased with the glowing comments from my Frank clients that when I slunk back to my desk she didn't even let me sit down, just ushered me straight downstairs and across the road to the champagne bar where we had two tall shimmering glasses each, served on pure white coasters next to bowls of fluorescent-looking wasabi peas. I don't get Tiger at all – one minute she's bitch personified, the next she's making jokes that don't quite cut it ("You're fired" emails for example – she told me she watched some TV show on catch-up last night and is hooked), the next she loves me but it's only because the clients love me. And that last point sums up Tiger – if I'm useful to her, if I'm making her money, then I could have two heads for all she cares, I could be shagging anyone. I could probably even have killed someone.

I drag myself back to safer territory. The biggest secret Simon's ever told me is that Tiger's real name is Sandra Balls and no wonder she changed her name. Simon made me promise, swear on my mother's life that I would never let on, but tonight the champagne had been tingling and fizzing and so when she told me I needed to come up with the goods again on Wednesday, in our major presentation to the car client, I leaned in tipsily and so nearly answered, "No sweat, Sandy," that instead I said I really needed to get home, we were having visitors, and I almost ran out the door before I disgraced myself.

I sit in the cab giggling at poor Sandy Balls – Simon told me it's a holiday park in the New Forest – and I'm sure the driver thinks, here we go, another drunk slapper, what's the world coming to, why can't laydees be laydees? He doesn't try to talk to me, thank goodness, and I look out the window at people who are in that in-between time, too late to be leaving work, too early to be going home drunk. We pass a cyclist with an enormous bottom, buttocks pumping like a squirrel's cheeks, and I turn around to see what her face is like, and she has such an expression of concerted effort, conviction, *destination,* that it somehow makes me feel inadequate sat here, a passenger just along for the ride, and a bitch of a one at that. I lean back and stare at the ceiling, willing the sudden dizziness to go away.

I get home about eight, it's quite early still. Angel is sprawled on the lounge floor in her soft white dressing gown, spotless and virginal, playing chess with Rafael, her Spanish hooker friend. He's absolutely brilliant at it, and Angel can never beat him although she's pretty good herself. She's drinking vodka, but she has it with cranberry these days, so her glass is thinly red, like watered-down blood. I decide to have tea and Rafael says he fancies a cup too, so I make it in a proper pot, and even put the milk in a jug, we're that civilised these days.

Rafael is a lovely boy. He's only 18 but looks younger, and he's told me he's been working for over three years already. He says he doesn't feel exploited, he figures that once he developed a voracious appetite for being buggered he thought he might as well get paid for it. I admire his entrepreneurial spirit in a way. Most of the punters are OK, he says, they don't give him any bother, and 90% are married so they need to be discreet. I thought about my father when he told me this. After Mum left and it all came out about Dad, his endless affairs, his penchant for prostitutes, I was disgusted. I wonder now whether they were always female – why would he pay for sex when he'd found it so easy to get women? I think to myself that I'll never know, that I'll never see my father again and I miss him suddenly, and think maybe I should have a vodka after all.

"Check," says Angel, triumphantly.

Rafael looks at the board for maybe four seconds. He swoops his bishop across to take Angel's knight.

"Checkmate," he counters and Angel stares wide-mouthed for an instant, and then she mock-screams and tips up the board.

*   *   *

I really am going to make an effort from now on, getting high before meetings is not how I want my life to pan out. It's time I grew up, got back some morals – I've become far too like my twin for my liking. I'm glad I'd resisted vodka after all and made a pot of tea, for me and Rafael, who despite his occupation is really quite a homebody. We settle down to watch a TV show about a couple who are turning a rotting old power station into a high tech vision of steel and glass, and it strikes me how smug they are, with their dream house-to-be, their Boden-clad children, how convinced they are that their lives are blessed and can be meticulously planned, and I wonder what future tragedies behold them and wish they would hurry up and happen. I don't like this side to myself, I didn't used to be like this, but I find I can't help it tonight.

Maybe it's because May the 6th is just four days away now.

As the programme finishes Rafael's phone buzzes and he checks his messages and gets up cheerfully and says, "Regular – I'm out of here, hasta luego," and he blows us a kiss and disappears off to some rendezvous I'd rather not think about. Angel goes to run a bath, she's working tonight too, and I flick to the news and a woman has killed her children in a hotel in Greece and I can't believe that someone could do something like that. The story depresses me further and I feel worn out from the day, worn out from my ruminatory journey to work, from the cocaine and the client meeting and the champagne with Tiger. I think I need a bath too, I'll have one after Angel: I feel grubby on the outside as well as the inside. And then I'll go to bed early and try to get some sleep, try to not think about Friday.

*   *   *

I lie in the bath and reflect on today, on the past nine months. I feel in some ways proud of myself, in other ways disgusted. I'm not like Angel, Angel has spent half her life mothering her own mother, no wonder she does some of the things she does. Angel has never been shown right from wrong. *I have*. Now that I'm established, successful even, I don't need to take drugs or steal any more. I don't need to differentiate myself so starkly from the girl I once was – I've done it, I've made it to the other side. I push up my knees and slide my back down the angled end of the bath and my skin creaks against the enamel. I keep on going until my head meets the water and I continue down and down and I can feel the suds popping above me and my skull resting on the bath's hard flat bottom. I stay like that until my head feels hot and bursting, and then for a while longer still. When it finally all feels too much I push forcefully with my feet against the tap end of the bath and shoot up out of the foam, and a wave cascades over the back of the tub, behind me, and water goes all over the floor. I grapple for a towel and bury my face in it. When I finally remove it it is wet and hot, from bathwater and tears, tears of renewal and absolution.

29

Dominic turned up at Caroline's dead on 7.30, she always had been impressed with his timekeeping. He was wearing a tight V-necked T-shirt and new-looking denim jeans, and although he was a carpenter he looked more like a male model. He'd been in charge of doing the sets for the students' end of year fashion shows, and all the girls had fancied him. But Dominic had gone for her, Caroline — they'd bonded over her epic spiders' webs — and he still seemed to be smitten, almost five months later: for some reason her poisonous comments and wearisome put-downs had either been ignored or passed completely over his head, and so she'd mostly given them up. It wasn't that he was stupid, he was just one of those people who seemed to have so much self-esteem he didn't take anything too personally. Caroline found her respect for her boyfriend growing as time went on, and it was a welcome change from the usual diminishment she felt, after the initial excitement, after she'd ground other men down, stamping out their confidence like a cigarette butt under her foot.

Dominic seemed in a good mood tonight, and although Caroline would have been happy to stay in, break the news to him at home, he was keen to go out. "I thought we'd try this new Italian place in Soho," he said. "I heard it's meant to be good. That OK?"

"Sure," said Caroline. She loved how Dominic took charge, didn't wait to see what she suggested, and she was glad of a strong man in her life for a change. As they walked towards the tube a black cab came past and Dominic hailed it, which surprised her – neither of them had that much money, it seemed extravagant.

"Don't worry, Caz," said Dominic and he put his arm around her and she could smell his cleanness and she thought, yes, maybe she could do this – be normal, have a proper relationship, be like other people. She may still be young but she'd seen a lot, she'd done her living already. No, it wasn't too soon. She leaned into him and felt surer about what she needed to tell him as the cab grumbled through the day-fading streets, towards the West End.

Caroline sat opposite Dominic in the blue-tiled restaurant and she sensed he was nervous, although she didn't know why – unless of course he'd guessed about the baby, was picking up on her agitation. Caroline normally would have played this situation quite differently: she'd have slammed down the test stick, picked up her mobile without even washing her hands, and said something along the lines of, "I'm pregnant. I presume you want me to get an abortion?"

This time she was thinking maybe she didn't want an abortion, maybe she was with a man who might actually love her, be pleased at her news. She fiddled with her napkin as the menus arrived. Dominic ordered champagne – he *must* have guessed somehow, she thought, and he was pleased, thank fuck.

The waiter set down two glasses and one of them looked dirty to Caroline, as if it had something in the bottom of it. She said nothing for a change, not wanting to make a scene, spoil the moment. As the bubbles rose skywards Dominic raised his glass and said, "Here's to us, Caroline," and he moved out of his seat, as though he'd dropped something, and as Caroline looked at him kneeling beside her there was a blast, a gust, and then both of them were on the floor. Pain flooded through her stomach. There was a long still pause until someone broke it with a prolonged agonised shriek, and then everyone was screaming, panicking, everyone except Dominic.

Caroline lay under the restaurant table and realised she wasn't seriously hurt, maybe something had fallen on her, and Dominic was already getting up, thank God, seemingly uninjured, but looking dazed and full of dread. Other people seemed winded and panicked, but not bloody, not limbless. Most of the plates and glasses had smashed and the furniture was everywhere, but otherwise there was surprisingly little damage. The screaming had subsided and people were subdued now, as though they didn't know what to do. There was pandemonium in the street outside, someone yelled that the whole front of the Admiral Duncan had blown in. Dominic picked a dining chair off the floor, sat Caroline down, and said, "Are you OK, Caz? It must be carnage out there, I'm going to see if I can help. You wait here." He kissed the top of her head and ran into the night, into the smoke and the screaming and the bent nails and the flailed flesh, and he didn't come back. Caroline sat shivering and blank for maybe

45 minutes, it was as if she couldn't process what had happened to her today: a thin blue line, a rumbling black cab, a sharp white sparkle, a grey stinking fug. As she finally realised what Dominic had been about to do before the bomb, Caroline went out to look for him, ignoring the bleeding people and the chaos, just wanting him, her almost-fiancé. The police were ushering everyone out of Old Compton Street, down Frith Street into Soho Square, where already they'd set up a makeshift camp for the injured. She shrugged off a policewoman, shrieking, "I've got to find my fiancé," and broke through the cordon. She stepped over bodies she didn't care were alive or dead; she just had to find him, tell him yes, tell him that amidst all this hate and horror there was a new heart beating, untainted and innocent, somewhere deep inside her.

She couldn't find him. His phone was going to voicemail. She decided to check if he'd gone back to the restaurant, maybe they'd passed each other in the mayhem, but it was dark there now and someone had locked it. The front of the pub next door was blown off and smoke and rubble drifted lazily into the dishwater sky. She didn't know what else to do, where to go, so she followed the last few people stumbling away from the pub, back to the square, where people were lain out and ambulance crews were tending to the injured. The mood was desolate. Caroline searched the square twice and still she couldn't see him. She was about to cut through the police cordon to the Charing Cross Road, give up, try to find a cab home, what else could she do, when she saw a dark head bending over a stricken figure, a once white T-shirt stained and murky. An ambulance man was next to him, pumping urgently.

"Dominic," she yelled, and as he looked up she saw that the young gay man in front of him had what appeared to be a hole in his side.

"Sorry, Caz, not now," he said and looked away. Something in Caroline broke.

"I've been fucking looking for you for hours," she shrieked. "How could you just leave me like that?"

"Shush, Caz," said Dominic, and his voice was weary.

"No, I will not fucking shush Caz, you cunt. You abandoned me, you just left me in that fucking restaurant and didn't come back for me, and I'm sat there waiting like a total prick, waiting to tell you I'm having your fucking baby." And then she ran, stumbled, across the lawn and out through the side gate of the square, ignoring Dominic's shocked appeals to come back.

Caroline was eventually picked up by a black cab outside a bar off Goodge Street, where people were laughing, drunk-bound, and although it was true they had heard some kind of explosion, were too busy shaking off the week to care what may be happening less than a mile away, or wonder why this dirty sobbing girl was staggering past them. The driver barely noticed her state either, it was par for the course for a Friday night, and he also was oblivious to the bomb – he didn't listen to the news, it was too bloody miserable. As she sat alone in the back the space felt voluminous, empty, like she might fall into the middle of it without Dominic there to keep her safe. How the hell had the night turned out so dreadfully, from a cab ride full of promise to a return one stained with grief. She knew Dominic would never come back to her, not after this, it was all ruined – by the tragedy that had enveloped them, by her sickening behaviour, the look she'd seen in his eyes.

Caroline found she needed to tell someone else her news now, make it feel real – she was so disorientated, maybe she'd imagined the blue line after all. She tried her mother but the phone was engaged for ages. She cursed and called her father and it rang and rang until going to answer-machine. She'd dialled the next number before she'd had time to think. As her twin sister answered Caroline didn't know what to say.

"Hi Caroline!" said Emily. "How nice to hear from you… Hello? Hello? Caz, are you there?"

"Yes," sobbed Caroline. "I'm pregnant."

"Oh," said Emily. She didn't know whether this was a good or a bad thing, what to say. "Why are you crying, Caz?" she said gently.

"I got caught in the bomb and then I lost Dominic and he was about to propose and he didn't even know about the baby then, and now I've called him a cunt. And, oh Emily I love him so much and I want us to have our baby and now I've lost him, I've lost him."

Emily had never had a call like this from her sister, she'd never turned to her before, and she felt absurdly grateful. She thought fast. Tomorrow was Saturday, she had nothing on she couldn't change, and besides she couldn't bear hearing Caroline like this.

"I'll come down, Caz," she said. "I'll get the first train in the morning."

"Oh," said Caroline. This wasn't what she'd planned, she hadn't wanted even to talk to Emily really.

"If you want me to," Emily said.

Caroline paused and she must have still been traumatised, because she found herself saying, "All right then."

"I'll see you in the morning," said Emily. "Bye, Caz, be strong, I love you."

"I love you too Em," said Caroline, and both girls hung up bemused, in shock, in tears.

Emily wasn't sure whether to go after all. Would Caroline really want her there, she hadn't seemed too keen when she'd offered: she usually rejected any attempts at friendship from her sister. Emily thought about calling before she set off, just to check, but was worried that might offend Caroline, as though Emily was trying to get out of it, and anyway the poor girl had been in a *bomb*, it must have been horrific. Emily had been devastated when she'd seen the news: she'd assumed Caroline was being melodramatic as usual, what with her boyfriend apparently proposing to her and the restaurant exploding and him disappearing like that, but the bomb part at least had been true. Her poor sister!

The train seemed to take forever, there were engineering works around Northampton, and when she finally arrived at Euston she followed the signs to the tube and tried to work out where to go. She didn't know London at all well and hadn't thought to ask Caroline, she just assumed Brick Lane would have its own station but now it seemed it didn't. She was deep underground and couldn't call her twin to check, and there were no guards to ask. She looked at the other people on the platform – there were two youths with back-packs, in baseball shirts and spanking white trainers who looked as lost as she did; a tiny old Asian lady in a beautiful orange sari teamed with black socks and sandals, who looked the other way as Emily went to speak to her; a sullen girl, dressed all in black with heavily-made up eyes, who'd prob-ably been out all night. Emily's only other option was a gor-geous-looking black boy, who wore gold in his ears and around his neck and when she plucked up the courage to ask him had a smile that made her want to take him home to meet her mum. She thanked him, blushing, and moved along the platform to study the map, to find out how to get to Aldgate East.

When Caroline opened the door Emily was horrified. Her eyes had blown up so badly that it looked like she'd been beaten up. She seemed angry to see Emily, and Emily thought maybe she shouldn't have come after all. Caroline's flat was eclectically trendy, all primary colours and weird objects and arty pornography. In the entrance hall three identical bowler hats hung in a line, above black and white stills of close-ups of monkeys, who looked pained, tortured, and Emily won-dered if they'd even been taken in science labs. She didn't like to ask, they made her feel uncomfortable.

Caroline just stood at the door, scowling. Emily brushed past into the tiny wonky kitchen and put the kettle on, while Caroline looked on numbly. She made the tea and stirred in two sugars for Caroline, it looked like she needed them, and as she put down the spoon she saw her twin crumple to the floor and start to keen, like an animal.

"Caz, come on love, it'll be OK," said Emily, bending down, putting her arms around her. As she helped Caroline up she saw a violent red smudge on the cold white tiles, like another bizarre work of art, and as she looked into what was left of Caroline's eyes, behind the puffiness, she understood.

30

I get through the rest of this tortuous week with no further run-ins with Tiger. The creative presentation for the new seven seater car went brilliantly well – the clients quite amazingly loved our very ropy quintuplets idea – and my team seem fine with my new status: they actually seem to respect me, even if I don't. I'm proud though that I've had no drugs since Monday lunchtime, and I've even managed to get Angel to swap vodka for tea this week, we're both officially on a health kick. Maybe I'm finally turning a corner, am through with the excesses that helped me survive.

I have just one more milestone to get through now, and it's the biggest one yet and it's this afternoon and I don't know how to cope, what to do, whether to embrace it or else push it away now that it's here.

Here.

Simon has promised to take me out to lunch to celebrate my first week as Account Manager and I've said yes, so I'll be with him throughout it, I can't face it alone. I know Tiger will bag me for it but just this once I don't care. Maybe I should have taken the day off, but what would I do on my own? How would I bear being inside my own skin? Being with Simon might help.

I check my watch. 11.07. Three hours seven minutes to go. The numbers are too concrete, I can't escape them. I'm hot and heady, can't concentrate. I feel my resolve drain like someone took the plug out, and I get up from my chair and head past Nathalie's desk, round the back of Luke's, towards those fabulous toilets. Inside my head I catch a glimpse of my husband and son, and then it's gone, but still I beg them to forgive me...

Simon takes me to a fancy restaurant down by Tower Bridge, and I think it's around here somewhere that Angel said she used to live, before she had to hide out from her murderous boyfriend at Finsbury Park Palace. I suggested to Simon we just go somewhere near the agency, there are hundreds of options, but Simon seemed to sense something in me today and said it would be nice to get out down by the river, it's a glorious day. I love Simon's old-fashioned vocabulary – things are always glorious or super, or conversely woeful or calamitous. He's a gentleman at heart, and maybe that's why he hasn't got the guts to up and leave his dreadful wife, it would be rather bad form. I know he's a little bit in love with me these days and I admit that I do feel something for him, but although he never asks me why he somehow knows not to take it further.

We sit by the open window and the Thames breezes in, and a bow-tied man tinkles on the grand piano and the atmosphere is exclusive, understated. It's lovely here, Simon was right. I forget myself for a while and we drink white wine and share a showy seafood platter, and when I check the time it's 1.45. Twenty nine minutes to go. To what? To a pointless anniversary on a doom-filled day. I can't help thinking that exactly this time last year, I still had a wonderful husband, a delightful son, I was pregnant again. I was happy, sickeningly so, and since then I have let them all down, in their different ways. I remind myself that thinking like that doesn't help anything and I say yes to a top-up of wine. I've done so well for so many months, I think I almost forgot that once I was Emily Coleman, but when it comes down to it I cannot forget this date. The more I've tried to forget it the more it has loomed, ominous and past-presenting. At least one good thing has come of this day though – I've given up drugs, yes, definitely, as of today. I feel proud of myself that earlier, at the agency, when I'd reached the toilets ready to snort my way into another little bit of forgetting, I'd thought of what day it is and of my darling little boy and what he would think of me, his mother, and I'd gone straight into one of those bright shiny cubicles and emptied the entire contents of the packet down the toilet, and flushed them away.

The pianist starts playing a song I've heard a thousand times but I can't think what it is, and it bothers me. I wonder what Ben and Charlie are doing now and I chase that thought away too. I hear a voice and realise that Simon is speaking.

"Have you tried the crab yet – it's rather delicious?" I look numbly at him and shake my head, my eyes desolate. He spots a weakness in me, an opening, and takes my hand.

"Why are you so sad, my darling Cat? You know you can talk to me. You can tell me anything – just as friends." And he says it with such tenderness and truth I feel tempted, more

191

than I've ever been, even more than on recent nights out with Angel, when I've been drunk and high and almost mad with the urge to tell her, I've held it in for too long now. I so desperately need to get through these next few minutes, maybe it would be better if I could talk about it at last, tell someone. I hesitate right on the edge of speech, as though forming the words might make it worse somehow, or better. It's like I'm standing high on a diving board, my body clenched and flexed and buzzing. Can I? Or can't I? I steady my nerves and step forward into the void.

31

Caroline breathed carefully into the phone, too lost, too damaged to think what to say. Dominic had taken two whole days to make this call, and in the meantime she'd lost their child. Both had been through traumas so great they no longer knew how to reach the other. Earlier that day Caroline had dug out the pregnancy test from the bathroom cabinet and the blue line was gone, and she'd begun to think she really had imagined it. She mourned the line, mourned the diamond in her glass, and she wondered where it was now, what had happened to it. But most of all she mourned her baby, what the line was meant to have become. In her other pregnancies the foetus had been a problem to dispose of, yet this one had been a miracle, a joining of herself with Dominic, a symbol of their love. But they both knew that love was gone and so was their baby, and nothing was going to bring either back. And the only other person who knew was Emily, and Caroline had never told her *anything* before. It felt strange that they'd become so close over this, although Caroline knew it was an anomaly, wouldn't last. Emily had been fantastic though, Caroline had to hand it to her, calm and non-judgmental, even when she'd described her vile outburst amongst the carnage in Soho Square. "It was your hormones, the shock, everything all together Caz, what do you expect?" Emily had said as she held her hand, and Caroline had found the contact strangely comforting. Maybe she should stop being such a cow to her twin, it might be nice to have her as a friend for a change.

After Dominic hung up, saying he'd call again soon, Caroline sat immobile. He hadn't even offered to come to see her, and she suspected he hadn't believed her when she'd told him about the baby, how she'd lost it, it seemed too convenient somehow. He did call though, as he said he would, a few times more. They went out for dinner each time and although always apologetic he was never on time again. The dinners were awkward, excruciating. Caroline insisted he come home with her the first time, and they tried to have sex but it was embarrassing, humiliating, and he didn't stay the night. Eventually Caroline couldn't stand the pretence, this imprint of their once real relationship, and she ended it late one night, by text. Dominic didn't object, and Caroline wondered again just what transformation had occurred in him the night of the bombing. Years later she heard through friends that he'd married someone called Martin, and that knowledge along with her lost baby haunted her forever.

32

I sit by the river and the sun is shining and I've decided to confide in Simon, so I start to open my mouth to say – what? That I'm not really Cat Brown, I'm Emily Coleman, that I'm a fake and a fraud and a deserter? Yes, why not, it might do me good to tell the truth at last. As the first words form I look down without thinking and there it is on my phone in all its digital unequivocalness:

14.14

May 6

I gag and scrape back my chair and run out of the restaurant as fast as I can. I hold the vomit in my mouth until I reach the river bank and then I spew, all over the railing, and it spatters back at me and I collapse to the floor into my own puke, and through my humiliation I wish for the millionth time I was dead.

I'm lying in bed at home in Shepherds Bush and although my clothes are gone my hair – or is it my mouth? – stinks of vomit. Angel is sat on a chair across the room watching telly, and as I stir she gets up and comes over to me. I feel ashamed, although I'm not quite sure why yet. I remember that Simon and – who? A waiter? A passing tourist? – helped me to my feet and staggered me along the river bank to where a taxi could pick us up. I wasn't unconscious (nor was I last year), but I was in the same hysterical state and Simon, I now realise, must have called a doctor to give me something, the drug fug is unmistakeable. It must be hours later now and I think with a lurch of Tiger, the awards do, and I'm suddenly back in the present, not stuck in my recurring nightmare, and I wonder whether I've passed a milestone and really will get better at last.

"I've got to get up," I say. "I'm meant to be at the Dorchester this evening."

"Don't be daft, babe," says Angel. "You're not going anywhere tonight."

A whole year.

It's as if I need to get up now, get on with the rest of my life, there's no time to lose. It's like I've moved beyond despair into – what? Acceptance? I'll never have my old life back and although I knew it before I don't think I felt it in my heart, even though I thought I did, if that makes any sense. I try to get out of bed but feel too groggy, and fall back onto the pillows. Angel pulls the duvet over me.

"You stay there, babe. I'm going to make you a nice cup of tea." She squeezes my hand and leaves the room, shutting the door gently.

I wonder how Simon knew my address, I've never got round to giving it at work, they still have my Finsbury Park one. He must have looked on my phone and rung someone. I only have people from the agency and clients in my phone, and a few vague friends like Bev and Jerome from the house.

And Angel. He must have thought that weird – hardly any friends, no Mum, no Dad. I've talked about Angel enough times and now I realise he must have been here at the flat earlier, they must have met each other, and I feel absurdly jealous.

Angel comes back in with a pink mug where the man gets naked if the drink is hot. I think she's trying to cheer me up and so I smile accommodatingly.

"You never told me Simon was such a looker," says Angel.

"Oh," I say. "D'you think so?" and I think again *keep your hands off him*, and I wonder what's the matter with me.

"He was really worried about you, babe," she continues. "Is he a tincy bit in love with you?"

"No," I answer, too quickly.

"What happened anyway?" she says. "You turn up here drugged up to the eyeballs and covered in God knows what. I thought we were meant to be getting healthy this week." Angel laughs nervously and I can tell she's worried sick about me, and it makes me more determined to show her I'm OK, that I'm through the worst. My phone rings on the bedside table. Angel gets to it before me.

"It's Simon," she says. "Shall I answer?"

"Yes," I say, meaning no, and for the first time I realise how dangerous it is to have a friend as beautiful as Angel.

"Hi Simon ... No, it's Angel... Oh, I'm fine, thanks (giggle)... She's just come round, she's OK, I think... Yes... No (giggle) I've told her that's madness... Oh. OK, that's kind of you, I'll ask her... Do you want to have a word with her?... Oh, OK, maybe see you later then, bye."

"What was that all about?" I say. The only time I've been

cross with Angel before is the day we went shopping and I found out she was a kleptomaniac, and I got over that pretty quickly.

"Simon says that if you feel better later you can always come down for a drink after the dinner. Apparently someone else can't make it now – Luke I think he said – so he said if I wanted to come with you that would be fine." She says it guilelessly, with no apparent agenda, and I feel ashamed at my jealousy. I have just two friends in the world and I don't want them to find each other, how childish is that? Maybe it's the drugs the doctor gave me, I really don't feel quite right. It's still May the 6th, I should be sad, sombre, but instead I feel mildly euphoric and groggy and paranoid all at the same time.

"I don't know," I say moodily. I swing my legs round to get out of bed and this time Angel doesn't try to stop me, she seems fine about me going out now.

"You have a shower," she says. "And let's see how you feel later." I grunt and stagger to the bathroom.

33

Emily stood staring into the cot at her sleeping baby, as if transfixed. She'd just opened the curtains and the little room was bright with late summer sunshine: it was time for him to wake up, they were off to see her in-laws in Buxton. She lowered the cot side so she could reach in and lift him out and as she did so the Winnie the Pooh characters on his mobile shook gently, as though they were awakening too. She hesitated before picking him up, examining him again, as if he were a miracle, which to her he was – perfectly rounded head with soft downy hair leant gently to one side, cheek so plump it was like a cushion for his shoulder; arms flung out as if in submission, elbows at right-angles so his little fists were level with his nose; belly moving up and down inside the plain white baby grow as his breath gently rasped (she'd never known babies snored); little fat legs splayed wide open, creased at the knees; the soles of his feet, in tiny white socks that were still too big for him, coming together and almost meeting. The cot was white, the sheet and blanket were white, he looked so clean and pure she wanted to stay in this moment, look at him forever.

Emily was amazed at how motherhood had affected her,

had made her see everything differently, more simply somehow. She hadn't even wanted to get pregnant really, and although Ben had been keen for ages she'd put him off – she hadn't wanted to upset Caroline, which she saw now was ridiculous. She loved everything about being a mother, the smells, the warmth, the unconditional nature of how she gave herself to her son, even when he'd driven her mad with his bawling, even when she was dog-tired from the day. She loved how having him had brought Ben and her closer, if that had been possible, and even Caroline had been wonderful about it. She didn't deserve to be this happy.

As the light gently woke him, he opened his eyes and blinked up at her and then instead of crying like he usually did his face split into a gummy smile and she leaned down and picked him up and held him as he cooed and gurgled. She thought then about how fast the time had passed, how she was meant to be going back to work in a couple of months, she'd booked the nursery place already. She'd probably have to wake him some mornings – she bet he wouldn't be smiling then – and it would all be such a rush to get him fed and dressed and out the door. As it drew closer she found she was dreading, a little more each day, the thought of going back. It was probably in this moment, sat amongst his teddies on the couch in his bedroom, in that beautiful moment of stillness, that she realised, and she wondered just how she was going to tell Ben.

In the end she just said it, later that night as they lay in bed, their feet kicking, pressing against each other's.

"Ben, I don't want to go back to work," she said.

Her husband shifted then and propped himself up on his shoulder, so he could look at her properly in the dusky light. He took her hand.

"I know I always said I wanted to, but now I can't bear to think of leaving him in a nursery. He needs me, his mother."

"Wow, you've changed your tune," said Ben and he leaned down and kissed her on the nose.

"You don't mind then?" she said.

"Of course not."

"We'll have way less money. What about our holidays, us getting a bigger house one day, running two fancy cars? We'll probably have to sell one."

"Emily," said Ben. "I couldn't care less. We have our family, that's all that matters."

"Are you sure?" she asked. "You're not just being bloody nice as usual?"

"No," he said. "I'd prefer it. I just never wanted to ask you, you didn't seem like you'd want to give up your job. I really couldn't give a shit about the money. We'll cope."

"I'll quote you on that when we're eating bread and dripping and have holes in our shoes," Emily said, but she felt so ridiculously happy she didn't even care if that's what they ended up doing.

34

I stand in the shower and wash the vomit from my hair. I feel strange still – empty, cleansed, I can't explain it. Free at last? I wonder what kind of drugs Simon's doctor gave me, why my legs are so wobbly and my mind is so still. I borrow some of Angel's pineapple face scrub and it zings my face but still I can't feel anything. Is it finally over?

As I step out the shower my legs feel stronger and I think of the new jade satin dress in my wardrobe, split to the thigh, my silver stilettos – maybe I should go out after all, it might even be fun if Angel's going.

Fun? Who am I kidding?

It's still only 7.30, we could be there in an hour, and anyway I'm hungry now. I hardly ate anything of the seafood platter, I was a lousy ad for their chilli crab claws, and the thought makes me giggle, and the emotion punches through the fog in my mind.

I swan back into my bedroom, where Angel is watching some terrible soap. I do a twirl in my towel. "Cinders, you shall go to the ball," I shout and Angel looks at me oddly, pauses for a long while, as if she's not sure what to do, and finally says, "OK, I'll go and get ready."

35

Until he tried to kill her, Angel lived with Anthony in a loft apartment at Tower Bridge. He'd met her playing poker with clients one night, and although Angel didn't usually pick up punters from the casino, it wasn't her style, Anthony was persistent. As he was leaving he persuaded her to give him her number, and then he called her every hour for the rest of the night, until she knocked off at six.

The next day 40 red roses arrived and although Angel knew it all seemed far too good to be true, she went online and looked up the number's significance and found it meant, "My love for you is genuine." Angel was flattered, fluttery, and found she couldn't say no when he begged her to call in sick the very next night. He picked her up in his Maserati and took her to dinner in a restaurant in the City with views across London. And then he took her back to his apartment to champagne on ice and floaty jazzy tunes she'd never heard, and when he led her onto the balcony overlooking the river to finally kiss her the perfection of the romance was complete. She stayed that night, dressed in one of his T-shirts, and he tucked her into his armpit like a precious doll, and she was the luckiest girl in the world.

Anthony ran his own venture capital firm. He was wealthy certainly (but, as she realised afterwards, in that precarious way ostentatiously rich people often are) and he was handsome, charming. Angel was besotted, and after just a few weeks she stopped going home at all, and she gave up working at the casino, and she lived like a princess, except there was a pea under her bed, waiting to be discovered.

Things started to change for Angel after the first blissful three or four months of living together. Anthony had already started taking her to client dinners, introducing her as "my little Cockney Angel," and although she thought it was a bit disrespectful she didn't take it too seriously, she was sure it was affectionate. She'd sit demurely with his guests in swanky restaurants and laugh in all the right places, throwing back her pretty head, exposing her slender neck, knowing the effect she had on these men, after all she was used to it. One night, when Anthony was outside taking a call, Angel had picked up from one of the guests that maybe things weren't quite so rosy at Anthony's firm, and so she'd asked him about it when they got home.

"What the fuck do you mean?" he said.

"Er, Richard was saying he was worried about the Fitzroy deal, I just wondered what he meant?"

"What the fuck's it got to do with you?"

Angel decided two fucks were enough. She stood tall, all five feet two of her. "Don't you talk to me like that," she said. "Who do you think you are?"

Anthony had given her a look of such pure hatred at this point that it turned her stomach even more than the swearing.

He reined in his fury and got up from the depths of the sofa and walked steadily towards the spare bedroom. He paused for a while at the threshold, as if relenting, and then he changed his mind and went in anyway, and he slammed the door so hard behind him that one of his jazz portraits in the hallway fell off and smashed, right across the gleeful smile on Charlie Parker's face.

36

Angel takes ten minutes to get ready, even though she's the type of girl you'd imagine taking hours. She has rung in sick – something she hasn't done in ages – and she looks stunning in nude floaty chiffon. Her blonde hair is swept into an off-centre bun at the nape of her neck and I don't know how she does it herself, with just three or four Kirby grips. I feel big and gangly next to her, like a giant runner bean in my emerald dress, and I try not to hate her.

Angel insists we order a cab, and when it turns up the seats are grimy and the car stinks of smoke and car freshener and I have to wind down the window and lean my head out to stop the nausea returning. It ruins my hair, but Angel just sits there, all chiselled cheekbones and slim silky legs and her chignon doesn't move a centimetre. By the time we arrive I'm sure my face is the colour of my dress, and I think perhaps I should have stayed in bed after all.

People are just starting their main courses and great armies of waiters and waitresses are descending on the tables like a culinary invasion, and Angel and I get in the way of the fillet steak in a cream and champagne sauce, or pumpkin and ricotta filo parcels for the vegetarians amongst us. I know this because

Angel gets Luke's dinner and he'd ordered the non-meat option, and I joke to her in a no-nonsense Northern way that that's why he's ill, he doesn't eat meat, the big wuss. "Shush," says Angel, smiling, and although it annoys me to be told off maybe I was a bit loud.

Simon seems delighted to see me, alive, bathed, back on my feet, but he seems even more keen to see Angel, and she sits down beside him and I get Nathalie. I'm sure it's me who's meant to be next to Simon – these things are usually boy girl boy girl and there are definitely name tags. I'm certain Angel's meant to be Luke. I suspect that Simon has swapped the tags and the thought makes me cross.

As I sit there moodily I feel like the world is wavy, not quite straight any more. I wonder what's wrong with me, why I'm so jealous of Angel tonight. There are so much more important things to be upset about. I realise for a moment I've stopped thinking about *it* although it's still the anniversary of it but the thought that I haven't thought about *it* makes me think it and I turn abruptly to Nathalie.

"You look nice Nat, love your dress."

"Thanks Cat, vintage – aka Oxfam!" She laughs, and then looks serious for a second. "You OK? Simon said you had a dodgy oyster at lunch – that must've gone through you quickly?"

"Er, yes," I say. "I'm feeling much better now though," and I tuck into my steak as I'm bloody *starving*.

The food's average and I'm getting a bit fed up now – Simon's monopolising Angel and although Nathalie's lovely I'm too grumpy to talk about clothes or celebrities or ads, and in truth I can't think of anything else to talk about today.

Tiger is the other side of the table, looking fierce and phenomenal, and although we don't speak she catches my eye and I know that Simon has confided in her and she gives me a smile of such kindness I didn't know she had it in her.

Angel turns to me then, and I can tell she's embarrassed by Simon's attentiveness and doesn't want to upset me, so she whispers, "I'm going to the ladies, you coming?" I know what that usually means, and I shake my head: I'm still being strong for my little boy, although what's the point, he won't ever know, I can't go back to him now.

So she gets up and goes on her own, and although she's so tiny everyone notices her as she crosses the room, maybe it's the way she walks, and she reminds me of Ruth, her mother.

Simon shifts across to speak to me. "How are you doing Cat? I was so worried about you earlier."

"I feel better now," I say, although the vacant feeling hasn't quite gone. "You seem to have hit it off with Angel."

"She is gorgeous," Simon concedes. "And anyway, you won't have me."

I look at him then and see the longing in his eyes, not for me or for Angel in particular, but just for love, for genuine giving-accepting all-encompassing love, like I once had with my husband, before Caroline, or was it me, destroyed it. I take his hand.

"Simon, I'm so sorry about earlier, I promise it won't happen again. I hope I didn't ruin your best suit, I'll pay for the dry-cleaning of course."

Simon ignores my attempt at humour. He looks at me searingly. "You were about to tell me your secret earlier, weren't you, Cat? What is it, you can still tell me. I'm sure I can help."

I look at him sadly then, as I know that he can't help, no-one can, and I also know that I'm back from the brink, it belongs in my past life, and I will never ever tell now, as long as I live.

37

As time went on Anthony became more and more unreasonable. If Angel burnt the toast, or he didn't like her outfit, or a girlfriend called her to have a chat, he'd go off on one, screaming and shouting, calling her names. Angel tried to stand up for herself, but it was hard, she was dependent on him now. She'd given up her job, her flat, her friends were drifting away, and what did she have? Beautiful clothes and expensive dinners, the most stunning view of the Thames, and a boyfriend who called her a cunt. She didn't even feel she could tell her mother – Ruth seemed delighted that her Angela had found such a charming rich lover, it was embarrassing to confess the truth. So Angel did her best to not upset Anthony, it really wasn't worth the trouble, and she rarely saw her friends anymore, she made sure she only wore clothes she knew he approved of, she never ever answered back, and when he started to tell her what she could and couldn't order in restaurants she didn't bother to try to assert her own opinion, she couldn't face the row.

Things may have carried on for a lot longer if Anthony hadn't stepped it up a gear. Instead of just flying into a rage and screaming obscenities, he started saying things like, "If you forget to put the dishwasher on again, I'll kill you, you fucking bitch." And then when that didn't fix her, he started ramming her up against the kitchen cabinets and spitting into her face as he said it.

Angel worked really hard to make Anthony happy – she didn't want to be like her mother, with a string of rubbish boyfriends and the occasional trip to A & E accompanied by a small scared child. Anthony was a lovely guy really, he'd treated her so well at first, hadn't he? Surely she could bring that back if she tried hard enough. Yet the irony was that the more she tried to placate him, the more she invited the eventual physical attack, and when it came it was merciless. Afterwards he sobbed and held her tight and promised to never do it again, but when Angel suggested she find somewhere else to live while he sorted himself out, he turned nasty again and physically locked her in the apartment and confiscated her mobile. She thought about standing on her marble-tiled balcony and yelling it to the river, that she was held prisoner here, but Anthony seemed to get wind of that idea and locked the terrace door too.

That first time he kept her prisoner for a week, until he was sure she'd learned her lesson. Although she was only locked up occasionally after that the fight had gone out of her – after all she must deserve it somehow. She lost weight and her hair became lank, and Anthony started telling her she was ugly and useless and that no-one else would want her and she even began to believe it. But when the beatings and threats to kill her became almost daily Angel knew enough was enough, it was time to act, and she hatched herself a plan.

38

Angel comes back from the toilet and she's in a good mood, her eyes are sparkling and I almost wish I'd gone with her. She sits the other side of Simon and starts talking to the H of CSGH and I can tell it doesn't take her long to realise that he's the hanger-on of the four, the one with no talent who just got lucky. Angel is so bright and capable, it's a shame all she does is work in a casino, she could do so much more, and then I remember the things she's endured and I think it's a miracle she's survived at all.

The waiting troops swoop again and deliver lemon tart with blueberries and crème fraiche, and for such a fancy affair they could have made a bit more of an effort with the menu. The awards bit of the evening is due to start soon and they've booked some chat show host from Channel 4, and he's being briefed by a stressed looking woman with a clipboard and heels she can't walk in. One of the waiters pours me more wine and he does it in a hurry, like I have no choice but to have it, and although I probably shouldn't I'm bored and moody so I take a sip and then another, but still I can't shake off the feeling that I'm only "almost here," I'm just observing. Simon's face looms large at me when I look at him, everything seems out of proportion, the lights that waltz around the stage as the presentation starts are screamingly bright, and I look down at my half-eaten lemon pie and feel bilious again. It must be the drugs the doctor gave me, they definitely haven't agreed with me, and as I don't know what else to do I raise my glass and drink.

The compere makes a risqué joke about what a bunch of tossers people in advertising are, but as he's in a room full of people in advertising it falls rather flat. Someone heckles him that at least they don't visit massage parlours, referencing his recent tabloid scandal, and he goes to walk off stage until Clipboard Lady manages to placate him from the wings.

The awards are interminable and I can't believe I'd thought it was so important to come, on today of all days. Frank is up for best TV commercial and when it wins I get to go up with Simon to collect the award. As I stand in my long green dress gurning at the camera, holding a plaque for an ad about underarm no-go zones involving runaway ponies, I think how ridiculous this whole world is and wonder how it's taken me so long to realise. I don't know why I've become so self-important, it's not as if I've been making movies or anything, we're not at the Oscars, I've just been trying to sell stuff. It's funny really.

The unfortunate compere makes another inappropriate ad-related remark as the next award-winner appears on stage in a voluminous orange dress, and people titter nervously. I've had enough. I look around the table and Simon is leaning into Angel, Tiger is looking bored and haughty, as if this is all beneath her, and I'm sure it is, and I long to get up and run across the room, to the safety of the ladies and the contents of my purse. And then I remember I flushed them down the toilets at work, and I don't feel so smug about it now, so I lift my glass instead and sip my white wine, and it's warm, but I sip again and again, I don't know what else to do with my hands. The room feels like it's moving away from me, like the floor is splitting in half and the stage is drifting off towards Park Lane and leaving me marooned here, on my advertising life raft in the ocean of my ruined life. I shake my head, and try to remember that this is meant to be a new day, a new start. *No it's not, it's still the same day, and anyway what difference does it make.* The brutality of the understanding that there is no neat finish, no end to the grieving, that I may have changed my whole life and let a full year go past but despair is part of me and always will be now, well that realisation exhausts me, and I close my eyes and lean forwards onto the table, my head turned neatly sideways, into the remains of my lemon tart.

39

Anthony had deleted all of Angel's numbers from her mobile a while ago, so she couldn't call any of her friends for help. He'd definitely track her down if she fled to one of her girl-friends' houses, and he knew where her mother lived, so she couldn't go there either. She just couldn't think what to do, she seemed so weak and useless these days. In the end she remembered that one of the bouncers from work lived in a house that seemed to have loads of tenants, most of them mad apparently, and from what he used to say there was nearly always a room available. One sparkling April morning, when Anthony was off to a meeting in the City and the cheery breeziness of the day had put him in better humour for a change, Angel made her move. She felt ghost-like, invisible as she walked along the river, terrified she wasn't meant to be there, worried that someone might report her. She told her-self not to be silly and carried on, head down against the wind. She walked through the Galleria and then cut up to Tooley Street, where she found a phone box, one of those old-fash-ioned red ones people used to use. She hadn't been in one for years, but the never-forgotten stink of old urine and dead saliva was so revolting it made her physically gag, and the cards on the windows were probably those of friends of hers. She called Directories and then the casino, and after nearly two minutes of ringing, one of the managers answered. When he asked who was calling, she said it was Angela and he put her through without comment, and she was lucky, Jerome was on shift. He'd been brilliant, she hadn't had to explain anything, and he told her to leave then, now, and so she'd rushed back to the flat and packed her favourite clothes and left everything else, and by the time she'd come out fifteen minutes later pale grey clouds were scuttering across the sun, and it felt colder, more ominous, and the quick-moving shadows were sharp, defined, landscape-changing. Angel flagged down a cab and it took her across the river, through the City towards Anthony, and then thankfully away from him again, along Upper Street towards Finsbury Park. She found when she got there that the house was a hovel, it had no river view or fancy porter to say, "Morning Miss Craw-ford," but it was safe and she was free, and so to Angel it was a palace.

40

Angel is shaking me gently and I can hear laughter, and as I sit up sleepily I realise that people are laughing at *me* this time, that wanker of a compere has singled me out for abuse now. I recover my composure and sit straight, feeling better in myself, like I've had a power nap and am ready for action. I couldn't care less what he's said or why people are laughing, what does it matter today of all days? I toss my head like a pony, and a little piece of pie flicks off and my ear feels sticky, but I'm still pissed enough to simply sip my drink and look nonchalant, and the conversation turns to the next tedious award.

"Are you all right, babe?" whispers Angel. "I think this is the last one, then we can go and sort you out."

"I'm fine," I say, and although I'm drunk I'm much more lucid, I think the doctor's drugs have worn off at last; it's taken this long though, they must have been mind-blowing. I look at my watch – it's still only 10.30. I smile beatifically around the table and they're all looking at me, but not with condescension or disdain, just concern, and I think they might be a nice bunch, underneath.

The compere delivers his final punchline and we all applaud

politely as he disappears off to his stalling TV career and night-time activities and I don't resent him for insulting me, just feel a bit sorry for him, like Emily would have. Angel takes my hand and we make our way over to the toilets, and I still feel green and bulky next to her, conspicuously tall, lankily lemony. People are looking at me. The side of my face feels glutinous. She helps clean the pie off me and then ushers me into a cubicle and I don't hesitate anymore, it feels like completely the right thing to do after all, our deserved treat after all those sodding awards. As we recross the ballroom I'm no longer gawky and bean-like, instead I'm verdant and lithe, like a long strand of seaweed swaying gracefully with the waves, rooted yet free. My dress feels dramatic and glamorous and my heels feel empowering instead of crippling and I'm sure that this time I'm turning heads for the right reasons. I sit back down at the table next to Simon and I beam a million dollar smile and he pours me a glass of the champagne he's ordered to celebrate our Frank win.

"Well done, my darling Cat. Are you feeling better now?"

"I feel great," I reply, and I do, Angel must have had some good gear.

"I've been invited to a friend's party later at the Groucho – do you feel up to it? I can only take you and Angel though, so please don't say anything to the others."

"Sounds fab," I say airily, and I take his hand and drag him to the dance floor where "I will survive" has just started playing. Surprisingly Simon doesn't object, the floor is already crowded, and I fling my arms above my head and sing along to every word, feeling liberated, strong, invincible.

41

After she'd finally upped and left her husband following his performance at Emily's wedding, Frances wondered why she hadn't done it years and years before. She'd never stopped loving Andrew, despite all his betrayals and humiliations of her, but she'd belatedly realised his personality contained a flaw which meant he would never lose his penchant for a pretty face or a large pair of breasts – or indeed for anyone who would boost his ego and help him forget he was a married man with too many daughters, a lacklustre career, a receding hairline.

Frances was well aware she couldn't stay with Emily and Ben for long, they were newly weds after all (plus Caroline kept coming round being far too friendly to Ben for anyone's liking) but the day after the wedding it had seemed like an instant solution to an overdue problem – the house was empty, she had the key in her purse, it would mean a clean break from Andrew – and she knew that Emily and Ben wouldn't mind, under the circumstances.

Emily had been as lovely as ever of course, and she'd helped her mother find a flat to rent and had even paid for it until the house sale went through. And now Frances had her own tiny cottage in the old town, and she liked it so much better than the house on the estate, with its square boring rooms and lethal glass doors. She joined a writing course and a yoga group, and found that people were friendly, and that some of them were on their own as well. She made particular friends with a woman called Linda from the writing group, and Linda was a widow who'd made a fantastic new life for herself and was doing a charity climb of Mount Kenya, and when she said to Frances, "Why don't you come too?" Frances had thought *why not*, and now here she was at Heathrow, almost a year to the day since she'd left her husband, and although she was worried sick about Caroline it was only for ten days, and she told herself that Caroline would be fine.

42

After one more song Simon shuffles me off the dance floor, and suggests we head off to his friend's party. I know inside myself that I shouldn't go, should go home to bed, it's been such a long and traumatic day – but I'm over-stimulated, wired, and I'm enjoying dancing in my long emerald dress. I know it's nuts, but I don't feel ready for the evening to end, I want to get past midnight now, into May the 7th, where I'm sure things will feel even better still. I've been less paranoid about Simon and Angel since my little nap at the table, and I let my hand rest in Simon's as we leave, and his hand feels warm and comforting. Angel is being as sweet as ever, and insists on holding my other arm, although I'm sure I don't need her to, I'm not that drunk or giddy any more, have definitely sobered up. Simon's driver is waiting outside the hotel and as we travel across central London the streets are clear and the car moves quickly, and the solidness of the big black limo, the heavy clunk of its doors feels reassuring, safe, and when we get to Dean Street I don't want to get out. As we pull up outside the club I think for an instant of Caroline, of how young she was when she was caught in the bomb round the corner, how she lost her baby and her boyfriend, and I feel achingly sorry for her suddenly, and almost forgive her.

The club is full of fashionable people and a smattering of celebrities, and although I try not to I feel out of place again, an imposter, which of course I am. Angel looks like she was born to be here, despite her accent, and she mingles easily, chatting for ages to the host, who it seems is a fashion designer with a store in Covent Garden. Simon takes me to the bar and orders more champagne and as I take my first sip I realise that it's just gone midnight and I'm inwardly congratulating myself on having made it to the day *after* when someone taps me on the shoulder and I turn to see a flamboyant young man with peroxide hair and heavily kohled eyes who says, "Caz, daaaarling, it is you! How amazing to see you," and he wraps me in a fragrantly light embrace, like I'm delicate, precious. I'm confused for a moment and then I get it – he must think I'm Caroline! I suppose it's a surprise that it's never happened before – and then I remember that awful day on Hampstead Heath and I can't believe I hadn't realised it then, that it wasn't me the man had recognised, he too must have thought I was her. I've forgotten I'm a twin, that I look like my sister, and I don't know what to say or do. Simon is looking at me but I think he's misheard the name and so I go with it.

"Hi," I say and inside I feel giddy.

"How *are* you? What are you up to these days?" asks the perfumed girl-man.

"Oh, this and that," I reply airily. "I'm based in Manchester now." I hope Simon hasn't heard this. "Sorry, must pop to the ladies, lovely to see you." And I walk over to Angel, whisper to her furiously and she reluctantly gives me her tiny pink silk purse, although she says I've had enough.

The second hit of the drug is more noxious, and I stagger in the cubicle, and decide that this time I really am going home, I cannot take any more for one day, Angel was right, I've had enough, what was I even thinking coming here? I'll walk over to Simon, tell him I'm not feeling well, and he'll order me a taxi while I wait outside in the air. Angel can stay if she wants, I don't want to ruin her evening. I wonder who else here may know Caroline, it is a fashion designer's party after all, and I kick myself for being so stupid. I look in the mirror and see a tall girl with flushed cheeks and glittering eyes, a red gash of lipstick above an emerald dress. I look pretty amazing, all things considered. I straighten my shoulders and turn to the door and as I open it my brain flips over, dumbstruck, as if it can't work out what's going on, can't work out why I'm staring directly into the eyes of my husband.

43

Frances found the trip up Mount Kenya exhilarating, life-changing. She'd never even travelled outside Europe before, never slept in a tent, never been at altitude, never gone up a mountain with a live chicken and eaten it two days later in a watery stew. She'd never before looked down across the plains from a freezing summit at five in the morning, as the sun is coming up, and acknowledge that *this* is living, this is why she was put on the planet, for her heart to beat loud and fast and free. She found the contrast between the hotly colourful landscape at the foot of the mountain and the sub-zero temperatures and steep ice walls at the top exhilarating, compelling. Despite the absence of any facilities, the rawness of the experience, she was hooked, and knew that these kinds of trip would be her thing from now on. No more bored weeks in Brittany or Cornwall with her philandering husband. There was another aspect of the trip that made her heart race, and that was one of the guides, and although he was twenty years her junior there was something about the set of his back and the way he commanded the group that made her achingly aware of where he was, *all* the time, and if he came near her or asked her how she was doing she blushed like a little girl.

She found the descent made her sad somehow, and when they reached the bottom, as the group drank local beer outside the huts where they'd sleep before returning to Nairobi in the morning, she felt like she never wanted to leave this mountain, this moment. So when at the end of the night he'd whispered his hut number to *her*, Frances, she was shocked but Linda said go for it and so she did and she spent a night of such glorious exhausting animal sex with this black god of a man that she thought if she never had sex again at least she'd had this.

44

The man stood in front of me is the Ben from years ago, the one I first met, not the sad broken Ben of now. I'm so confused from the drugs and the drink and the events of this never-ending day, from having just been mistaken for Caroline, that I can't work out what he's doing here, transported in place and time. I seem to have lost all sense of reality and I just stare at him and he stares at me, at my brittle eyes and red gashed mouth. The electricity I feel is as fierce as the moment I fell in love with my husband, just before that disastrous parachute jump, as he strapped me in to my harness and sent firecrackers up my thighs. I try to recover myself and wrench my gaze away, look down at my feet, at my silver stilettos that will transport me away from this crazy crazy day. I feel like I must get out of here, I mustn't bump into anyone else who might know me or my twin, who occupies my darkling inner world. I take a step forward and stumble in my heels, and he catches my arm and says, "Are you OK?"

"Yes," I reply. "I just feel a bit faint, I think I need some air." And this beautiful past-haunting boy takes me by the arm and guides me ever so gently through the crowds, past the bar, past Simon and Angel, and out into the coolness of the midnight street.

"I think I need to go home," I say. "Would you mind calling me a taxi?"

"Of course," he replies. "But it might take a while, are you OK to stand?" I nod but I'm leaning on him heavily, drooping. "Maybe it's easier if we flag one down. Do you think you can walk a little? We'll find more cabs out on the Charing Cross Road." So we walk slowly along Old Compton Street, past the rebuilt Admiral Duncan, and people are staring but I don't know why, I think I'm walking OK now we've got going, I'm no longer faint or staggering. When we get to the main road, there are no black cabs, and so my new friend flags down a mini-cab, one of those dodgy ones that charges a fortune, and as I go to get in he stops me and says, "Look, I'm worried about leaving you like this. My place is only round the corner. D'you want to go there, just until you feel a bit better? I can make you a cup of tea if you'd like."

I still don't know his name but the day has been so long and surreal that I find myself saying yes, he doesn't seem like an axe murderer, and so he asks the cab driver to take us to Marylebone, and when we get there his flat is above a shop of some kind and it's amazing – huge and stylish and beautifully furnished. I sit on the couch and feel safe at last, as though I'm finally where I'm meant to be today, and all I want to do is curl up and go to sleep.

"Sorry, I don't even know your name," I say, and he looks at me oddly and says, "I don't know yours either."

"I'm Cat," I say.

"And I'm Robbie," he replies.

"Pleased to meet you, Robbie," I murmur, and I smile shyly and shut my eyes.

45

When Frances got back to the hotel in Nairobi, there was a message waiting for her. "Hi Mum, call me asap, love Ems." Frances felt sore and slightly embarrassed, as if her daughter would guess down the phone line what she'd been doing all night with her olympian tour guide. She felt that familiar feeling of dread as she dialled and knew it would be about Caroline, and she didn't want to be transported back to drama and turmoil, she wanted to stay out under the African sun forever.

The line took ages to connect, and then Emily took ages to answer. Frances had been right, it was about Caroline. She'd been arrested for drink driving, had been two and a half times the limit, and then she'd kicked up a huge fuss at the station and they'd kept her in a cell overnight until she'd sobered up and calmed down.

"I didn't know whether to ring, Mum, but Caroline says she wants to go straight to rehab this time which I think's a really good thing, and, um, well, she says she hasn't got any money. Me and Ben can manage some of it, but it's quite expensive."

"Tell her to go, and don't you worry, I'll sort the bill out," said Frances, although she didn't know where the money would come from. But it was the least she could do for her daughter – after all, how Caroline had turned out was all her fault. At least they were closer these days, thank God. She wondered whether the treatment would work this time, whether Caroline would ever be better, or whether there would always be some illness or addiction for her to have to fight. The thought saddened Frances as she walked from the lobby and sank down into her sun-lounger. She was so far from her child, her child who needed her, a forever useless mother lying by a pool in Africa, with aching insides and the sweet smell of sex still lingering in her nostrils.

46

When I wake up there's a duvet covering me and I'm lying stretched out on a sofa and I've no idea where I am. I tentatively recall the events of yesterday: the abortive lunch with Simon, my horrendous breakdown, the afternoon spent comatose in bed, the dreadful awards event, my crazy unhinged behaviour, the party at the private club... being mistaken for Caroline! Slowly the last part of the evening unfolds in my mind, and I finally remember the stranger I went home with. I look down at myself and I'm still in my green dress (a good sign), I'm still in his living room (another one), but he's not here. I'm embarrassed that I must have passed out – how long have I been here? What time is it? The clock on the wall says 6.30. Is that morning or evening? Yes, it must be morning, Saturday morning. My mouth feels dry and my head feels nuclear, the pain is terrible. I sit up and clutch my head and try to work out the best way to get out of here. He seemed very kind, and doesn't appear to have molested me, so maybe I ought to just go, but leave him a note, to thank him for his hospitality. Or perhaps I should poke my head around his bedroom door, just to say bye? What the hell is the etiquette? I know how I'll look out on the street in my satin dress and smudgy makeup, I should call a cab – but I have no idea where I am, what address to say. I desperately need some water so I pull myself up and stagger across the room and into the hallway. The kitchen is opposite and it's colossal and uber modern, with an island in the middle and four tall moulded white stools lined up neatly along it. I find a tumbler on the drainer and turn on the tap and it sets off a pump that groans through the flat. I panic, turn it off and gulp the water in one. I'm still wondering how to make my exit when I hear movement and Robbie appears in the doorway, in a white T-shirt and boxers and he's shaking the sleep off him.

"I'm sorry I'm still here," I say.

"I'm not," says Robbie. I look down, embarrassed. I'm aware of him in a way I've not been with anyone except Ben, and I feel treacherous, and the thought is ridiculous.

"Would you like some tea?"

"It's so early, you should go back to bed," I say.

"No, no, it's fine," he says, and he goes over to the kettle and as he passes me I feel a physical pull towards him, as if he's a magnet, and the sensation skims all the way down the front of my body.

Robbie confuses me. He's good-looking, caring, rich presumably, surely too good to be true. His kitchen is immaculate, it's like it's never been used. He makes two mugs of tea, and we go into the lounge and I sit awkwardly on one couch, with the duvet bundled next to me, and Robbie sits on the other. I stare into the brown froth that has formed round the edge of my mug where Robbie has stirred the milk in. I don't know what to say or where to look and my head is still throbbing.

"Do you have any headache pills?" I ask, mainly to break the silence.

"Sure," says Robbie, getting up, and as he passes by me I hold my breath again, he's just so attractive. I press the pills he finds me out of their silver foil and gulp them down with my tea although he gave me a glass of water, and it's hot still and burns the back of my throat.

"I'm not hungover as such," I say. "I just had a bit of a fraught day yesterday, that's all."

"That's OK," says Robbie. He pauses. "Look, I'm tired and your head hurts, so I hope you don't mind me asking... er, would you like to come and lie down, and we can just go back to sleep? It'll be much more comfortable than in here."

I don't answer.

"Or there's the spare room if you prefer," he added.

I try to think. I know I should go home, but when I'm upright my head throbs so much I can't face the cab ride. I want to go back to sleep. I think he's to die for. Maybe I could take up his offer of the spare room, but something tells me that would be a waste, but of what I'm not sure.

"That sounds nice," I say in the end, politely, like he'd asked me to tea. "Would you mind if I borrowed a T-shirt or something though? I'm desperate to get out of this dress."

"Of course," says Robbie, and as he gets up and leads me towards his bedroom I know emphatically that this moment is key, that I'm moving with this man I've just met into yet another new stage of my life on this earth.

47

Ben did his best to carry on with life after Emily left. He tried not to blame her, tried to understand why she'd done it, and in a way knowing that she'd planned it, had taken her passport and emptied her bank account, made him feel better somehow – at least he knew she was out there somewhere, not lying dead and unfound in some lonely wood or stinking ditch. Other times he felt unbelievably angry at her, at her cowardice for leaving him and Charlie, for them not facing things together. She'd got it all totally wrong – from the moment they'd met, they were meant to have been *forever*, for better or worse, that was what was supposed to have happened in their story – but it was like the planet had turned in on itself, had become a kind of sick anti-world where since *that* day everything had gone wrong and there'd been nothing Ben could do to put it right. He'd tried tracing her of course, but the police had done little more than be sympathetic, so he'd searched out every single one of Emily's friends and no-one knew anything and he could tell they weren't lying. In desperation he'd taken time off work, and had driven to Devon and West Wales and around the Peak District, going into hotels and pubs and tea-rooms they'd once visited, furtively pulling out a beautiful picture of her and then feeling like an idiot when they'd look at him as if he were mad and say things like, "Sorry sir, I can't help you." His in-laws were no use either – Frances had Caroline living back with her, having split with her latest boyfriend (who'd been unfaithful apparently) and she was worse-behaved than ever; and Frances seemed so lost in dealing with her youngest daughter and managing her own grief that she had nothing to offer Ben. Poor Andrew was a mess, he seemed to be fading, receding into himself, and Ben rarely saw him these days – he just took Charlie over every now and again but Andrew didn't seem much interested in even him anymore.

Only work and Charlie kept Ben going, once it was clear Emily really wasn't coming back. He arranged a rota of care and his parents stepped in and were brilliant, and although they never said it he could tell that they thought it was no wonder their daughter-in-law had run away, just look what kind of family she came from. They'd always loved Emily for herself, he knew that much, but they'd been disgusted by all the goings on at the wedding, and had never quite stopped worrying about the impact such a family might have had on the mother of their only grandchild. Ben would sit alone on quiet nights and wonder that himself too. Just why had Emily left? Was it *only* because of what had happened, or because deep down she was so damaged by her family after all? She'd always seemed so sane, so compassionate, so weirdly like him – and that was what had drawn him to her in the first place, from the time he first saw her standing there in the office car park, obviously terrified, kicking her feet into the tarmac while they worked out who was going in which car to the airport. As he'd said hello he'd experienced a thrill of recognition of something in her, and that for him had been that. She'd seen right through him on that first day of course, aware at once that he was smitten, but the fact that she then doubted it, couldn't see how stunning she was, only made him love her more. At the time he'd thought he must have imagined it, but later in the afternoon, after he'd strapped on her parachute, she'd straightened up and looked at him, bewildered almost, and the look seemed to be one of realisation, and then it had turned to embarrassment, and she'd stumbled away from him as he'd carried on rigging up people willing himself to concentrate, he couldn't be distracted doing up parachutes.

He'd kicked himself afterwards for not being more friendly on the way home, but he didn't know how to manage his feelings, he'd never been lovestruck before – he hadn't thought those kind of things really happened. It was only when they finally, fantastically, got together months later and she'd told him about herself, said she had an identical twin, and one that didn't even like her very much, that Ben was certain she needed him as much as he needed her. It was like in some ways he became the twin she'd never had – her soulmate, her best friend, the one who knew what she was thinking, the person to whom she could say the absolute truth of how she felt, no matter how weak or mad it may have sounded to someone else: he had always got her, understood what she meant. The fact that they were so madly attracted to one another had seemed almost a bonus, even though Emily used to tease him that she fancied him *despite* his profession and geeky pastimes, and he would tease her back that if ever she went off him there was always a replica of herself who he was sure would have him. And they would both laugh at their mischievousness, and the absolute sureness of their feelings for each other.

Ben often found himself thinking back over his and Emily's lives together, when Charlie was asleep and he was sat alone on the sofa, the same one on which he and his wife had cuddled up in the showroom, Emily kicking her shoes off, curling like a cat, making sure it was comfortable enough to buy – it was too expensive to make a mistake, she'd said at the time. Recently Ben had hooked up the TV to his computer so that it played endless photos from their vast collection, and he'd sit there mesmerised by the random images – an arm's length snap of their windswept faces on an unknown winter's beach in Devon; Emily in front of the Doge's Palace in St Mark's Square, on their second wedding anniversary; Ben holding Charlie by a river near Buxton, in case he tried to jump in; Emily looking more stunning than he knew she could on their wedding day, the sea glinting approvingly behind her; Emily cradling their baby son in Frances's tiny rose-filled back garden; the pair of them on honeymoon in Sorrento, holding hands in front of earthy pink and orange buildings that jumbled down to the water; Charlie and his best friend Daniel cuddling on this very couch; Emily laughing as she watered the flowers with Charlie by her side, soaked; Emily looking serene in front of a red-columned temple in Knossos, neither of them knowing she was pregnant; all of them tucked up together in bed on Christmas morning, Charlie sitting on Ben's head. The images floated tantalisingly across the screen, giving Ben just enough time to place them, date them, before they drifted off again and a new one glided in. Ben would watch for hours, thinking *just one more and then I'll move*, until his bones grew cold as the darkness settled, but he couldn't pull himself away to even put the heating or the lights on, it was almost like she was talking to him from afar, saying *remember this time or that moment* and he found it strangely comforting. But there were other times when an image would appear that seemed so vivid, so taunting, that he still couldn't believe that she'd abandoned him, on top of everything else, couldn't believe that he didn't know how or where she was, and he would capitulate to his anguish and lie alone on the floor and sob and beat his fists, helpless in his grief, like a little child.

Ben coped better than anyone thought he would after the initial shock had faded, as the leaves fell and the year sighed its way out – but the thought of Christmas was excruciating, and so his parents had put their foot down and arranged a trip to a tiny hotel they knew in the Highlands, and the weather had been unseasonably lovely and they'd all got on with it, and even managed to enjoy it somehow. They'd set off from Manchester early in the morning, and within four and a half hours had found themselves driving along the banks of Loch Lomond, and when they stopped to give Charlie a break the air was so thin and pure it was like Ben was breathing properly again, taking the air into his lungs willingly for a change instead of through obligation to Charlie. It was a good call on his parents' part – the hotel was warm and posh in an old-fashioned, shabby way, with no past history to sideswipe Ben, and the owners adored Charlie, he was just so cute, and they made a huge fuss of him, constantly giving him biscuits, and for a change no-one minded. Charlie seemed to almost have forgotten Emily up there – he loved running free alongside the loch and chasing the ducks – and his mischievousness, his unmitigated joy at the beauty of life kept them all going. The change of routine made even Christmas Day bearable, and Ben found himself almost relaxing, but he found he couldn't quite shake off his need to be always looking over his shoulder, in case she was there, in case she'd suddenly appear out of the mist and crouch on those long lovely legs with outstretched arms, so Charlie could run to her, leap into her arms and show her that he loved her still, even though she had left him.

48

Robbie's bedroom is painted slate grey, with bleached floors and furniture and crisp white bedding, and it's stylish and androgynous, but stark, like the kitchen. I wonder whether he's done it himself, or whether he has an interior designer, or worse a girlfriend, but I don't like to ask, now's really not the time. He gives me a T-shirt and it's a fancy label, and it feels nice when I go to the bathroom and put it on. It's short on me, my legs look longer than ever, and I pull it down at the front self-consciously as I walk back into the room. Robbie looks at me but says nothing, and when I get into the bed he puts his arms around me and holds me gently, unthreateningly, and my body feels just right, fusing with his, and the pain in my head starts to subside.

"It's so refreshing," he says quietly, "that you take me exactly as I am."

"Of course," I murmur, and I lie contentedly next to him and for the first time in a whole year I feel perfectly at peace, safe – loved even. It's extraordinary, and I know it won't last – he's so much younger than me, could do so much better – but somehow we've found each other, and I'm certain that for whatever reason it's what we both need right now. I'm so warm and comfortable I drift off to sleep and for a change my dreams are gentle, untroubled, and when I next open my eyes it's much much later and Robbie is sitting next to me on the bed, dressed, and he's made me another mug of perfectly-coloured tea.

"Would you like some breakfast?" he asks. "I've been out and got eggs, bacon, sausage, muffins, the works."

"Why are you being so nice to me?" I ask.

"Why not?" he says. "I was bored at that party anyway, it's not really my scene, and then I didn't want to put you in some dodgy cab on your own, you obviously weren't well, and when you passed out on my couch I could hardly throw you out, could I?" He smiled. "And then I thought you might feel better if you went to bed for a while, and now I'm hungry so I'm going to make breakfast. What's so nice about that?"

What's so nice about *that*? I can't think what to say, so stick to safe territory.

"Would you mind if I have a shower first?"

"Of course. D'you want to borrow some clothes?" Robbie crosses the room and opens a door into a separate dressing room, and all his clothes are arranged neatly, colour coded. He pulls out some jeans and a couple of shirts for me to choose from, and gives me the biggest softest bath towel ever.

The shower is vast and fierce and as I stand under the deluge the last vestiges of my headache travel down my spine, through my limbs and pour down the plughole. As I wrap the towel around me I feel a pang of fear that this is all too good to be true, something's not right, I don't deserve this. I still haven't called Angel to let her know I'm safe, but when I check my bag my phone's dead and I don't know her number, and my disquiet deepens.

I dress in Robbie's jeans and a pale pink polo shirt, pull my fingers through my wet streaky hair, and join him in the kitchen, where the smells of frying tomato and smoked bacon mingle and make me realise I'm ravenous again. I sit timidly on one of the mushroom stools and I'm too high up, don't know what to do with my feet, and I fidget like a toddler.

Robbie smiles and gets plates from the cupboard. He goes to the fridge and takes out two pale blue eggs and cracks them into the bacon fat and the hissing fills the silence. He cooks confidently and when he serves up my breakfast it's beautifully executed, like in a restaurant. We sit side by side at the counter and eat politely, silently. The attraction I feel to him is tight, like a rubber band. Outside it's muggy and what with the fug from the cooking I start to feel heady again.

"Would you like to go in the lounge?" asks Robbie when we've finished. "I'll make us some coffee."

"OK," I say, squirming down from the stool and padding back to the living room. As I sink into the sofa there's a loud crack of thunder but I must have missed the lightning, and then rain is galloping down the windows, thrashing on the roof, and the air temperature drops. Robbie comes in with two mugs of milky frothy coffee, sets them down on the table, then goes over to his iPod and puts on Eva Cassidy. He sits next to me on the enveloping couch and finally we look into each other's eyes and I feel lust and despair and, yes, *love*, tender pure love for this man I've just met. There's something strange about all this, but I cannot work out what it is, and despite my worrying about Angel worrying about me, about where I've got to (now there's a laugh, there's only half a dozen people in Manchester who've been doing that for months) I decide to go with it and the moment feels special, rarified, still. I never want it to end, I want time to stop right here, before it all goes bad again. I stare deep into Robbie's eyes and it's like looking at Ben, but the Ben who was innocent still, the *before* Ben. Eva's tones and the beating rain make my heart stop and I can't breathe properly, and after at least a song and a half of this Robbie finally moves towards me, slowly, gently, and when he kisses me his taste is warmly of coffee and bacon and his mouth is tender, unhurried, genuine.

I look at my watch and it's nearly lunchtime. I try to move but I want to stay. "I really should get out of your way soon," I say and as I speak my lips move against his. "I'm sure you must have plans."

"You know what, I've had a bit of a full-on week," says Robbie. "And it's a revolting day – so what I'd really like better than anything right now is to sit here and listen to music and maybe watch a movie later and just shut the world out." He pauses. "And if you could stay and do it with me that would be even nicer."

I hesitate. I try not to think of the real Ben and Charlie and where they are, what they're doing. I worry about Angel worrying about me. And then I make my decision. I pull away and take his hand and kiss it all the way along where the palm meets the fingers and I look at him, not shy any more, and say, "You know what? That sounds just perfect."

49

After the success of the Highlands, the new year came and the winter months dragged listlessly by. Then before Ben knew it, it was nearly May and he was forced to confront the biggest milestone of all, the anniversary of the day his life had changed forever. For this he found he wanted to be completely alone – he couldn't face having even Charlie with him, not without Emily there, so he left him with his parents and drove into the Peak District. He got out the car and walked – in as straight a line as he could, although he didn't know why – for hours and hours, veering off paths, beating through brambles, crossing fenced-in fields, hauling himself over rough rocky terrain. He'd originally thought about climbing Kinder Scout, where he'd proposed to Emily (and she'd laughed at him for getting down on one knee, before getting down herself and saying yes please) but he couldn't face being up there without her, and besides he didn't want to risk seeing anyone. His walking was relentless, meditative, and he almost forgot the time, forgot where he was – he even forgot Emily for brief seconds, what they'd had and what they'd lost. He knew Charlie had sensed the date too, although Ben couldn't tell him of course, he wouldn't understand, but he seemed upset when Ben dropped him off, not howling exactly but crying pitifully, which in a way was worse. Ben carried a small tent on his back and when it was late and almost dark he stopped and pitched it beside a gently-flowing river where there were no sounds besides the burbling water and the occasional shriek of an unknown bird. He lay awake half the night and *almost* enjoyed the feeling of being all alone in the world out there, of having the time and space to grieve and breathe, and when he awoke he felt oddly refreshed, relieved that he'd got through the day and arrived on the other side, as sane and intact as he could be.

50

Robbie doesn't ask me any questions about myself and I don't like to ask him anything either, although I'm curious at how he seems so young and can afford such a swanky place, how he's such a good cook, such a gentleman. We find we like the same music and we lie together on the couch and listen to the Doves and Panics and Libertines, to Oasis and even Johnny Cash, but when he puts on Radiohead I cringe and tell him I don't like them. Robbie says nothing, he seems to understand, and he puts on a playlist instead and after a while that song from The Wannadies comes on, and as the chorus kicks in he looks straight into my eyes and doesn't flinch and I feel like my heart is going to break. The rain hasn't stopped and the temperature has dropped further, but we don't care as we gaze at each other and cuddle and snog the afternoon away like a pair of teenagers. Robbie seems happy for us to stay on the couch, to stay dressed, and the desire in us builds and crunches through our clothes, but neither of us has the inclination to take it any further right now, and so we don't.

51

Ben asked his parents if they'd mind having Charlie the next night too, the Saturday night, as it had taken him ages to find his way back to his car, and by the time he'd arrived home with scratched-up legs and feet covered in blisters he'd been too exhausted and wrung out to cope with looking after anyone, even Charlie. He closed the curtains and ordered a curry and settled down to Saturday night telly – something he used to claim he hated, but which Emily had always loved and insisted they watch, and secretly he'd quite enjoyed it too, not that he would ever admit it of course.

It wasn't the same watching on his own, without laughing at the tears pouring down Emily's cheeks and her telling him to shut up, she couldn't hear what the judges were saying. He found himself wondering where she was right now, what she was doing – and without Charlie there to restrain him, make him put on a show, he felt the same thumping grief as on the day he'd looked under the bed and realised their leather holdall was gone, that she was gone.

The doorbell rang. Shit, it must be his curry, he needed to get a grip. He swiped at his eyes and grabbed his wallet.

As he opened the door he stopped, staring at his visitor like he couldn't believe it, his mouth hanging open, foolish almost. What was going on? Where was his curry? *Had she come back?* His heart leapt as if he'd been shot, and then it crashed, like he was on the floor dying.

"Oh," he said.

"Can I come in?" said Caroline. "Maybe I shouldn't have come, but I tried you last night too, and I just needed to see you, to say sorry."

"Sorry for what?" said Ben, and he knew he was being rude.

"Please let me in, Ben. You're not the only one who's suffering, maybe we can help each other."

"I don't think so," he said, but he stood aside and she walked in anyway. He followed her into the living room and as she took off her coat the doorbell went again, and this time it was his curry, but his hands still shook as he paid the delivery boy. In the kitchen he divided the food onto two plates and there was plenty for them both, he'd ordered much too much as usual. He grabbed himself a beer, and then hesitated – maybe he shouldn't drink it in front of Caroline, wasn't that a bit taunting, but then he thought, fuck it, and he poured her an orange juice, that's all he had in the way of soft drinks.

Just as he'd loaded up the trays Caroline teetered in on her heels and asked for a wine glass, and out of her handbag she produced a bottle of white wine wrapped in red paper, misting it was so cold. She must have bought it just now, the insensitive cow, from the off-licence at the end of their street, but as he was tired and uneasy he said nothing, he really couldn't face a fight. They ate in silence in front of the TV, while a man ate golf balls and an old woman danced with her poodle, and Caroline's skirt kept riding up as she balanced her tray on her naked thighs. By the next ad break she'd finished her wine although the glass she'd poured herself had been massive, and she asked him to get her another.

Something in Ben broke a little then and he got up and stormed into the kitchen, into the fridge, and he ripped open another beer and tipped up the can, poured the liquid down his throat, as fast as he could, why the fuck not? The fact she'd gone to *that* off-licence had made him so explosively angry he needed to obliterate the feeling, smash it to pieces, and as he gulped down the alcohol he realised he wasn't even angry with her anymore, he was angry with the whole horrible world.

52

Much much later it has grown dark, but we still haven't moved from the couch. We've half-watched two movies, we've kissed and groped through countless albums, and I've fallen more than a little in love with him, have fantasised just a teeny bit about a new life together, maybe one day us even getting married, becoming Mrs – who?

"What's your surname, Robbie?" I say through my bruised pumped up lips.

Robbie looks uncomfortable for the first time. "Uh, it's um, Brown," he says.

I stare at him. "That's my surname," I say. "Wow, it's fate," and I laugh.

"I'm hungry," he says quickly. "Do you fancy getting a takeaway?"

"There must be loads of places round here, what about going out for something?" I say.

"I'd rather stay in with you," he says. "It's raining outside, I've got some champagne, we can just chill – plus you won't need to worry about what shoes to wear with that outfit." He looks at me in his too-big jeans and shirt, and he has a point.

"OK," I say, and I don't mind, in fact I prefer it.

"Is curry all right?"

"Perfect," I reply. "You choose, I like everything." He rummages in a drawer for a leaflet, and when he orders he rattles it off as fast as he can and his voice sounds a bit weird, high-pitched for some reason.

He disappears for a moment, and comes back with a bottle of champagne and two tall glasses. The sight makes me think longingly of Angel's pink silk purse, and I realise with a lurch that I never gave it back to her. I picture the pair of us last night in the toilets at the Dorchester, of how quickly I broke my promise to my boy, and then I think about how I turned my back on him anyway when he needed me most, so what difference does one little line make every now and again?

Although the need in me is expanding now, into every last crack in my messed-up mind, I worry about Robbie and what he'd say. Somehow he doesn't seem the druggy type, and I'd hate him to think less of me, so I push the thought of the little purse away again, as far away as it will go. *If it wasn't in my bag I'd be fine now. Just pretend it's not there.* Robbie fills our flutes and toasts us, toasts the last 24 hours, kisses me again, and the thought of the drug drifts hazily away.

When the doorbell goes Robbie jumps up and says, "I'll be back in a minute, would you mind getting that," and he shoves a £50 note into my hand and heads to the bathroom. I buzz up the man smiling into the video screen, and he delivers aromatic food in smart cardboard boxes that I dish up onto white square plates in the gleaming kitchen. Robbie reappears and we take the food into the living room and sit back and stuff ourselves, it's like we're starving, and as we eat we watch

Britain's Got Talent, and it feels so nice, a proper Saturday night in, like I used to have with my husband. I find we laugh at the same jokes, make the same kinds of comments, and whenever I look at him, my stomach tingles and my pulse goes crazy, until I have to look away. Robbie opens another bottle and we lie down and the drink has had its effect now, and so eventually he pulls me up and leads me to the bedroom and this time we don't just lie and cuddle, we're ready, it's like we've known each other forever, and it's fucking wonderful. It's like Robbie is some amazing gift from God and being here in this moment, it all just feels right right right. The only thing missing is that extra buzz and when I finally give in and suggest the cocaine we're both a bit drunk, on champagne and love. Robbie looks at me for a long while and then he says, "For you I'd do anything," and I don't know why but it doesn't feel sordid with him, in his fancy apartment in Marylebone, it feels exciting and glamorous and mind-blowing. Hours later we finally fall asleep and when I wake up the dawn is peering through the half-opened shutters, and I am lying guilt-ridden and Robbie is lying dead.

53

When Ben came back from the kitchen he was still fucking fuming, but he was almost as angry with Emily now, for leaving, than with Caroline, for coming. It seemed too much to bear at this time of all times to have to confront someone who looked like Emily, sounded like her, yet wasn't her. *She shouldn't have run away, how self-centred was that?* He was so drunk now it was like his wife's absence was a physical void, as if his stomach had been gouged out and there was nothing but a gaping hole where his insides should have been. He put his hand to his midriff – yes, he was still all there, he hadn't been cut up in the night. He glared at Caroline lounging on his sofa in her too-short skirt, and wished she would just fuck off, what did she want anyway. He went over to the wicker chair that he swore he hadn't sat in since that first magical night at Emily's flat, years ago now, and it was so battered and uncomfortable to sit in, they really should get rid of it. No, *he* should get rid of it, there wasn't a *they* anymore. He wished again that Caroline would just take the hint and get the fuck out of there, but he was reluctant to ask her directly to leave, in case she made one of her scenes, and he couldn't face that tonight.

"Where've you been?" said Caroline, and her voice was slurred.

"In the kitchen," Ben said, and he wondered dimly how Caroline was also drunk, he'd only just brought in her second glass of wine – but he hadn't spotted the half bottle of whisky empty on the floor.

The TV continued its fake emotional assault on them. They watched a little girl with a big voice murder a Whitney song, and then a group of grown men in dungarees dancing with wheel barrows, until Ben thought he really couldn't stand any more, he had to go to bed, and on impulse he pressed the remote and the screen went black. The silence blared. Caroline huffed and as she turned to glare at him he realised she looked ill again, pale-faced and fragile under her makeup.

"What did you want to talk to me about?" he said eventually – maybe she'd leave once she'd told him. Caroline bent her head and twisted her fingers.

"I wanted to say sorry," she said.

"About what though?" Ben persisted.

Caroline looked awkward. "About what happened," she said. "I'm sorry about everything."

"Not as sorry as me," Ben replied, but he said it without pity, just bottomless sadness.

"Do you think she'll come back?" Caroline asked. She waited as the question spun around the room and he took so long to answer that she thought he hadn't heard her.

"No, not now," he said, and it was the first time he'd acknowledged it and it was devastating, so he got up to leave the room, he couldn't cry in front of Caroline of all people, but he stumbled over the whisky bottle and fell awkwardly, almost on top of her. The sofa was low and deep and squashy and although he tried to get back up it seemed too much effort all of a sudden, and so he slumped there, drunk and defeated.

Caroline shifted over and put her arms around him and held him quietly while he sobbed, out of his mind on beer and grief and loneliness. He found her touch weirdly comforting – although she was so different in temperament to her twin, she felt like Emily, even smelled like Emily, as well as looking like her, obviously. Ben hadn't held anyone except poor Charlie for so long it was disorientating, and reminded him of happier times – so when she started stroking his hair and saying there, there, it would all be OK, he even thought in his drunkenness that maybe she *was* Emily, and when she leaned in to kiss him he let her and he even kissed her back and it all became so urgent and animal-like it was as if he didn't even notice that it wasn't his wife, but her flawed malignant twin, until it was too late. Afterwards he realised what he'd done and screamed at her to get out and leave him the fuck alone, and then he staggered from the room and fled upstairs, slamming the door behind him.

54

Gorgeous Robbie has blood congealed in his nose, the bed is cold and his skin is blue. There is absolutely no doubt he's dead. I don't scream, instead I leap out of the bed and run to the window, naked, panting – like a dog. I am so horrified I can't think straight. I cannot, *cannot* look at him again, the image is stuck in my brain and I know it's another vision of hell that I will never be rid of, another life I have ruined, for daring to love him. I gag at this thought, but manage to hold the vomit in my mouth long enough to reach the bin and then it spews everywhere and I sink to the floor, and for the second time in two days I'm covered in my own sick and I wish this life would just hurry up and end now. As I stand up my legs are wobbly and my chest is rising and falling faster than I knew it could, and my breath is getting shallower and shallower until I know I'm hyper-ventilating but I can't seem to stop. What can I do? Who can help Robbie? (*No-one, it's too late.*) Who can help me? (*Ditto.*) I can't call Angel, Simon, not even my mum or dad, my phone is dead and I don't know any of their numbers. There are only two numbers I know off by heart that could possibly help me – my old house in Chorlton, and 999. I desperately want my husband, I want

Ben, he'll know what to do, and so I dial the Manchester number almost without thinking, and as the call connects I remember myself, what on earth would I say, and after three rings I hang up. My hands are shaking but I just about manage to call 999 and after a few seconds an efficient sounding operator comes on the line.

"Fire, police or ambulance?" she asks.

I don't know. He's dead, I know that much, what good can an ambulance do?

"Hello?" she continues. "Do you want fire, police or ambulance?"

I pant and talk at the same time. "There's somebody dead here."

"Are you sure? Are they still breathing?"

"He's cold and blue. I think that makes him dead." And I start to give great gusting sobs down the line, for Robbie, for his poor lost life. It's horrendous.

"What's your address, love? Tell me your address."

"I don't know. I'm somewhere in Marylebone."

"OK, we'll get that number traced. Stay on the line, pet, try to calm down. What's the deceased person's name?"

"Robbie. Robbie Brown."

"And your name?"

"Catherine Brown."

"Are you his wife?"

"No," I wail. "I've only just met him." The room starts to whirl and I assume I'm fainting and then I realise it's the blue lights down in the street and the police are here already.

Thank God. Until I remember I'm still naked, covered in vomit, and I run to the bathroom, am in and out the shower before it has time to get hot, and by the time I've wrapped one of Robbie's sheet-sized towels around me, the police are banging on the door.

I open up just before they're about to break it down, and they storm straight past me and one of them heads to the bedroom. Within a couple of seconds he calls, "Jesus Christ, come and look at this Pete."

The policeman called Pete goes towards the bedroom but stops stock still, at the threshold, as he sees poor dead Robbie, the drugs paraphernalia on the bedside table. He lets out a cry of horror and then turns to look at me, and there is hatred in his eyes.

55

In the night maybe someone had come in and cleaved Ben's head in two; and then he remembered Caroline turning up, the amount of beer he'd drunk, what he'd done with his missing wife's twin sister. He felt disgusted, repulsed, but there was no time to get to the bathroom, and he vomited endlessly into the waste-paper basket until there was nothing left apart from spice-reeked bile in his throat. Thank Christ Caroline hadn't followed him up to the bedroom, hopefully she'd have gone by now – she wouldn't hang around surely, not after how nuts he'd gone afterwards. No, he'd never see her again, not ever, no matter what might happen in the future.

Ben lay in a stupor for hours and hours and when he finally got up it was lunchtime and Caroline had left, thank God. He had a shower hotter than his body could bear and scrubbed himself raw, but still he felt dirty, wrong in his skin, defeated: Emily would never come back to him now. He didn't know what to do with himself. All he could think of was to clean up, try to remove every last molecule of evidence, make it not true. He threw out the congealed remains of the takeaway, loaded the crockery and glasses into the dishwasher and ran it on its highest setting, even though it was half-empty. He disinfected the coffee table; got the vacuum and hoovered the carpet; sponged and blow-dried and turned over the cushions on the sofa, stained as they were with shame. He threw the beer cans, the whisky and wine bottles into the recycling bin and when he was finally done he made himself a strong black coffee, sat down and turned on the news. When the phone started ringing he ignored it, in case it was Caroline, but then he changed his mind – what if it was *her* – but it cut out anyway before he could get to it. He still wasn't thinking straight and so when he saw Caroline's face staring out at him from the TV screen he thought he was mistaken, hallucinating even. Then when he realised it was definitely her he couldn't take in the pictures or the words and he wondered blankly what had happened, what terrible thing she'd done now. It was like his mind had too much information to process and refused to reboot, and it was only when they said it a third time, Catherine Brown, not Caroline Brown, that he realised he had finally found his wife.

56

Pete and his colleague don't know what to do with me, still in my bath towel, and after some anxious conferring and calls for back up they finally tell me they're arresting me on suspicion of murder. The words don't make any sense to me, so I nod and let them caution me, I don't give a shit what they do to me now. *Poor poor Robbie, so young, so full of life, what the hell have I done?* I start sobbing again. A woman police officer arrives, I think they called her specially, and she takes me into the bathroom to search me, and I drop the towel and all she can see are my long white legs and my torso patterned with tiny shiny rivulets of sick. It takes all of 10 seconds and then she says I can get dressed, but after more whispered debate she tells me I have to put on clean clothes out of Robbie's wardrobe, we mustn't touch anything to do with the crime scene. That's what she calls it, a crime scene, because a murder has been committed, by me apparently. Finally the policewoman, butch with her clumpy boots and short sensible hair, cuffs my hands in front of me, and she seems apologetic almost – she knows I'm not up to fighting or running away – and the metal feels cold and alien and painful, and yet it comforts me. As they finally lead me barefoot from the flat, down the lushly carpeted stairs and out onto the morning street I feel small and frail next to the police officers, as if I've shrunk a few inches in the night. As the one called Pete marches me to the police van I see the waiting photographers and realise this is a news story. I will be found now, my family will know where I am, discover what I've done, know that I've ruined yet another life. They must be taking me to a police station, and the thought makes me faint.

In the van I'm put in a cage, like an animal. I'm so low down I can smell the diesel fumes, can feel the road close by, beneath the slack motion of the van's suspension, and I start to feel nauseous again. I'm so defeated I try to lean my head back, but funnily enough there's no head rest, so I lie it awkwardly against the side of the van and at every bump it hits the metal, hard, and the shot of pain is dull although it should be electric, and I know I deserve it. I'm hazily aware of stopping for traffic lights and changing lanes and rounding corners but I feel a weird out of body sensation, as though I'm looking in on myself, am some villainous protagonist in a movie. After maybe 10 minutes the van picks up speed and it absolutely hammers round a corner, turning left, going briefly onto two wheels or so it seems, and now it's a right hand bend, and then the brakes are applied and it yanks to a halt, and I hear some talking through the window, and now we're off again, more slowly this time, and after a few more yards we stop and the back doors are being opened and the pin sharp May sunshine, fresh after Saturday's rain, floods into the van, into my eyes, and I close them quickly, there's no place in me for brightness.

I'm told to get out the van and as I do so I stumble and brush against the door and get black grease on Robbie's jeans.

For some reason this bothers me so I say sorry, I'm not sure to whom, and try to brush the mark off, and the woman PC says, "Come on, madam," not unkindly, and she holds my shackled arm and leads me towards the steps that take us up into the massive building. We enter reception, if that's what you call it in a police station, and there are officers everywhere, staring at me, I seem to be a big story for some reason. I'm buzzed straight through and am taken into a hideous little room that stinks of misery, and they send a doctor and ask me all these questions about my health, my mental health, whether I've ever self-harmed, whether I'm suicidal now. It's depressing. I tell them that it depends what their definition of self-harm is, but they just look at me stonily and when I refuse to be drawn on whether I'm planning on killing myself they mark something down on their pad and move on to asking me if there's anyone I'd like to be informed of my arrest. I almost think that's funny, presumably the whole country knows by now, judging by all the photographers outside Robbie's flat, and I wonder vaguely how they got there so fast. When they ask me if I want a solicitor I'm too tired to think and so it feels easier to say no. So they take me to a cell and when they finally leave me alone I find that I'm beyond feeling, beyond caring, I'm in a place deep in my mind that feels safe and warm, where nothing can go wrong, because it already has, every last thing that can.

57

Angel was so busy chatting to her new friend Philip that she didn't notice for ages that Cat wasn't around. She'd assumed Cat was with Simon, and so when instead she'd spotted him talking to a willowy woman with glossy black hair cut straight across her brow, Angel went over and asked him where Cat was. Simon hadn't seen her leave either, it had been crowded in the bar and he'd been waiting to be served, so when by 1.30 Cat still hadn't come back Angel tried to call her, but her phone just went to voicemail.

Oh well, thought Angel, and she guessed she'd just see Cat at home. But she was a bit annoyed that Cat had left without saying goodbye, especially as she'd taken her pink silk purse – Angel was feeling a little edgy now, and wasn't sure who it would be OK to ask in here. In the end she went to rejoin Simon, and drank more champagne which took her mind off her purse, and when Simon asked her if she'd like to come back for a nightcap, he was staying at a hotel just round the corner, she thought, why not, he was attractive and besides it would save her a cab fare, and so they left together and Angel hoped afterwards that Cat wouldn't mind.

58

Many hours later I sit on the edge of my very own bunk in a cell in Paddington Green Police Station and I'm still trying to digest the fact they think I'm a murderous drug dealing tramp. *Am I?* What with the terror of waking up next to a corpse I'd completely forgotten the implications of what we'd done together, how we'd shared Angel's drugs, that it was me who'd given them to him. *That I have caused his death.* I shiver uncontrollably, it's cold in here, my police-issue white top and trousers are far too flimsy, and I realise that my pathetic attempt to run away from the past, to start a new life, has failed, back-fired, caused yet more misery. I've been strip-searched again, by two officers this time, and the snail trails on my body are still there and the rank smell of sick is lodged forever in my nostrils. At least I can give up now, I really am past fighting for survival, but the irony is I think my erratic answers earlier mean they've put me on suicide watch, so someone keeps peering through the grill every 15 minutes. It would be quite funny really, if I hadn't killed someone. A fat-faced policeman looks in on me yet again and I look blankly at him for a while, uncomprehendingly, like a gorilla in a zoo, and then I turn my face to the wall.

59

When Angel got back at lunchtime on the Saturday and it was clear that Cat still hadn't come home, Angel started properly to worry. Although she'd never liked to ask (she'd assumed Cat would tell her when she was ready) she'd always sensed a strange sadness in her friend, and after the drama of yesterday she wondered just what the truth was and what Cat had done now, whether she was OK, or whether perhaps she should call the police.

Don't be daft, thought Angel. She wasn't Cat's mother, she probably just went home with someone. But the feeling wouldn't go away and when Angel went to work on the Saturday night she left Cat a message asking her to call as soon as she got home, and she wrote down her number on the back of a gas bill and left it on the table by the front door, in case Cat had lost her mobile, maybe that's why she hadn't called.

It was from one of the customers at the blackjack table that Angel first overheard the shocking news that Roberto Monteiro was dead. So when she finished her shift she pulled up the BBC news on her phone to see what had happened, and that's how she found out her best friend had been arrested for murder.

60

I'm sobbing quietly now, as if it has finally hit me. I regret everything I've done these past two days, every last thing. If only I'd been sensible, like I used to be, taken the day off work, stayed quietly at home. If only I'd been brave enough to get through it on my own. If only I'd not gone out for lunch with Simon, what an insane idea, as if I could possibly have enjoyed myself. If only the doctor's drugs hadn't turned me manic, crazy. If only I'd stayed in bed all evening instead of going out again, what the fuck was I thinking, and to a pointless awards dinner of all things. If only I'd not gone on to the party, not met Robbie, not had Angel's drugs on me. If only if only if only. And now because of me one of the country's brightest young footballers is lying dead and blue in a morgue. When the police said it was Roberto Monteiro it all made sense at last – why people were staring as we walked to find a cab; why he was so keen for us to stay in rather than go out and be recognised; why he seemed so into me, who didn't have a clue who he was, knowing I must have liked him for himself; why he was wealthy and yet so young. He just didn't seem like a footballer to me though – I thought footballers lived in home counties mansions, not central London apartments, and I know this is prejudiced but he seemed far too cultured, too much of a gentleman. His sister's a model apparently, it seems she's a friend of the fashion designer's and that was why he was at the club. He was injured, recovering from a knee operation, and so would have been allowed to be out, even on a Friday night. I only know all this because I overheard the policeman called Pete telling someone outside my cell, and he was almost crying, he must be a Chelsea supporter.

Of course I've heard of Roberto Monteiro, everyone has, but I've never been into football and although it sounds silly, out of context in my over-wrought state I just did not work it out. I'd even laughed with my husband one time, shortly before everything went wrong, at how much Ben looked like him. I almost laugh now, I feel hysterical, maniacal, mad. What did Robbie see in me, I wonder? Was it just that I didn't know who he was, or was it more than that? And what did I see in him? Was it only that he looked like my husband? I suppose I'll never know, and then the tears come, big fat generous ones, for Robbie, for his youth and promise and beauty that will never be fulfilled, and that makes me think of everything else that has happened and I curl up tight on the filthy bunk and wish the world would just fuck off and go away.

61

Caroline had felt a peculiar sense of triumph when she'd fucked her twin sister's husband. She'd thought he was fair game, Emily had abandoned him after all, and the fact that Ben's desire for her, Caroline, had been so intense and all-consuming, well, it had made her feel powerful, magnificent, in that moment of release for them both, the ultimate triumph in her lifelong competition with her sister. Immediately after-wards though, when he'd pushed her violently off and leapt to his feet, glaring at her with revulsion before bolting from the room, she'd realised the depth of his disgust for her – that their act had turned to hate not love, that she'd achieved nothing. Her heart tightened as she poured another drink, and she wondered why she was so unlovable. What was wrong with her?

Caroline stayed on Ben's couch all night and drank herself stupid, and in the morning she crept upstairs to his room and stared at the slammed door, willing him to come out. She debated opening it herself and just barging in, but the handle was hanging at an odd angle, as if it was about to fall off, and in the end she thought better of it, he *had* been quite scary last night – and so she turned on her heel and staggered out into the street. She swayed the hundred or so yards to the end of the road and stopped outside the off-licence, with its green steel grill snapped shut like teeth, and she stood at the kerb and teetered as a bus crashed past. Eventually she crossed when there was a break in the traffic, and stumbled along the side street opposite, not knowing what to do, where to go. She perched on a garden wall and buried her head in her jacket and began to sob, loudly, theatrically, and she'd been there for maybe five minutes when two lads in United shirts swaggered by, and said, "Cheer up love, you could be a Chelsea supporter," and when she looked up at them bewildered they laughed and said, "Haven't you heard – Roberto Monteiro's dead."

62

I've been alone in this cell for hours, with just my toxic thoughts and the every-15-minute sight of a bored-looking policeman to distract me. Eventually I guess I doze off, and only wake up when a meal gets dumped through the hatch. My jailer tells me they're still collecting evidence so won't be interviewing me for a while. I don't acknowledge that I've heard what he's saying, I don't mean to be rude but I don't care whether they interview me ever, I don't care if I never leave this cell again. The meal they give me is a supermarket ready meal, a lasagne they must have removed from the packaging and microwaved themselves. I haven't eaten since the curry last night, and although I'm not much interested in living anymore my stomach continues to defy me, it's rumbling, and so I take a few mouthfuls and it's actually quite nice, and I end up eating it all which dimly surprises me. They've only given me a plastic spoon, I obviously can't be trusted with a knife and fork, and when I've finished eating the uniformed officer demands I give him back the spoon, as though it's precious, so I hand it through the hatch to him. I lie down again and nothing happens for more long hours, apart from at some point there's some shouting and swearing outside, some heavy scuffles, and then I hear another cell door slam and some pitiful high-pitched wailing starts up, and it must be someone different as the shouting voice earlier had been low-toned and threatening, although I had no idea what language it was in. It grows dark and I use the toilet in the corner of the cell and even in the gloom I can see it's shit-smeared and disgusting, and then I lie back down and go to sleep.

When I wake up it's light and a microwaved breakfast gets shoved at me, and I almost wonder whether to ask what's going on, what will happen next, but I feel too listless, apathetic, I just can't be bothered. Instead I sit up and take hold of my inadequate implements and smash the food down my throat like a toddler. Before I've finished the door opens and a young man in very clean jeans and a pressed striped shirt asks me to get up, they're ready to interview me. It must be Monday morning – I should be in work, they'll all be there by now, talking about me, I must be the biggest story ever. I get up and my bones feel old. The police officer asks me to follow him and he leads me along the passage, past other wretched prisoners, and someone is ranting and swearing and begging to be let out, he says he needs to feed his dog. I feel sorry for the dog, pining somewhere, hungry, and it makes me cry. The thought of another police interview, a year after the last one, is torture now it comes to it, and I feel so guilty and bereft, about Robbie this time, I can barely stand, but I do my best to keep up and we walk through some double doors and along another cheerless corridor and enter a small windowless room that contains a desk, three orange plastic chairs and a big old-fashioned tape machine. The detective tells me to sit, and he takes one of the seats across the desk from me, and he looks too immaculate, too newly-laundered for these surroundings.

I lean back and again I look in on myself, as though I'm watching an actor still, and the sensation makes me feel dispassionate and strangely calm. We wait, how long, maybe half a minute and then another plain-clothed officer comes in, a woman this time, and she sits down and they start the interview, and although they ask me again if I want a solicitor I don't care what happens, so I say no, it's OK thanks.

I answer all the questions they fire at me, about how I met the deceased, how I came to be in his flat, what we'd been doing for the last 36 hours. I realise that it sounds nasty, sordid, and I want them to know that actually it wasn't like that at all, it was romantic, special, as nice a way as any to pass the time if you have to end up dead. (I start sobbing at this point, and they have to stop the interview for a few minutes.) When I've quietened down they ask me about the drugs and I tell them they were my friend's and that we only did a tiny little bit, we were busy, and at that they stop me, and say, "Do you mean to tell me that you supplied the substance to Mr Monteiro?" and I answer, yes, I suppose I did.

Although I don't want to think about any of this, what's the point, it won't bring him back, they ask me more questions, about who my friend is, how I met her, what she does for a living, what her full name and address is, that kind of thing. I realise too late that I should have said the drugs were mine, but they press me and I can't think of what else to say so I tell them the truth and I feel bad that now I've got Angel

273

into trouble too, dragged her into this whole sorry mess. Finally they stop the interview and take me back to my cell. They don't tell me what will happen next, they just lock the door and leave me there, so I lie down, on my back this time, and stare at the ceiling, try to arrange my thoughts. Do they really think I killed him? *Have I killed him?* He was an adult, he took the drugs willingly, didn't he? Was there something wrong with the drugs? Was it the drugs that killed him, *if so why aren't I dead?* I'm sad for myself now, but most of all I'm sad for Robbie, that he is dead, another life wasted, and I'm sad that my life really is over this time, there's no way back from this.

I have no idea what time it is. One of the uniformed officers opens the cell door and asks me politely to come with him, as though we're in a hotel and he's showing me to my room – he must be newly qualified, he has that air about him, it's sweet really. I swing my body off the dirty bunk and sit on the edge and toss my head between my legs, as if I can simply shake off the filth and the shame. The officer waits patiently, and when at last I get up he leads me from my cell and takes me down long cold corridors to another room, maybe the one where I first got booked in, although it all looks the same to me, grey and grim. Here yet another plain-clothed officer awaits me, and he says something like: "Catherine Emily Brown, I am hereby charging you with possession of a Class A drug, namely cocaine. You will be bailed to attend magistrates' court and must return on the day you are summoned."

I look at him uncomprehendingly. Where was the word *murder* in his statement? What does he mean by *bailed*? My left cheek starts pumping, and it's never done that before. My mouth falls open and I'm aware that in my thin white sleep-suit, with my twitching face and heavy eyes weighed down with misery, I appear like I just don't get it. So he tries again. "Miss Brown, what I am telling you is that you are free to go."

There's a problem of what to put me in. My beautiful green dress has disappeared – it got taken for evidence and now no-one seems to know where it is, although they assure me it will turn up at some point, and at least they give me my shoes back. I don't want to leave in my police-issue pyjamas, I don't want to actually look like a criminal on the loose, even if I feel like one, but the clothes they offer from the lost property department smell revolting. In the end I decide the white outfit is best after all, with my heels, as long as I can order a cab, I'll have to ask for one at the front desk. They press the buzzer and that's it, they let me go. I am back on the other side of the counter, the free side. There are people thronging about, it's busy and someone takes my picture. I startle, not from the flash, but because there in the corner, looking older and thinner and infinitely sad, sits my husband.

Part Three

63

The world outside the taxi looks overly bright, overly busy, too alive for my brain to comprehend. I sit hunched against the window, facing inwards, moving with the car and my husband from the west of London to the north. I'm not looking good, but I don't look that bad either. I'm just another young woman on bail, in a white police suit and silver stilettos. I was arrested on suspicion of murder yesterday, but although I'm free for now I know I'm more trapped than ever. The cab is dim and ominous-feeling, despite the freshness of the day, the sunshine outside, another glorious May morning they would have said on the radio.

It's funny how easy it is, when you have no other choice, to slip back into your old being, into your old name. Ben still calls me Emily and I don't bother correcting him, what's the point of trying to be Cat Brown now I've been found, now I'm forced to face my past? I didn't want to leave with Ben, but also I really desperately did. When I'd seen him waiting there in the police station my heart had leapt and sunk at the exact same time – leapt that maybe he did still love me, after all, sank that how could he forgive me for all I have done?

I sit quietly in the cab and wish I could evaporate, take my leave like a fading spectre or dying soul, not have to face the look of disappointment and loss in Ben's eyes, the final death of the last bit of his love for me. Ben sits straight and says nothing further than what he'd said in the station: "Hello Emily, I think it's best if you come with me," and then he'd taken my elbow and steered me gently but precisely through the waiting press pack and into the taxi. When his hand touched the thin cotton of my top my whole body had jerked, like I'd been given an adrenaline shot, like my life had maybe restarted. That strange illusory sensation I'd had since my arrest had lifted and I saw myself clear and unfettered for the first time in days, since before the anniversary, before May the 6th, and what I saw beneath the grief was a tiny bit of hope.

Ben takes me to the small hotel in Hampstead where he stayed last night, after he'd dropped Charlie at his outraged, disapproving parents and travelled down on the first train he could get, to find me before I was lost again. The hotel is clean and basic, serviceable, but it feels too plain, too character-free to be the back drop to our finale. I'm relieved he hasn't brought Charlie of course, it would all be too much for him, but I find that I ache to see him, that now I've seen Ben I somehow have to see Charlie too, to hold him, cuddle him, tell him I'm sorry, and just as soon as I can.

When we go up to the room it is neatly blank, void, free of our history, and maybe it's not such a bad place after all. Ben suggests I have a shower, so I do as I'm told, and as I undress I realise I'm filthy, in fact I stink. The shower is like shots of steel and I have it bruisingly hot, bruisingly hard, it's what I deserve. When I come out I'm red raw, shy in my towel, but I have nothing else to wear. Ben looks me in the eye and says he'll run to the high street and pick me up something as long as I *promise* to get into the pristine white bed and rest, watch telly, whatever – do anything but bolt while he's gone. I look straight at him and I promise, and he shuffles awkwardly by the door for a moment, as though he doesn't know whether he can trust me, and finally he says quietly, "See you soon, Emily," and although I wonder briefly whether I should leave while I have the chance, I lie down on the bed and sleep takes away my decision.

I hear the firm click of the keycard and the heavy door opens, and Ben is back although it feels like he's only just left. He has bought me some clothes and they suit Emily, not Cat, but I don't mind, not really. I wrap the towel back around me, I'm still absurdly self-conscious, and go in the bathroom, where Ben has laid out the clothes for me, and when I come out I look innocent and new in my dark blue jeans and white cotton shirt. I sit awkwardly on the bed and look at my hands, at my dirty nails that the shower didn't get to, at the space where my ring used to be. Ben sits on the desk chair and we don't know what to do, how to take it further. There's so much to say how do we possibly know where to start? After long minutes of silence, of twingeing loneliness, Ben opens the conversation. He gets straight to the point, this is no place for small talk.

"Emily, you have to tell me what happened that day. I didn't want to push you, I thought you'd tell me in your own time, but then you ran away and left me. You owe it to us both to talk about it, even if you have nothing else to do with me ever again."

I look at Ben and I know that he's right, and even though I've recently been arrested on suspicion of murder, of a famous footballer no less, *this* is where the real story is, and I have kept it in for far too long. I look at the love in his eyes and it gives me courage, so after yet more long minutes of gaping silence I finally open my mouth and start to speak.

64

15 months earlier

There was such a selection of chicken Caroline didn't know where to start. Breasts, skinless breasts, value breasts, thighs, wings, drumsticks, diced, free-range, corn fed, organic, whole birds, quarter birds, poussins (whatever they were). Caroline shivered as she slunk up and down the aisle, past pallid flesh gleaming under shiny packaging and glaring lights, all the way to the tills and back. She couldn't remember now exactly what the recipe had specified, she'd just written down, "Chicken, 300g," under the onion and above the soured cream. In the end she went for breasts, skinless, free range, but not organic, those were extortionate. Caroline worked methodically down her list – milk, cheddar, goat's cheese, yogurt. There was so much choice it took forever to work out what she wanted, make sure she got the right type, right size, best value, the one which was on offer; it was like a giant mathematical treasure hunt. She carried on to the next aisle (tinned tomatoes, beans, ketchup, herbs, pasta) and found bizarrely that she was enjoying this: pushing her trolley, working the aisles, consulting her list, proving at last she was a real person in a proper relationship, not a sad ready-meal-for-one shopper or, worse, a hopeless anorexic who bought nothing but fruit, diet Coke and chewing gum.

After an hour and a half she was nearly done. She reached the final aisle, the drinks section, and picked up a pack of beer for Bill and three bottles of tonic water for herself, relieved that she'd been able to resist the rows and rows of alcohol, she'd come so far lately. Her trolley was almost full now and she wondered briefly how much this was all going to cost, but it didn't really matter, she felt pleased with herself, grown-up. As she reached the tills she scanned her list to double-check she had everything.

Soured cream! She'd forgotten the soured cream. Shit, she thought, that's way back at the beginning, and she needed it for the chicken dish. She felt a pin prick of irritation at the base of her neck, where she held her tension, but recovered herself as she glided the trolley the length of two football pitches, a beatific half-smile fixed on her face. The temperature was several degrees lower back here and she shivered again, and not just with cold. When she couldn't find any kind of cream, let alone soured – just the vast lines of yogurt, milk and every type of cheese that she'd agonised over earlier – a sharper shard of temper struck further down her neck, in between her shoulder blades this time. Surely cream should be round here somewhere? *Where the fuck is it?* The super-market was so monstrous, so full of every kind of everything you could possibly need, it felt overwhelming now, not enjoyable anymore. She hunched into her trolley and looked for someone to ask. The goosebumps on her arms were plainly visible – she had to get out of this fridge aisle, it was ridiculous how cold they kept it. She looked up and down its cathedral length – no-one – and so she left her trolley and stomped off round the corner, past the pies and pasties on the end display, to the meat section. A man in a thick blue fleece was sat low on a footstool, laying out packaged lumps of bright red flesh so vivid they looked alive still.

"Excuse me," she said, unable to keep the impatience from her voice. The man carried on with his stacking.

"Ex-cuse me," Caroline said, louder this time.

The shop assistant glanced up. He was bald, younger than she'd assumed, with a dark goaty beard that looked lost amongst his fleshy jowls, and a small pursed mouth – like a vagina, she thought bitchily.

"Can you tell me where the soured cream is."

"Aisle 32," mumbled the man, looking down at his steaks again.

"Where's Aisle 32?"

The man jerked his head towards where she'd just come from and continued his stacking.

"I've looked there," Caroline said. "Will you please just show me?"

He looked up and his expression was openly hostile now, and she thought at first he was going to refuse. Holding onto the lowest shelf for leverage, he humphed his fat frame off the stool and got to his feet, moving lumberingly round the corner like an awakening bear. He waved his arm vaguely, and went to head back to his special offer sirloins.

"I've already looked there," said Caroline, and this time she couldn't help herself. "Why can't you stop being such a rude lazy arse and help me? Isn't that your job?"

The man stopped. "Madam, I'm going to have to report you to my supervisor if you speak to me like that again – employees here are entitled to be treated with respect."

"Fine," said Caroline, and she was yelling now. "Go and get your stupid supervisor and I'll tell him what a lazy ignorant tosser you are." She realised that other customers had stopped their trolleys and were staring at them both. The man walked away, towards the tills, and Caroline was left with her heaving trolley, but no soured cream still, and everyone staring at her. Shit, why had she let a loser like that rattle her? What if a security guard appeared and asked her to leave? How dare he threaten her?

As the other customers started to move again, carefully keeping their distance, Caroline made her decision. She abandoned her trolley right there, in the middle of Aisle 32, and fled down to the checkouts, along the back of the tills and out into the half-hearted warmth of the early summer's day. She stumbled to her car and roared out the car park, so furiously a mother had to grab her toddler out the way. She drove wailing down the main road back to north Leeds, accelerating and braking crazily, and if she missed any of the lights she screamed and slammed her fist against the door repeatedly, until it throbbed. When she got home she lay on the sofa and sobbed into the cheap black leather, until eventually she stopped and turned on Countdown, to help her calm down before Bill came home.

That night Caroline ordered a takeaway. She told Bill sorry, she'd been too busy to get to the supermarket like she'd promised. Bill said it was fine, he was happy with Chinese.

*   *   *

Caroline never went to a superstore again. She discovered a medium-sized supermarket, in a nicer part of Leeds only 15 minutes' drive from the house, and she went there instead. There was less variety, which in her opinion was a good thing: the products they did have were fine, it took a quarter of the time to get around, and she didn't freeze like she had in the larger shop. She realised that being cold made her anxious, it reminded her of how she'd felt at 15, when she'd weighed less than six stone and could never get warm. Maybe that's why she'd flipped out that day in the dairy aisle, because of the cold. It was a one-off, she was sure of it.

Although Caroline didn't much like shopping anymore she enjoyed cooking these days. She'd bought a few recipe books and took an unexpected delight in having tea ready for when Bill came in from work. It was as if her issues with food had turned in on themselves, and she grew to love cooking the most sumptuous meals, the more calorific the better. Bill had asked her sometimes why her own portions were so tiny, or why she didn't touch the chocolate profiteroles she'd slaved over, but she'd just get defensive and deny everything, and so in the end he'd stopped asking.

On the Friday before Bill's birthday Caroline had done her weekly shop that morning, and was making beef stroganoff followed by banoffee pie for tea. She loved doing something special on a Friday, and as Bill was normally home by four they could eat early and snuggle up on the sofa to watch a movie. Sometimes she couldn't believe how much her life had changed – how her chaotic life of crises and drama had been replaced by the steady domesticity of hers and Bill's life together. It was true he wasn't as trendy or edgy as her previous boyfriends, nor anywhere near as good-looking as her nearly-fiancé Dominic, but he was a good steady man who loved her, and that was enough these days. She was through with melodrama, definitely so, happy in the tiny terrace they shared, with its newly fitted kitchen and knocked through front rooms and gas effect log fire; she had a part-time job in a designer fashion store in the city centre, and OK, the money wasn't great and it wasn't where she'd once been, not even as good as the job she'd had in Manchester, but it would do for now. She and Bill weren't well off exactly, but they could afford nights out whenever they fancied it, and the odd weekend trip away. And anyway this more relaxed lifestyle meant there was a greater chance of her falling pregnant, not that she'd quite got around to telling Bill about those plans yet. Caroline smiled to herself.

As she heard the key turn and the front door shudder, she was stretched out on the couch watching Deal or No Deal. (She'd got herself scarily addicted to that show – it seemed she always needed to be addicted to something, and if now it was cooking calorie-laden seventies-inspired meals like her mother's and watching vacuously rubbish game shows, surely these were better than her previous vices?) She turned the TV down a little and heard the double thud of his shoes coming off, the rustle of his jacket, the noise of his feet on the stairs, the long and splashy sound in the bathroom, the flush of the toilet, the turning on of the pump that worked the taps. Normally he poked his head round the door to give her a kiss, he must have been desperate for the loo. Oh no! The contestant hadn't take the "Deal" just now, the whopping £38,000 he'd been offered by the banker, and now he'd lost the £250,000 prize. He'll almost certainly end up with less now, the moron, she thought, doesn't he realise it's a pure game of playing the odds? She turned her head and smiled as Bill finally came into the room.

"Hi, love," she said.

"Hello," said Bill, and leant down to give her a quick kiss. Caroline's hand snaked around his neck but Bill stood up. "I'm tired, love," he said. "How's your day been?"

"Fine," said Caroline. "I spent £76.38 at the supermarket, I'm getting much better at budgeting. Dinner will be ready at five – we're having one of your favourites."

Bill sat down in the big easy chair, although he normally sat on the end of the couch so Caroline could put her feet in his lap while they watched the last few minutes of the game show together. He's tired, she thought, it's been a long week. He picked up The Sun.

"Aren't you watching this? It's at the exciting bit."

"Nah, I'm a bit bored of it to be honest."

Caroline shrugged. "Emily rang this morning. She's invited us to the christening, it's on June the 6th, she's said they'd better get on with it before his voice breaks," and she laughed.

"OK," said Bill, and continued reading. As she watched him Caroline thought again how nice it was to have someone to take to her nephew's christening, someone who was steady and pleasant and who definitely wouldn't make a scene. He looked good in a suit too – although she did notice his girth was expanding a bit, maybe she'd been over-feeding him. Bill was an almost-handsome man: regular features, everything in the right place, an impressive physique; but his hair was thinning a little and his head was ever so slightly too big for his body. But he wore clothes well, was interested in them – that's how they'd met, through him coming into the store where Caroline worked. His openness about fancying her, pitiful at first, became flattering after a while, and when he'd eventually asked her for a drink she found herself saying yes, she supposed so. That first evening was pleasant rather than scintillating, but she'd agreed to another, after all there was no-one else on the scene, and soon they were sleeping together, and to her surprise he was *amazing* in that respect. She took to staying more and more often at his house, which he'd renovated himself, and before long she'd bought a new toothbrush and left some clothes there and was hardly ever going home. Her latest therapist had told her to accept people as they were, and she'd embraced the advice, embraced Bill's imperfect looks and eager love for her, their life together. For the first time ever she was properly, sensibly happy, she was sure of that.

"£10 – what a total loser, he could have had 38 grand!" she shrieked.

Bill looked up at Caroline. "I don't know why you watch that crap," he said.

"It's part of my routine," she said, still not rising to him, surprising herself. "I know it's pointless, but I just can't help myself. I'll go and cook the rice – dinner will be 10 minutes."

She swung her forever legs off the sofa as Bill watched her. Then he turned off the TV and shut his eyes.

Caroline had already laid the table: taupe oblong mats with silver round ones on top, matching cutlery. She was about to light the candle, but something stopped her – Bill didn't seem in that kind of mood, and besides the nights were drawing out now and it wasn't nearly dark enough. She poured Bill a beer and a tonic water with ice and lemon for herself. She drank tonic in vast quantities these days: it felt like a real drink almost, and it seemed to help somehow.

Bill sat down and she dished up the stroganoff. "Thanks, looks great," he said. As they ate there was a hint of awkwardness to their silence, unusually for Caroline she couldn't think of anything much to say. She got up and put the radio on, and they listened to mediocre easy listening, Zoom by Fat Larry's Band and an unfamiliar Michael Jackson ballad. As Bill stood to clear his plate, he said, "By the way, I promised to pop round to Terry and Sue's this evening, they've still got a problem with their boiler."

"I thought you'd fixed that?" said Caroline.

"The pilot light keeps going out, so they have to keep relighting it and it's a hassle. I shouldn't be long."

"OK, which movie do you fancy watching later?"

"I don't mind – you pick something. I'd rather get fixing this boiler out of the way so I can relax. I'll see you later." He squeezed her perfect rear perfunctorily and left.

Sue and Terry lived next door. Sue was loud and super-cheery, and she always wore the same thing – leggings and smock-like lace-up tops, which showed off her huge bosom, wench-like. She wore her hair short and was out of proportion, her body massive and her feet and head tiny either end. Terry was well on the way to obesity too, but their two boys were solid rather than fat, and totally football mad, and Terry was always ferrying them off to training or matches, he was a real pushy dad according to Bill. Caroline had never met anyone like Sue before – loud, overweight, under-educated

– and she barely said hello when she saw her in the street, and she assumed Sue had spread the word of how stuck-up she was as no-one else was very friendly either. When half-thoughts surfaced of what was she doing here, living with a man like Bill, with Sue and Terry for neighbours, she pushed them resolutely down. She was good at living in denial. She was happy.

Caroline lay in bed restless, Bill snoring lightly beside her. It was five in the morning and she couldn't sleep. She looked in the half-light at the pale boring walls, the horizontal striped curtains that she knew in daytime were deep blue and aqua and just the wrong side of garish, at the country-style ward-robe, and she wondered again how she'd ended up here, in this house, in this life. She rolled over onto her stomach but that hurt her ribs, despite the softness of the mattress, so she sat up and turned on the spot lamp on the bedside table, angling it away from Bill's eyes, and although he stirred a little he didn't wake up. She watched him sleeping, his big hairy chest rising and falling, like a laid-out independent mammal, quite separate from his handsome square face – and then she turned away to retrieve her book from down the side of the bed. She'd been living officially with Bill for over six months now, and it was going well, he brought out the best in her, calmed her down. The rest of her life was OK too – she enjoyed her job, had made some new friends – but there was an unease she felt and she wasn't sure what it was. Was she succumbing to this life because Bill was who she really wanted, because she was where she ought to be, or was it because she felt it was time to settle down and he'd happened to come along? Her desire for a baby surprised her – as did her uncomplicated love for her only nephew across the Pennines in Manchester. Although she knew she'd been a complete bitch when Emily was pregnant, amazingly her bitterness and jealousy had vanished once the baby had been born – he was pure, unadulterated, adorable. He even made her feel closer to her twin, closer to wanting what Emily had, closer to making her, Caroline, feel that life could turn out normal and that she could perhaps live the kind of ordinary happy life that other people did. She'd even started to chart her temperature now, although she hadn't quite told Bill yet, and she always ensured she was at her most desirable at exactly the right times. She sometimes worried that Bill had twigged though – he seemed so much less enthusiastic about sex these days, maybe men have a built-in radar for ulterior motives. They had talked about starting a family, she reassured herself, in fact he'd been the one who'd suggested it, but as she lay there now she realised he hadn't mentioned it in quite a while. Caroline felt sure he wouldn't mind once it happened though, not once there was a baby growing inside her.

As Bill continued sleeping she studied him again, noticed the dimple in his chin, the shadow thrown long and sharp by the focussed light of the spot lamp, the kindness around his eyes. So what if he snored, she'd get used to it. She moved towards him, wrapped her body around his comforting bulk, and although he grunted and half-shook her off she stayed there, until she drifted off herself.

The doorbell rang just after Bill had left for work, and Caroline was up for a change, already on her second black coffee.

She assumed it was the postman – who else would be calling this early – so when it was her neighbour Terry she wasn't expecting it.

"Yes?" she said.

"Can I come in?"

"Bill's not here."

"I know, it's you I want to talk to."

Caroline felt uneasy. Terry looked awful, what could have happened that he wanted to talk to her about? She was annoyed, she needed to wash her hair and it took ages to blow-dry, it was so long these days.

"You'd better come in," she said, and ushered him through to the kitchen. She didn't offer him a drink – she didn't want to prolong his visit, they had nothing to say to each other.

Terry pulled out a chair and sat his huge behind onto it, at an angle away from the table, and he looked precarious, like he might tip off. He stared at her but still she didn't comprehend. "Well?"

"Did you know that your Bill is carrying on with my wife?" he said at last.

Caroline looked at the browning cactus on the window sill behind Terry's vast expanding outline. That plant needs water, she thought, it's dying.

"What do you mean?" she said.

"Exactly what I say. Your Bill and my Sue, they're having an affair."

Caroline struggled to find any feelings, she was so taken aback. The first one that hit her was revulsion. How could he sleep with that whale of a woman, with her massive rolls of fat, hanging like flesh jewellery around her neck and wrists, her horrible heaving bosom. The second was inadequacy – what with her skinny frame and supermodel's chest she was the antithesis of everything Sue was. The third was confusion – how, when, where? And then she remembered the boiler, and the leaking tap, and the broken oven, and realised for the first time that it was always on Friday nights, after they'd had dinner but before they watched a movie together and, depending on her charts of late, even had sex themselves.

"Caroline?" Terry said. "Are you all right? Here, sit down."

"Where are you on Friday evenings? Where are you and the kids?"

"We're at football training, we don't get back 'til eight. That's when it's been going on, and sometimes in the mornings too, according to Sue."

It all seemed so obvious now, but Caroline had never remotely suspected because she couldn't imagine *anyone* finding Sue attractive, let alone Bill. She thought now of Sue's sparkly eyes, her pretty fat face, her infectious laugh, and she felt fucking furious. Bill knew she never spoke to the neighbours if she could help it, there was no reason for her to ever ask Terry how his boiler was, as if she cared. He'd been getting away with it, right next door, right under her perfectly turned up nose.

Caroline couldn't bear to hear any more. She moved towards the door. Terry stood up and followed, as if an invisible cord linked them, all the way to the front door. "You'd better go now," she said, and her voice was over-loud, harsh.

Terry started snivelling. "She says she wants to leave me, to be with Bill."

"Well, that's up to her," said Caroline. "It's nothing to do with me how she feels."

"Are you some kind of robot?" said Terry. "Don't you even care?"

"I don't know," said Caroline simply, and she shut the door.

Caroline meant to ring in sick, but she hadn't managed it. Instead she found herself sat in the kitchen, rooted, literally unable to move, staring at the chair Terry had occupied, which was still pushed out at an awkward angle, making the place look untidy. She felt frozen – not sure how to feel, what to do, where to go. After perhaps two hours she finally felt able to stand, and she went over to the cutlery drawer and selected a small lethally sharp knife with a cruel curved end, a parer she thought it was called. She studied the knife, held it at every angle, until finally the sun outside, beyond the dying cactus, caught its steel rivets and flashed warning signs at her. She looked at her wrists – the veins stood proud, livid, like blue scars. She felt the point of the knife against her chin, her cheek, her forehead, her neck, her wrists again. She left the kitchen and made her way precisely, carefully upstairs to the bedroom she'd shared with Bill only a few hours before. She sat on the bed and stared sightlessly at the vile orange pine wardrobe for long absent minutes; she gazed longingly at the three inch blade, admiring its beauty, feeling its potential; she held it to her wrist again and pressed, just a little; she returned her eyes to the wardrobe.

And still Caroline sat there, doing nothing, feeling nothing, undecided still.

At long long last an emotion kicked in. It was pure unfettered rage.

With a guttural roar she hurled herself at the wardrobe, yanked it open and attacked the contents, knife held aloft, like a dagger. The more she ripped and scraped through his shirts and jackets and jeans with her tiny lethal weapon the more angry she felt, and her screams of rage and abuse could be heard by Sue next door, curled up weeping in the adjacent room, like a giant bean bag. Finally Caroline stopped, and she knew she had to leave before Bill got home, before she did the same to him, before she ripped his heart out. Grabbing her bag and phone and car keys she fled from the house, her breath jumpy and unregulated, her eyes wild but dry.

65

I lie in bed, content and drowsy. Ben has just got into the shower and I enjoy that brief interlude, before the little voice calls "Muuuummy," and it's time to get up. The sun is rampaging through the curtains and it feels warm already, but nicely so, snoozingly so. It's a Thursday morning in early May, and I can't help but feel how unbelievably lucky I am, with my gorgeous husband and beautiful boy, living in our lovely cottage in this amazing part of Manchester, so friendly and laid-back, so full of life, close to the city centre yet also near to the wilds of the Peak District where we love to go on the weekend. I can't believe that one random decision – to go parachuting of all things – has led me to here, to right now, to this bed in this house, with the memory of my husband warm inside me, and my child still sleeping obligingly.

I must have dozed off because now it's 7.30, I really must get up, but my mind keeps drifting – I think it's the sunshine, I swear it's rained solidly for a week, and today's the first proper Spring day after a cold hard winter. I can't stop feeling ridiculously grateful to the whole entire world, maybe it's my hormones, I was like this last time. I'm not even worried about my nutty family for a change, they seem to have all settled down at last, with Mum climbing mountains and Dad finally picking himself up after the shock of the divorce, and taking up badminton of all things. And Caroline is perhaps the greatest surprise of all. Yet another stint in rehab seems to have worked this time, thank God, and she seems at peace with herself at last. She has a nice partner Bill, and OK he might not be as glamorous as her previous boyfriends, but he's real and decent and seems to love her. I'm so pleased for her. We don't see her much now she's in Leeds, but when we do it's nice – she seems to have taken to Ben finally, and adores our darling child. Best of all, I've stopped worrying about upsetting her at last – my fretting about getting married or pregnant in case I offended her used to drive Ben mad. In fact I feel all right telling her about this new baby, hopefully she'll be pleased from the start this time, she seems to love being an auntie.

I sometimes wonder how amidst all my family's dramas I've turned out so normal, how I've been able to cope with Caroline's various crises and my parents' divorce without any of it affecting me that badly. It's not that I'm hard-hearted, or at least I hope I'm not, I just seem to have a very solid core somehow. And of course I was lucky I met Ben, and he has been that person who complements me in every way, and to this day makes my heart soar and my flesh sing, and I wonder whether other people's marriages are like ours.

The sing song cry comes at last, and I am glad of it, can't wait to see his little face still crumpled from sleep explode into a smile of love, for me, his mother. I pull back the duvet and almost run from the room.

★   ★   ★

It's just gone two now, I've given Charlie his lunch and we're dressed and *finally* ready to go, only a few minutes later than planned. I've collected all the paraphernalia you need to take a two year old to the park – nappies, wipes, snacks, change of clothes in case he jumps in the puddles, bread for the ducks. Although I adore being a mother, I'm not great at the practicalities, am in no way one of those super-mums who finds time to purée freezerfuls of organic food whilst holding down a directorship. Never mind, *love is all you need*, that's what I tell myself anyway, how I make myself feel less inadequate, and love is what I have tried to give him, from the moment they handed him to me in the delivery room. My only child has been adored from the start.

As we're about to leave there's a knock at the door, and I assume it's the postman, but instead I'm shocked to see Caroline, looking pale and uncharacteristically scruffy – it's a Thursday afternoon, shouldn't she be in Leeds?

"Hi, Caz," I say, flustered. "How... how lovely to see you." She stares at me, mute, so I say, "Are you OK?" and go to hug her but she shrugs me off. Although it's true we were closer for a while, more like you'd expect twins to be, when she turned to me after the bombing, it didn't last long, I guess we're just too different. In fact I've long since given up trying with her, and I feel guilty now. She still hasn't said anything, and I wonder again what's wrong.

"What are you doing here, Caz?" I say carefully. "Is everything OK?"

"I'm fine," she breezes, but I don't believe her. "You off out?"

"Yes, it's such a lovely day we're off to the park." I pause, and although for some reason I don't really want to, I find myself asking if she'd like to come.

"Ooh, happy families, how super," she says, but then she smiles and I'm not sure if she's being bitchy or just being Caroline. "Sure, why not?"

So she takes Charlie and I take the buggy, it's a long way for a two year old to walk there and back, and we set off down the sun-filled street. The blossom on the trees is pink and tissue-like, as if God stuck it on in the night, and it contrasts with the flat mid blue of the sky, and although I still think the world is a fantastic place a sense of unease has wormed into my day.

Charlie is dawdling, checking out every tree, every puddle, every gate, and Caroline lets him, it seems she's in no hurry either. I'm in front, pushing the buggy, and the rhythmic bumps of the paving stones under the wheels sooth my nerves. I feel slightly calmer, less anxious now. I'm a few yards ahead of them, near the junction and I'm daydreaming, planning our route, trying to decide whether to go to the swings or the duck pond first, it'll be nice to show Caroline. Maybe we could pop into Unicorn later and get something for tea, she'd like it in there, perhaps even have coffee afterwards at the new cafe opposite. I'm oblivious to what she and Charlie are up to, I'm distracted by my plans. So when above the noise of the traffic I hear something behind me, a crash and a splintering of glass, I don't know what's happened but I just know it's not good, and I turn and look back up the road, towards my sister and Charlie.

A half bottle of – what, vodka? – lies smashed on the ground. *She must have had it under her coat, she must have dropped it, she's still drinking, she's drunk*. The thoughts come all at once. Great jags of glass soar up from the pavement where the base of the bottle is still intact, and the angles catch the sunlight and glint menacingly.

"Mind Charlie's paws," I shout, but I'm too late, the puppy steps on a shard and lets out a pitiful prolonged howl. It makes holes in my soul. Caroline just stands there, looking down at the glittering pavement as Charlie whimpers, his paw held aloft, like in evidence.

I start to run towards my sister and my poor bewildered puppy – and then I remember Daniel, I'd just let him out of his buggy so he could walk a while, but again I'm too late, I know I am. I turn and see my son, just ten yards away from me, standing, *teetering*, on the edge of the pavement, outside the off-licence at the end of our street, right where it meets the busy main road.

"Daniel!" I scream, and my little blonde boy, so vivaciously alive, so full of potential, turns around and gives me the biggest cheesiest smile of utter utter joy, he loves buses. Then he turns back and looks across the road at the people standing at the bus stop opposite. Their expressions are horrified, their arms are waving in windmill patterns of helplessness.

Time slows down, as if the wind has dropped. I see the beautiful blue of the sky, like a backdrop, the gesticulating arms and mouths, slow and silent. I see a cyclist slide past, this side of the road; watch him look back at my son, over his shoulder; see him wobble, push his bike to the ground, but I know there's no point, he won't get there either, and I can't bear it. I watch a bird fly across the scene, so slowly it might fall out of the sky. I see Ben this morning, kissing

Daniel goodbye, ruffling his hair, saying, "See you later, little man," but he won't, he was wrong. I watch myself as they put Daniel to my breast, the flood of love thumping through me. I see the back of my son, his cobalt blue puffer coat, his little beige cords, his new navy shoes, his golden blonde hair. I notice the colours somehow, and they are gorgeous in the sunshine.

And then I pull myself together. I start to run towards my boy as the blood drains down my body and leaves my limbs shivery, but before I can get there Daniel waves cheerily at the people at the bus stop and takes one more step, into the road.

There is no room in my heart for anything other than silence. The quiet is oppressive, it is grief distilled, and it is unbearable. It is universal, I suppose, that moment of bereavement. It makes the whole world stop, for how long I cannot tell you, an excruciating respite from all that's to come. And then the screaming – within me or outside of me? – starts, and it doesn't seem to stop.

Ben takes me in his arms now, in our anonymous hotel room so far from Chorlton, and we weep together for our son, perhaps for the first time. Although here is the only place I want to be I still feel lost and desperate and as if the world has turned on the wrong axis somehow and day has become night and good has become evil. I've never vocalised what actually happened before and the sobs resonate out of the room and down the corridor, the horror is as big as a bus, as big as the number 23 that hit my beautiful boy in front of my very own eyes, that turned his blonde hair and blue eyes into blood and mush and unravelling brains.

Ben says nothing and holds me and we cry and cry and we're both weeping for our dead son and for our own ruined lives, just when everything had all felt so utterly perfect. I was never superstitious before but maybe Daniel's death was a sign – don't wish for too much, don't expect too much, life doesn't work like that. Eventually we lie down together on the hard white bed and somehow we manage to fall asleep, still wrapped in each other's arms, still wrapped in misery.

66

They must have drugged me but still I wake up screaming. I shriek and shriek, it's horrific but I can't seem to stop. Ben rushes to my side and his face is ashen and the grief hangs around his eyes, and even in my delirious state I realise I've broken his heart too.

"I'm sorry, so sorry," I sob and then I continue shrieking again. It seems my mother is also in the room and she rushes off to fetch the doctor, to give me another shot of something I suppose. When I cry and say, "Where's Caroline?" everyone looks at me like I'm mad, and then I remember Daniel's little smashed body again and I howl like an animal. The doctor comes eventually with his glinting needle and the image recedes again into the inky depths of my consciousness, to be lodged there forever.

It is three days later and I'm no longer in hospital, no longer sedated, and Ben tells me gently that I need to talk to the police, have to make a statement. "Will Caroline have to go too?" I say, and again Ben looks confused, and says, "What's Caroline got to do with it?" I think then that perhaps I imagined it all, maybe I wasn't watching Daniel anyway, maybe my twin sister is in no way implicated, *wasn't even there*. And then my sanity kicks in and I know that of course she was there, but it seems no-one saw her behind me, they must have been too fixated on the excruciating scene in front of them – the annihilated toddler, the maniacal mother, the distraught bus driver – to clock a clone of myself bolting in the other direction. When I notice Charlie limping ever so slightly I dully check his paws, and there in the front left one, gleaming like a diamond, is the end of a tiny sharp shard of glass. I pull it out and Charlie yelps, and I decide there's no point complicating things, what difference does it make now, it won't bring Daniel back, and I put the shard in the bin.

I wake up early and my belly aches and my world feels empty, although Ben keeps telling me, quietly, sensitively, that we mustn't give up hope, we have another life to think about. I shuffle to the toilet and as I sit down something feels wrong and I stand up again and screamingly bright blood is gushing down my legs. I screech for Ben and he comes running and I unlock the toilet door and stare up at him, naked yet gaudy, painted with pain. He looks at me with such devastation that I realise I've let him down again now, that now I've taken both his children from him.

How I make it to the funeral I don't know. I'm still bleeding and can barely stand but I make it there somehow, I have to say goodbye to my boy. Everyone looks at me as if *what was she thinking, not holding his hand by such a busy road*, and the shame feels livid. No-one can comfort me. When I see my little boy's coffin, white and gleaming like a brand new shoebox, draped with flowers – someone had thought to get pink, Daniel's favourite colour – I grab Ben's hand for support and squeeze it hard. His hand doesn't respond, not for at least half a second, and I realise with a shock that *he* blames me too. I feel like I'm going to pass out but we get through the service and when the coffin starts moving away from me, travelling ominously behind the curtain, that's all I can cope with and I scream and scream and as Ben tries to restrain me I run down the aisle towards my boy, and then I change my mind, what good will it do, I'm too late, again, and I turn on my heel and run the other way now, out of the chapel into the grim grey world where the sun will never shine again.

67

On a rainy and blustery June morning, just over four weeks after his son had died, Ben went back to work. He didn't have to, his boss told him to take as long as he needed, but he didn't know what else to do. He couldn't reach his wife, she seemed lost to him now, and he found that he seemed to annoy her somehow, whatever he said, whatever he did, and he thought maybe it was better to give her some space for a while, let her have some time to herself. He simply didn't know how to cope with her, his own grief was so agonising, and he found he needed the distraction, craved the safety of the neat columns of numbers, the debits and credits that he was meant to balance, as if any of it mattered. Going to the office was painful: not the work itself, but the pitying looks from his colleagues who meant well but didn't know what to say, and so pretended instead that nothing had happened and said nothing about any of it. Even worse, they would try to censor their own conversations when he was around – would chat about what they'd been up to at the weekend, and studiously fail to mention their own kids, and Ben knew they were doing it for him, but he wanted to yell at them that it didn't make it any better and to stop being so bloody stupid, but of course he didn't.

He was lonely, wherever he was, whoever he was with. He felt the anger build inside him, and more often than not it was aimed at his wife. She still refused to talk to him about it, tell him how it had happened, and although he never wanted to push her, he couldn't help sometimes wondering what the hell she'd been doing, how could she not have been watching their son on the Manchester Road – it was so busy, he was only just turned two – and the more he tried to suppress the thought the more it grew inside him, creeping and insistent and insidious, like moss under a dank dead tree. It didn't help that Emily seemed to hate him now, seemed glad that he'd gone back to work, and he wondered what he was doing wrong – after all he had no blueprint of how to look after the mother of his dead child.

He couldn't understand Emily's sadness about the unborn baby either. Last night, on the first occasion he'd tried to talk to her about what they might do next, Ben had tried to be practical, had even suggested tentatively that they could maybe try again soon – Emily seemed to find it easy to get pregnant, he'd said, this time next year everything might be different.

"What do you mean?" she'd said quietly, her body tight and clenched as she perched on the silver wicker chair by the window. "How can I even think of having another baby? You think I can just replace Daniel? Replace my unborn child?"

"No, of course not," Ben had said. He'd hesitated, aware that carrying on could be dangerous. "But we didn't actually know the baby, so it's not like we've lost him like we've lost Daniel."

"Yes we HAVE," she'd cried then. "We've lost his first smile, his first steps, his little personality that never had the chance to grow. You don't understand do you? I should be twenty weeks pregnant, halfway to holding him in my arms, he should know the sound of our voices by now, but he doesn't, because he is *dead*. A week and a half ago it should have been Daniel's christening, but we had to cancel that because *he's dead too*; tomorrow Daniel should have been going to Nathan's birthday party, the present's still upstairs; in July we should have been taking our son on his first proper beach holiday, he was so excited to be going on a plane. Every single day I should be making him breakfast, getting him dressed, playing with him, taking him to playgroup, bathing him, reading to him, putting him to bed, looking after him, loving him. Do you want me to go on?"

"No," Ben had said. "I don't. Why are you acting like it's all my fault? What have I done?"

"Oh, nothing," Emily said. She stood up. "You've been a bloody saint, as usual. It's me who's the villain round here, isn't it? *She should have been watching him,* that's what YOU think, that's what everyone thinks. You think it's all MY fault, don't you?" She had looked at him with hatred then, or so it seemed. "DON'T YOU?"

Ben had been shocked – Emily never shouted, had always been so mild-mannered even when they argued, it was like he was looking at a stranger. Her face was twisted and ugly, and he tried to suppress the rage he felt, his sudden urge to grab her by the shoulders and shake her, shake some sense back into her. She saw his hands clench as he got up to leave the room and she ran at him then, beat her own fists at him, out of control suddenly, and he'd tried to stop her, pin her arms against her side and hold her tight until she calmed down – and maybe if he'd succeeded it might all have been different, but she shook herself free and flailed at his face, catching him with her nail, and as he let her go to cup his ear, contain the squelching blood, she ran from the room.

Ben stared rigidly at his computer, trying hard to send his thoughts away from their confrontation last night, back to his spreadsheet, but he found his heart was racing and his palms were sweating again, so he stood up abruptly from his desk, saying he was popping out for a sandwich, although it wasn't even 11 yet. Out on the street he turned blindly right, in the direction of his favourite cafe; then right again into Rochdale Road, on automatic pilot now, not thinking at all; but then as he went to enter the cafe someone was coming out, and although he already had his hand on the door he found he couldn't face it after all, and he turned abruptly away, onto New George Street; and when he reached the end of there he took another right, randomly, he had to go somewhere. He slowed down at last. He needed to ring her.

"Hello," she said, and her voice was cold.

"Hi," he whispered, barely able to get the words out. "Are you OK?" and as he said it he regretted the question.

"Oh, yeah, great," she said and he winced at her sarcasm.

"I'll come home early, I'll cook dinner," he said. "What do you fancy?" and again he wished he could take back his words, unsay them.

"Nothing," she said eventually, but she wasn't bitter this time, just blank, which was worse in a way.

"OK, I'll work something out."

Emily said nothing.

"What are you doing?"

"Nothing."

"It's a lovely day, maybe you could do a spot of clearing up in the garden."

"What's that supposed to mean?"

"Nothing. I – I was just trying to think what might make you feel better."

"Ben, nothing will make me feel better," she said, but the way she said it wasn't self-pitying or accusatory, just desolate. Her voice was thick. "I've got to go. Bye."

"Bye," he said, to a dead line, and he stayed mute and stupid on the pavement opposite the old fish market, staring up at the sculptured panel of the woman with a babe in arms and a little boy by her side, until he could tell someone was staring at him, perhaps wondering whether to ask him if he was all right, and so he moved at last, fast and purposefully back to the office, his sandwich forgotten.

68

"At what point did you first think of leaving me?" says Ben. We are lying side by side, not touching now, and it is late afternoon in the hotel in Hampstead, and we are both staring at the ceiling, as if maybe the answer lies there.

I take ages to answer. "Probably that moment in the chapel," I say. "When you didn't comfort me, that's when I thought it was over for us, that you'd never forgive me. I didn't know then how it would happen, but I just knew Daniel's death would destroy "us" too."

Ben looks at me puzzled. "When didn't I comfort you?"

"You wouldn't hold my hand, you didn't respond," and as I say it out loud I realise I haven't been entirely rational.

"Don't get me wrong," says Ben. "Of course I was angry. At you, at the world, at the bus driver. The only person I wasn't angry with at the time was Caroline."

His face grows troubled. "So that's what she meant when she said sorry."

"What do you mean? When did she say sorry?"

Ben takes a breath and tells me that on the anniversary of our little boy's death he went to the Peak District and walked for hours over mountains and across fields, and then camped alone, it was all he could face without me, without Daniel. Then on the next night, he'd been at home on his own and Caroline had turned up to say sorry for something, but he didn't know what, there were so many things she could have been apologising for. He tells me quietly that he'd let her in and got paralytic with her and that they'd ended up having sex – my husband and my own twin sister.

"Emily, I'm so so sorry," he says. "I just missed you so much I almost convinced myself she was you. I thought I'd never see you again, and I was trying to get back to you, back to us somehow. And then when it was over I had to face up to the fact that it was her not you, and it felt like I couldn't hate the world or myself any more." He stops and looks desperate, like something irrevocable has broken inside him.

Although I'm horrified, repulsed, mad at him, I work it out instantly. "So this was Saturday night?"

"Yes," he says, and it feels insane but I tell him unflinchingly about meeting Robbie and how much he looked like him, Ben, and that despite all the bad stuff I've done since I left, the first and only time I had been unfaithful to him was exactly when he was having sex with my sister.

Ben is silent for ages. "I can just about stand you being with him," he says. "If that's how I was able to find you."

"But look what I've done. I've killed him. He's dead now, and he didn't deserve that," and I start to weep again, for Robbie this time, another bright boy whose life has ended because of me.

"It's not your fault, Em. He took the drugs willingly, didn't he, there must have been something else wrong for him to die like that."

314

I haven't thought of that and it's probably true, but it doesn't make me feel any better, it still feels unreal, nightmarish, a further descent into hell.

Ben changes the subject. "Emily, I need to know. Why did you leave me like that? If you owe me one thing it's to tell me that. It seems like such a shit thing to do."

I look at my husband. "First I lost Daniel, and then I lost the baby, I just couldn't bear losing you too. And I know I pushed you away, but I was so certain you didn't love me anymore, that you blamed me, that it made it worse and worse and I became convinced that you hated me. And then we seemed so far apart and I'd become so mean and hostile I thought in my madness that you and Charlie would be happier without me, that if I left completely then one day you'd be able to meet someone else and start a new family. We were both just so unhappy by the end. And I knew that the new house you wanted to buy wouldn't have made it any better either. All it would've meant was that I wouldn't have had to walk twice as far to get anywhere, to avoid the dark patch on the road they could never get rid of. But it still lives on in my mind Ben, it's never going to be gone, not ever. So it seemed easier to just leave, to try to start all over again, I honestly thought I was doing the right thing for both of us. It was either that or...," and I stop.

"I know," says Ben, and he turns on his side and looks at me, but I keep on staring at the cold blank ceiling. He hesitates but I know what's coming and I don't know how I feel, I'm still in shock I suppose.

"Emily, do you think there's any way you and I can ever be happy together again?"

315

I take ages to answer, my mind is too scrambled, I don't have a clue what to say.

"I just don't know. Too much has happened, it's too soon to think about. Poor Robbie has only just died." I feel Ben tense and I know he's jealous. My eyes fill with yet more tears, sad for them both. I struggle to continue. "And anyway it's so complicated: I have a new name, a job, a court case to get through, new friends, I'm a different person now." I see the hurt in his eyes and it's agony to witness. I pause.

I still can't think what else to say, so finally I say what I really think, what I've wanted to tell him since I first saw him again, sitting alone in the police station.

"Ben, I still love you, I've never stopped loving you, I just don't know whether we can simply start up all over again, after everything that's happened. And whatever you say someone else is dead now, probably because of me, and he was massively famous and people adored him. I'm going to be a public figure of hate. I don't know how I'm going to manage that. I don't know how I'm going to manage yet more guilt."

"Will you at least try?" he asks, and despite myself I find myself nodding and the tears in my eyes are ones of happiness this time.

69

On the Tuesday morning after my release on bail Ben takes me to the flat at Shepherds Bush so I can collect my things. I realise I still haven't been in touch with Angel, not since Friday night, just before Roberto Monteiro had escorted me out of the Groucho. I'm nervous, I don't know how she'll be with me, especially as I gave the police her name, told them it was her drugs that Robbie took. The flat feels quiet and I assume she isn't home from work yet, but as I hesitate in the hallway, her bedroom door opens and she comes out, her hair a golden mess, fluffy dressing gown as white as ever.

"Cat, babe, what on earth happened?" she says, and she comes over and gives me a hug of such sweetness that I think maybe the police haven't contacted her after all. "Why the fuck didn't you call me?"

She seems to have only just noticed that I'm not alone, and so she smiles and holds out her hand and says, "Hello, I'm Angel."

"Angel, this is my husband Ben," I reply, and she squeals and says, "Jesus, Cat, can you stop springing this stuff on me. First you're arrested for murder, and not just any murder, only the biggest football player in the whole flippin' country, then you put the police onto me, you cow, and now you tell me you're married. What the hell's next?"

"My name's not Cat, it's Emily," I tell Angel, and that's the moment I properly make my decision, to cross from my new life back into my old one.

70

I stand with my hand on a bible and although I'm no longer a believer I have somehow in the confusion agreed to make an oath, and so I promise Almighty God to tell the whole truth and nothing but the truth and the God bit makes me feel uncomfortable. I find I don't mind telling the truth these days though, I know that lying has got me nowhere. The court is a modern informal-feeling room, more like a school hall, not at all like the courts I've been in before, but it's rammed with reporters, and it's only by looking across at my husband and him giving me a small smile of support that I find the strength to not buckle at the knees. I'm wearing a navy fitted jacket and a cream skirt and my hair is pulled back neatly, my lawyer told me to make sure I look serious and contrite. That's easy, I just ensure my exterior matches how I feel inside.

"Catherine Emily Brown, you are hereby charged with possession of Class A drugs, as discovered at Flat –, 87 Marylebone High Street, London at 06.45 on Sunday the 8th May 2011. How do you plead?"

"Guilty," I say, and the single word resonates loudly across the room and makes me feel spacey, euphoric.

The judge pauses before starting a lengthy pronouncement on the evils of drugs, and I find it incomprehensible that this is me, Emily Coleman, once an upstanding lawyer, here on the wrong side of the dock, being lectured about my criminal activities involving illegal substances – but thankfully not about murder. This is just the latest episode in my life over the past year or so that I find hard to digest, ever since the hideous annihilation of my precious son started a train of incredible events that took me away from myself, but now seemed to be turning full circle, bringing me back to who I really am – Emily, wife of Ben, mother of Daniel (deceased), mother of unnamed baby (miscarried). Although I'm trying my best I find I cannot concentrate on what the judge is saying, my mind keeps drifting – back to the main road in Chorlton, over to the death bed in Marylebone, on to the doom-filled church where I said my wretched farewell to my boy – and so when I hear the gasps from the gallery I don't know what's happened but I assume it must be bad, and it's only when Ben tells me afterwards I discover that all I got is a fine, a measly £180 fine, and it's over.

71

Three years later

I sit alone in the pews in the flower-filled church, and the scent reminds me of summer meadows from long ago, from when I was a little girl. The church is beautiful, with a soaring stained glass window, but the brightness of the colours make me think of Daniel lying like a smashed toy in his cobalt blue coat, covered in blood, so I try not to look at it. The lectern is golden, in the shape of an eagle, and the eagle is standing upright, and its little fat legs remind me of Daniel's, but its face is mean and beaky and I can't look at that either. I still find it hard to go into a church, ever since the funeral.

I'm wearing a black silk dress from my agency days, feeling self-conscious that I'm on my own, it's the first wedding I've been to since my divorce. Maybe I should have agreed to be Matron of Honour after all, but I felt too old, too frumpy, too bowed down by life to feel like I'd do a good job of it, and the bride didn't seem to mind. I keep turning round, looking down the aisle to see if she's coming, she's fashionably late as usual. I catch the eye of Angel's old friend Dane, who's hard to miss, massive in an ostentatiously bright blue suit and crimson button-hole, bald head gleaming blackly, and he makes me think of Daniel too. I give him a little wave, and he recognises me and after the initial shock he waves back and blows me a theatrical kiss. Angel's mother Ruth sits in front of me wearing deep vivid red, the colour of the blood that courses wildly through her veins, and she looks as sensational as ever.

I feel close to tears, and I'm not sure whether it's just because of Daniel, or because it's a wedding, or whether it's knowing that people have recognised me and are looking, whispering. I wonder whether it will ever end, being pointed out as the woman who caused the death of 24-year old Roberto Monteiro, the unfulfilled football genius, even though the post-mortem proved what Ben had always thought, that the drugs had had nothing to do with it, that Robbie had died from a rare heart defect that no-one had known about until it was too late.

I look towards the altar and the groom's still standing there patiently, noticeably nervous, and next to him stands his best man, Jeremy, and he looks so smart and handsome it's hard to fathom he's the same lanky boy who long ago flung himself upside down out of a plane, and scared me witless.

I turn to peek back up the aisle, the bride is unacceptably late now, the vicar's looking agitated, but at last the music starts up and as I look again she comes into view and I feel like I cannot, *cannot* believe my eyes, because there is my ex-husband walking straight towards me, and now he has seen me too, for the first time in nearly two years. My whole face feels like it's burning and I put my head down and sharp angry tears claw at the backs of my eyes, begging to be let out. Angel is on his arm, looking like a vision of virginal loveliness, younger than her 27 years, a frothy halo of white silk tulle framing her blonde tumbling hair. I have never hated her more than I do at this moment.

The service is lovely but to me it's interminable, and although I try to stay calm I find that when it's over I can't think of anything else to do but leave. I can't possibly go to the reception in this state. I'm sure Angel won't mind and anyway after what she's done today I don't much care, and so whilst everyone is milling about outside, waiting to congratulate the bride and groom, I duck around behind the church, through the gravestones, and make my way quickly to my battered black Golf. I kick off my heels and as I start the engine I can barely see through my mascara and the rhythm of my sobs is in tune with the car. The car-park is at the rear of the church so I have to drive round the front past the people, it's the only way out. I drive as steadily as I can and I feel like I'm going to make it without anyone noticing, until I see someone in a morning suit run out from the throng and manage to get in front of my car and I'm shocked when I see it's him, he'd looked so appalled to see me. He signals frantically for me to stop, and I panic – what does he want? I have to get out of here, I just can't face him, not now he's with someone else, and my foot wavers – my God, the moment lasts forever – my foot wavers between the accelerator and the brake.

Part Four

72

I stand at the edge of the road outside the off-licence at the end of my old street in Chorlton and nothing much seems to have changed. No-one pays me any attention, I'm just a 40-something woman with my husband stood next to me, looking like we're waiting to cross at the lights. As I stand silently in the rain my body feels unconnected to my mind and I realise I'm swaying and that if I'm not careful I could lose my balance and pitch forward into the road. My husband seems not to trust me, and he takes my arm and holds me tight, like you would a child, like I should have done with my own child so many years ago.

It's funny how hard it is, when it really comes down to it, to move on from a tragedy that will always define you. You need a bucket load of determination and a resolve to never go back to the scene of the original devastation, to leave that place behind. Or that's what I thought for such a long time. But standing here now I wish I'd come back years ago. Seeing the buses clattering past, and how easily it must have happened, how one smashed bottle can be the difference between life and death, makes me realise that tragic accidents like that occur every single day around the world, and this knowledge has finally helped heal me. A mother who lets her concentration slip for half a second, with her toddler in the bath, or at the edge of a pool or by a busy road is not incompetent, not evil. These things happen, and 99 times out of a hundred it doesn't matter, fate intervenes and the child is OK, and the odds don't work so maybe there is a God, after all. My darling Daniel was the one in a hundred it wasn't OK for. I weep for him now, quietly, calmly, but I know he's at peace, next to his baby brother, I'm sure it was a he.

My son is not the only person I'm mourning today, not the only one who has died here, at this exact spot. I'm also weeping for my twin sister Caroline, who last week on the 10th anniversary of Daniel's death stepped in front of her own bus-shaped destiny, has left her own gruesome mark on the ground here, and who we buried at lunchtime. When I got the call from poor long-suffering Mum I wasn't really surprised, I knew long ago that Caroline's life would never be a happy one. But I also knew that this was her own way of finally saying sorry, of trying to make amends, that it is she who has forced me to face up to what happened, to come back to this spot and say goodbye to them both. I'm grateful to my twin sister in a strange sort of way, her final step has released us both – her from a lifetime prison of addiction and turmoil, me from my ten year sentence of anguish and guilt. As I stand on this miserable, rain-sodden corner I feel the forgiveness flood through me, of her, of myself, and the feeling is one of lightness and brightness, as though four sparkling angels, one for each life lost, have left my shoulders and flown free above the dark streets of Chorlton into the ever-expanding sky. After long healing minutes, serenaded by honking horns and

squealing brakes, beeping crossings and wheel-splashed puddles, I finally sense it is time to leave, and we turn wordlessly
together and head back to our car.

73

I leave the gravel footpath and I miss the reassuring sound of the crunching underfoot, reminding me that I'm real, that I'm really still here. I move quietly amongst the wild flowers, moving with the breeze and the bees from the magnificent Georgian house down to the playground next to the running track. No-one pays me much attention, I'm just another well-dressed mother, with an ageing labrador and two young children. I went back to Manchester for the first time in ten years yesterday, for my sister's funeral, and perversely today I feel as if my steps on earth are that bit easier. The breeze feels cold and cleansing, despite the sunshine, despite the early promise of the mid-May morning, and the weather suits my mood of absolution.

It's funny how easy it is, once you actually finally confront something, to move on right away from it, to leave it behind at last. I knew I couldn't face going back up north on my own, so my husband came with me, obviously, and Mum, and of course my dear friend Angel, the only person other than Simon who has straddled both my lives and knows me as Cat as well as Emily. In fact she still calls me Cat, and none of us minds, although the children do sometimes ask. I'll tell them the whole story one day, I owe them that.

It's ten years now since Daniel and my unborn baby died, six since I remarried and I thank God for the two little girls we've been blessed with. I'm glad they weren't boys, I think that would have been harder, but I admit it was an unwelcome shock at first when I found out I was having twins. At least they're not identical, and they share a closeness I never had with Caroline, thank goodness, and I adore them both, exactly the same.

I suppose looking back it was inevitable Ben and I would get a divorce. I guess it was too much to expect that we could just carry on after he found me again. It was all too hard: the horrendous publicity, what with the media digging up the whole sorry story of Daniel's death and my desertion of my family; the strain of being an ongoing hate figure (although Roberto Monteiro was always a hero, he has absolute cult status now, another God-given boy who will never grow old); my struggle to come off drugs, it turns out I did have a problem after all. But those things were nothing compared to our grief for our dead children and my terrible guilt about Robbie, who I think I loved a little, not just because he was so like Ben, but for himself too. Ben and I were both jealous of each other's lovers, although we didn't like to admit it – I may have slept with the most desirable man in the world, but he slept with *my sister*. It was too grim. I think the clincher was Ben's anger at my running away, he couldn't help himself, once the relief at finding me had faded, and we found ourselves descending into petty rows about everyday things, fights full of rage and jealousy and abandonment. When after nearly a year it still wasn't working it seemed easier to split than to keep on trying, although he didn't want to at first – but finally I left and went to stay with Mum for a while. I think we were both just worn out by the end.

As we walk further down the hill into the fields I let Charlie off the lead and he bounds off, more slowly these days, he's nearly eleven now. I find my thoughts wandering still as I let the girls run: I'm a bit easier with them of late, slightly less panicky, less paranoid that they'll be stolen or drowned or run over.

It was Angel who engineered my next marriage. Who would ever have thought she'd end up with one of Ben's friends, another boring parachuting accountant at that? But she went for counselling and has given up drugs and stealing and sleeping with men for money, and I'm happy for her. She was always going to marry well, she's one of those girls, and now her bastard rich boyfriend has been replaced by her adoring rich husband. She spotted Tim's potential and he has turned out to be such a catch, and he treats her like the fairy princess she is. I don't know how she gets away with it, but Tim just accepted her past life, he was that puppy-struck from the moment we introduced them, that first Christmas after Ben found me. It took her a while, and a few of his City promotions, to fully come round to Tim, but now she shows him the loyalty of a lioness to her cubs, like how she is with me. She doesn't work in casinos any more, of course, she gets her kicks these days out of 10,000 foot free falls over southern Spain and from trading shares on her laptop – Tim taught her, and she's quite brilliant at it, she always did have a sharp brain.

I could not believe her cunning over her wedding though, that trumped anything else I'd ever known her to do. OK, she didn't have a father to give her away, but choosing Ben? How ridiculous. How calculating. She knew we'd be forced to confront each other, that we wouldn't be able to get away, although my God I'd tried.

My mind meanders back to that moment seven years ago when I was sat slumped in my car wondering what on earth I was going to say to my ex-husband, who I'd just very nearly run over in my bid to escape from him. Although I only had seconds all my thoughts came rushing past, like an auto cue on fast forward – how could Angel do that to me, her supposed best friend? Why was Ben running out to speak to me, what could he possibly want? Does he really think I'd run him over, surely he knows I was just trying to get past him, escape? What the hell was Ben doing giving Angel away? Why is Angel such a stinking liar, why did she swear that he was working overseas, that he couldn't make the wedding? Who's he here with, where's the new girlfriend I heard he has now?

I'd had no time to work out anything before the passenger's door was yanked open and Ben piled into the car, bigger than I remembered. He was making sure I couldn't get away I suppose, if I drove off now he was coming with me. I must have been in shock. I sat looking straight ahead, out the windscreen, over the faded black bonnet he'd so nearly ended up on, my breath shallow and jumpy. Ben was raging, hopping mad like I'd never seen him.

"What the fuck are you trying to do, you maniac?" he yelled in my face. "You could've killed me." And then he obviously realised what he'd said but he carried on, his fury hadn't burned itself out yet.

"What are you doing here anyway? Angel said you were volunteering in Malawi with your mother." I remember snorting at this, at Angel's level of conniving.

"Don't laugh, it's not fucking funny. Are you trying to ruin this day for everyone, like your sister tried at our wedding? Why can't you just leave me alone? Why do you keep tormenting me?"

I snapped then. "*Tormenting* you? I'm not trying to torment you. I didn't want to see you either, I can assure you. Angel swore on her life you wouldn't be here. D'you think I wanted this to happen? I just wanted to go home, I wasn't trying to run you down, I'm not that insane, I was just trying to avoid THIS." And as I spat out the last anguished word I twisted and looked at him for the first time, full in the face, and it was like my heart had just taken another 90 degree turn, back into unconditional love for this man I used to be married to, and he saw it in my face, I couldn't disguise it, and he leant across the car and grabbed me, not tenderly but with rage still, and he kissed me like he was trying to kill me, and then I was kissing him back and we were pulling across the car at each other so hard, so clumsily, so fucking furiously that we forgot completely that everyone, including his soon to be ex-girlfriend, was watching.

Charlie is lying down in the long grass under a tree, it's too hot for him already, and the girls are turning cart-wheels and I call to them to mind where they put their hands, there are nettles just here. I missed Charlie so much in the two further years Ben and I were apart, it's lovely to have him back. I'm

334

so glad we decided to make our new home together in London, where Ben was living anyway – I moved straight back in with him the week after Angel's wedding, it's like we both felt we had no more time to lose. And after a few months we bought a tiny house not far from that hotel in Hampstead, the one where we stayed when Ben first found me. Our original attempt to try neutral territory, in a little Cheshire village, never had felt right, we're city people really, and Manchester wasn't an option either. But I love it here. Who'd ever have thought you could feel so at one with the earth in the middle of this monster city?

I still see Simon occasionally. It's wonderful to see him so happy now he's finally split from his wife – he waited until his son was 18, which is typically honourable of him, and his girlfriend is gorgeous. I'm lucky to have Mum nearby too these days, now she's moved down to see more of her grand-children, and although she's devastated about Caroline of course, hopefully it will be easier in the future – at least she won't have to worry anymore, and she's sure that Caroline is at peace at last. Dad seems to have coped OK too so far, his new wife has been fantastic, and perhaps one day we'll see that it's a release for all of us.

I don't feel anger or guilt about Caroline anymore. I found it so hard to forgive her but it seems she never forgave herself, and ten more years of misery and self-abuse are at least over for her, my poor tortured twin sister. Ben kept his promise to not see her again, so I barely saw her either and although it makes me sad to think it, perhaps what's happened is how her story was meant to end.

I walk with my girls down between the ponds, and I call

Charlie and I stoop to put him on the lead, I don't want him to chase the ducks. As I look up I see my husband walking towards me, he must have finished his swim early, and he has the weekend papers and coffee and fresh buns from the café by the tennis courts. My heart swoops and soars and our twins yell, "Daddy," and Charlie breaks free from my grasp and runs like a puppy again. Charlie speeds towards him and Ben catches him by the collar and then the twins are there too, and I watch my family fall in a crumple to the soft grass, and laughter sounds across the sweet air.

Author's Note

I wrote *One Step Too Far* in early summer 2010 whilst my mother was inexplicably becoming unwell, encouraging her to read chapters of it to keep her going, not knowing quite where it was going myself. I wrote it anywhere and everywhere – propped up in bed, in friends' gardens watching our children play, in hospital, on the plane to Dublin where I was working at the time – always driven to finish it for her although I didn't want to know why. I completed the first draft a few days before my mother died. This book is for her.

Sylvia Blanche Harrison
7th September 1937 to 3rd July 2010

Acknowledgements

My huge thanks to my very earliest readers: my mother, my husband and my friend Claire Lusher – and the ones who followed thereafter: Kathy Weston, Alice Baldock, Anna Jachymek, Claire Heppenstall, Donna Malone, Angie Starn, Gail Walker, Dave Sheehan, Val Young, Nicola Young, Nicole Johnschwager, Garry Boorman, Claire Smith, Mary Bishop, Colin Sutherland, Chrissy Paech, Joanne Doran, Sandie Kirk, Dave Martin and Annabelle Randles for your encouragement, support and most importantly candid feedback. A special thanks to my friends Alli Campbell, Tracy Morrell, Bex Davies and Catherine Burkin who as well as reading the book gave me so much practical help and showed unwavering belief in me. My just as great thanks to Kavita Bhanot and Becky Swift at The Literary Consultancy, who I really couldn't have done this without, and to Arabella Weir for pointing me in their direction. To my darling son and to shuck for the very first and very last cover designs. To the professionals who helped me begin to have a clue what I was doing: Heather O'Connell, Stephen Bass, Jeff Taylor and Kristina Radke, and to Matthew Bates, Gary Rosenthal, Susan Kirby, Scott Pearce and Laila Hegarty for your help in putting me out there. To the agents and especially Penny Faith and Deborah Wright who gave me such insightful feedback. To Lyndsey Kilifin and Angie Greenwood for you and your book groups' support. To Jacky Lord for giving me my love of the English language all those years ago, and to Clare Johnson, Harriet Lane and the people I wrote with on Thursday afternoons in Highgate for reigniting it. To the friends who've listened to me go on about this book for so many years. To Karen Seskis who showed me what can be done if you try hard enough. To my dad John Harrison, my brother Stuart Harrison, my sister-in-law Angeles Borrego Martin, my dear neighbour Connie Bennet, and the rest of my family who have pulled together over the past few years, I love you. And to all of you who've helped me along the way: everyone who has supported me on Facebook and to my new band of readers and cheerleaders – thank you thank you thank you.

Book Group Reading Notes

1. Can anything justify a mother leaving her child? Do men face the same level of disapproval when they do it? How does that affect our view of Emily throughout the novel?

2. Can people really walk out of their lives without trace and survive?

3. The impact of parents on children is well-known. How do sibling relationships affect how people develop?

4. What do you think of Finsbury Park Palace and its occupants? What impression of London are you left with?

5. Why does Angel behave as she does? Why did she stay with Anthony for so long? What motivates her in life?

6. There are three mothers (Frances, Emily, Ruth) in this story. Discuss them and the differences between them.

7. What transformation in Emily's personality occurred on 6th May 2010? Is she still fundamentally the same person?

8. How did you feel when the truth of Emily's past was ultimately revealed?

9. Did Ben and Emily's relationship have any hope of surviving after he found her again?

10. Emily says, "Don't wish for too much, don't expect too much, life doesn't work like that." Is she right?

11. Is there a religious message in this story? If so, what is it?

12. The author wrote One Step Too Far as a love story. What do you think will happen next? How will Ben and Emily's lives turn out?

A SERPENTINE AFFAIR

by Tina Seskis

Seven old friends.
One annual reunion.
Countless feuds.

How do friends stay friends for more than 25 years when there is so much to feel aggrieved about? Juliette and JoAnne have never got over one of them sleeping with the other's boyfriend. Sissy secretly blames someone for the death of her husband. Natasha knows one of them is having an affair with her partner. Siobhan annoys everyone. Katie is annoyed by everyone. Camilla desperately tries to keep the peace.

So when their picnic in the park goes horribly wrong and one of them ends up in the Serpentine, who knows what really happened? And just what secrets from the past are about to unfold, changing everyone's lives forever?

Publication date Autumn 2013.
Sign up at tinaseskis.com to get a free preview right now.